NORA WOLFENBARGER

The Promise

The Blackbird Series – Book One

D1279299

First edition

This book was professionally typeset on Reedsy.
Find out more at reedsy.com

Contents

Acknowledgement	V
CHAPTER ONE	1
CHAPTER TWO	4
CHAPTER THREE	8
CHAPTER FOUR	18
CHAPTER FIVE	28
CHAPTER SIX	33
CHAPTER SEVEN	37
CHAPTER EIGHT	38
CHAPTER NINE	47
CHAPTER TEN	54
CHAPTER ELEVEN	61
CHAPTER TWELVE	73
CHAPTER THIRTEEN	83
CHAPTER FOURTEEN	90
CHAPTER FIFTEEN	97
CHAPTER SIXTEEN	102
CHAPTER SEVENTEEN	109
CHAPTER EIGHTEEN	114
CHAPTER NINETEEN	118
CHAPTER TWENTY	124
CHAPTER TWENTY-ONE	130
CHAPTER TWENTY-TWO	136
CHAPTER TWENTY-THREE	143

CHAPTER TWENTY-FOUR   144

CHAPTER TWENTY-FIVE   151

CHAPTER TWENTY-SIX   156

CHAPTER TWENTY-SEVEN   165

CHAPTER TWENTY-EIGHT   174

CHAPTER TWENTY-NINE   183

CHAPTER THIRTY   191

CHAPTER THIRTY-ONE   197

CHAPTER THIRTY-TWO   204

CHAPTER THIRTY-THREE   209

CHAPTER THIRTY-FOUR   212

CHAPTER THIRTY-FIVE   216

CHAPTER THIRTY-SIX   222

CHAPTER THIRTY-SEVEN   228

CHAPTER THIRTY-EIGHT   235

CHAPTER THIRTY-NINE   238

CHAPTER FORTY   243

CHAPTER FORTY-ONE   252

Acknowledgement

I would like to give a special acknowledgement to Goldie Edwards. She guided me through the swamp, boosted me up when I was down, and gave me a gentle nudge when I needed that too. She is the greatest mentor a person could ever have.

My writer's group also deserves a generous amount of credit for helping me pull this project off.

I also owe a great deal to my beta readers. They are a wonderful bunch.

This book is a major accomplishment for me, and I couldn't have managed without the support of my children, Brian and Jessica. I love you both more than you can imagine.

My husband deserves the most credit. He encouraged me, gave me great ideas, and told me when my own ideas weren't so great. Men like Larry are few and far between. He allows me to live on the edge of insanity. I love him for that understanding.

1

CHAPTER ONE

1988

"Grandpa, don't die."

Breath wheezed in and out of the old man's smoke-ruined lungs. Twelve-year-old Silas Albert shifted from foot to foot. This man who had taught Silas to bait a hook, sort truth from lies, and how to appreciate the value of a dollar, was suffering, and Silas didn't know what to do.

"Come closer, Silas. I don't have many words left."

Silas forced his rubbery legs to carry him deeper into the sickroom. He'd been here many times, but his grandfather had only been *sick* then. The acidic smell signaled something new. Something worse. Water flooded Silas's mouth. He swallowed again and again.

I won't let him see me hurl.

The puke urge passed, and Silas willed himself across the floor. He perched on the edge of the bed. "Don't say that, Grandpa. We haven't caught the biggest catfish in Missouri yet."

A smile flickered on the old man's face, softening the ridges of his wrinkles. "You're a good boy, Silas." The papery-thin eyelids drifted shut.

1

Silas's heart crashed against his rib cage. "Grandpa—wake up." He shifted and the mattress bounced.

The eyelids flew open, the room silent except for his grandfather's ragged breathing. Beyond the door, a cat meowed.

"You take care of those you love—don't you, Silas?"

Silas picked at a loose thread on his shirt, glanced toward the darkened windows, and then to the closed bedroom door.

"Don't be scared, boy." The old man's gaze held his, the once piercing brown eyes faded and weak.

Silas squared his shoulders. "I'm not afraid, Grandpa."

"That's better. Now, listen to me." His grandfather paused for a breath. "Remember the warehouse in the West Bottoms?"

"Where you let me run the freight elevator?"

His grandpa's chin lifted a fraction.

"We found a blackbird there with a broken wing. You helped me make a splint." Silas searched for words to keep his grandfather talking—and alive. "She hatched six babies. A big black snake tried to eat them, but she pecked his eyes."

"That's right. Your sister named the momma bird..." A spell of coughing ended in a froth of red spattering the old man's lips. "Audrey."

Silas nodded. He dug deep and resisted turning away. Little remained of the brave firefighter and the shrewd invester his grandfather had been. "We named the warehouse, *The House of Audrey,* after that blackbird." Silas busied his hands, tucking the quilt around his grandfather's shoulders. "Remember? You said it stood for the house of noble strength. We still need to hang the sign you made."

"You'll have to hang it for me. When I'm gone...that building will be yours." A gasp dry as the desert wind snatched at the old man's words. "Make me a promise. Can you do that?"

"I'll try."

"Give The House of Audrey a heart."

"But how? Buildings don't have hearts."

"Find a way." A frail hand, road-mapped with the raised blue rivers of a long life, found Silas's smaller one. "Promise?"

Silas choked back a sob. "I promise."

The faded brown eyes brightened. Silas's pledge appeared to have boosted Grandpa's strength. "I'm leaving you and your sister a little money as well. Use it wisely." Grandpa's voice rang clear and strong. He smiled as though satisfied he'd closed another great business deal. "Now, give me a hug, and tell your parents I want to see them."

That was the last time Silas saw his grandfather alive.

A week later the family lawyer came to visit. Silas found out his grandfather was a shrewd businessman indeed.

A little money turned out to be ten million dollars.

2

CHAPTER TWO

2019

One hundred and fifty miles east of Kansas City, Carla Beecham cowered in the corner of her candle-lit dining room. Gravity dragged blood from a split lip down her chin. The back of her skull throbbed in the fashion of a dozen bass drums. She touched the lump, her fingers coming away sticky. The police would find a good-size piece of her scalp on the cabinet door handle. She'd be dead by then.

Her husband moved in again. A mirthless grin showcased his perfect, chemically whitened teeth. He tipped his face down as if he intended to kiss her.

Carla shielded her head with her arms. "Stop, I'm begging you. I'm sorry. I'm sorry, I won't do it again." She had no idea what she'd done to set him off—this time.

Hot breath fanned her skin as his vile laughter filled the room. "You don't look sorry enough—not yet."

Russell's fists slammed her ribs. She buckled and fell to the floor. Moans burst from deep in her throat. A vicious kick landed the toe of his handmade Italian shoe in the pit of her stomach. Fiery pain exploded through her body. Vomit squirted from her mouth. She rolled on her side and pulled her knees to her chin. He moved again and she peaked to see if he was picking up the gun from the table where he'd left it earlier. Instead, her husband picked up a plate of food from the cherry dining room table.

"You expect me to eat this?" he screamed, dumping the contents on her head.

So, today the food was the problem. She expected the plate to slam into her skull next.

Instead, he stroked the fine bone china as though seeing it for the first time, then carefully returned it to the table.

Of course, Russell Beecham III wouldn't break a piece of his mother's precious Wedgewood.

A cool draft touched Carla's skin. The candle flames flickered as the table she'd so carefully set for her husband spun. She squinted her one open eye, to settle the rotation. A gasp burst from her throat as three human figures slipped out of the shadows. Masked and clad in skin- tight black clothing, they glided soundlessly toward her. For a moment, hope of help rose in Carla's chest, and then faltered. Was she so confused from her injuries and so desperate to escape Russell's battering that she imagined a rescue? Her heart filled with despair. With her luck, Russell had arranged a new and horrific way for her to die. At her husband's direction guns, knives, or a taser would appear from the multiple pockets and holsters worn by his henchmen. Or—these were black angels, and she was already dead? The devil's helpers here, assigned to throw her into Hell.

The lead figure broke the silence. "Carla?" The sound was low, throaty, and clearly female.

Carla whispered, "Am I dead?"

Her husband spun toward the stranger's voice, slack jawed. "Who are you? How dare you break into my home?" His eyes turned deadly. "Do you know who I am?"

Battle-ready, the fighters created a human wall between Carla and her husband. "You are nobody when you abuse another." Defiance in a soft falsetto exposed a *don't mess with me* attitude—and a second woman.

Carla struggled to raise herself to one elbow. Her muddled brain attempted to sort good from bad. She wasn't dead, the pain was too great. *Good.* These women dared to stand between her husband's fists and her. *Another good.* "Help me," she begged.

"We will," the second woman replied.

"No, you won't." Russell Beecham's voice was cool and controlled. "My wife had an accident, that's all."

"Abuse is no accident."

The outline of the third warrior wobbled in Carla's vision. Even with only one good eye, she recognized curves that men didn't have.

Russell raised a hand a gun held tight in his grip. "Maybe not. Neither is breaking and entering. You just gave me the excuse I needed to get rid of this worthless cow. Here's tomorrow's news. *'Man protecting his home from intruders, kills his wife by accident.'* Sad. Oh! I almost forgot. *The* burglars were killed as well."

"Not this time." Gloved in black leather, a hand snuffed out the candles.

Carla cradled her ribs and curled into the fetal position, anticipating a gunshot. Her heart pounded. The scrape of leather across the floor, thuds followed by a grunt of pain, and the overhead light switched on. Carla blinked. Her husband lay on the hardwood floor, bound and gagged. A breath of time passed. Her abuser's eyes bulged. He bucked and twisted, but the restraints held. The wood beneath Carla's body vibrated with his rage.

A warrior knelt at her side. "I'm sorry we didn't get here

sooner," the women said. "Where are you hurt?"

"How did you know I needed help?" Carla gasped through the pain racking her body.

"Someone who cared called a hotline."

3

CHAPTER THREE

2019

I wait in the dark. The sky is inky and moonless, perfect for the job that must be done. Dressed from head to toe in black, my figure blends with the night. Non-reflective goggles cover my eyes. I control my breathing. The woman will be along soon. She's not a bad person, but her death is necessary. The fury of purpose burns inside me like hot coals.

A chemical-soaked rag makes a lump in my pocket. A baggie allows only a faint fruity aroma to escape. The smell mixes with the pungent odor from an open can of tuna. A smell cats love.

The cat's meow causes an old fear to visit my chest. I shove it away, tightening my jaw behind my mask. The cat comes to the scent of fish. I force myself to stand still as the animal rubs against my legs.

The old woman will wait on her front porch for her friend Abbey Bryant and Abbey's cat. Neither will ever arrive.

* * *

Detective Silas Albert prepared the stub of his left arm and attached his prosthetic. At the same time, he listened to an update from Big Bertha. The sophisticated computer had been specially programmed to support The House of Audrey. Thirty years after his grandfather's death, Silas imagined his smile and an approving nod from heaven. Carla Beecham was safe, thanks to The Blackbirds. Silas's efforts were indeed giving the old warehouse a heart.

He returned his focus to the medical examiner's report. If only this case had ended as favorably. The city had plenty of murders, but this one had him by the gut. History told him bad things happened when his gut got involved.

For the tenth time he studied the facts. According to the ME, the dark-skinned Jane Doe's cause of death was murder by asphyxiation. No wounds, and only moderate bruising. Why hadn't the victim fought back?

"Silas are you listening?"

The aggravated voice of the detective's niece, Lila, jolted his thoughts away from the report.

"I really want to go on this float trip."

"No," he said. The word snapped through the kitchen of the loft apartment Silas and Lila called home. Ignoring the instant pout of her glossed lips, he stirred his coffee, pinging his spoon against the heavy crock cup. He sucked in the strong aroma of the steaming black coffee, gathering his defense. Lila wouldn't give up without a fight.

"Too dangerous," he said firmly. "It's been raining for a week. The river will be wild." Raising the cup to his lips, he made the slurping noise, the one Lila hated. A few drops fell to his tie. He dabbed at them with a napkin.

"Quit being such an old mother hen," Lila said.

"Did you get that line from Grandma?"

"Oh, come on Silas." A strand of long blonde hair twirled between Lila's fingertips. "It's not raining now, and we're not leaving until Friday. That's four days. By the time we get to the campsite, the water level will be down." She stuck out her lower lip and dragged a long face. "Please. I won't take any risks."

"The puppy-dog look doesn't work when you're seventeen. Like you weren't taking a risk last night? Racing on the boulevard for God's sake."

"I should have known someone would tattle on me." She crossed her arms. "I thought you agreed, if I didn't get a ticket for a month, you'd let up on having your cop cronies watch my every move."

"One of my cop *cronies* cut you a break," Silas said, passing his good hand over his balding head. "He could have hauled you to jail for that little trick. Instead, he followed you home just in case you hit an innocent pedestrian. I have an idea to take your keys."

She blinked, the only sign she recognized the risk of losing her driving privileges.

His throat tightened. What had he been thinking when he bought her the 1953 Studebaker, loaded with a 2017, LS6 Corvette engine? His friends on the force thought the car was ugly and not at all a car for a sixteen-year-old. Silas knew it fit Lila to a T. He could still see her knuckles turning white the first time she popped the clutch. He'd taught her to drive like a cop. Now, she loved the thrill of surprising a non-suspecting racer by blowing their doors off. In a demented way, he was proud of her skill. Once he realized she was racing, he'd determined the talent might save her life.

"I don't have to drive to get where I want to go," she said haughtily.

He sighed. "No. I guess not, but until you're eighteen, I'll be approving the places you go, and floating down the White River at flood stage is not one of them. Remember those bodies you found in the Little Blue last year?"

Her face paled. She remembered. They both did. Prolonged time in the water did unforgettable things to a body. He wasn't playing fair, but where Lila was concerned, he used whatever card he had up his sleeve. His phone vibrated. He pulled it from his pocket, glad for the momentary reprieve. "What?"

"You were right, Silas," Hadley said. "we've got another one."

Silas's blood chilled. He knew immediately what his partner meant. In his peripheral vision, Lila stepped closer, leaning in to hear the conversation.

"Male or female?"

"Female," Hadley replied. "Same items left with the body."

"Where?"

"Vietnam Veterans Park. North end."

"Pick me up."

"I'm two blocks away."

"Why aren't you at the scene?"

"What is this, fifty questions?" Hadley quipped. "I read your mind like usual. Even though with your advanced age, there isn't much there to read."

Lila giggled.

Silas shot an evil eye her direction.

"See," Hadley said. "Even Lila agrees with me."

"Don't get me in this," Lila said.

"So, Boss, do you want me to pick you up or not?"

"I'll get my walker and meet you down front." Silas disconnected.

"You think it's related to the others?" Lila's pout had disappeared. Her dove gray eyes sparkled.

"Stop. It's not right for a person to love crime."

She handed him his shoulder harness. "Must be in the blood," she said. "Do you have your vest on?"

"This isn't an extra layer of fat," he said, patting his belly. "Who's the mother hen?" He raised the scar where his left eyebrow used to be.

"You really should change your tie."

"The victim won't care."

"The chief might."

Silas frowned. Chief Cartwright and Silas interacted like gasoline and matches. It was better to keep them separated, to keep one from blowing the other up.

"Wait." Lila ran from the room. A door squeaked and then slammed. She returned, holding his best tie. "Here. Stick this in your pocket, just in case." Lila tilted her head and for an instant, Silas saw his sister. The same eyes and hair. The resemblance didn't end there.

Like her dead mother, Lila was a mixture of tough sweetness. Silas could stare down a killer, negotiate a hostage situation, or talk a person out of suicide, but he had been dough in his sister's hands. Lila embodied her mother's ability to get her way, but she had achieved a master's level. She liked living on the edge, driving him crazy with her lack of concern for her fragile health.

"If I promise not to float the river, will you let me go? Some of us want to pick up trash."

"Pick up trash?" Silas rolled his eyes, thinking of infection.

A car horn blared from the street below.

"We'll talk later." He shrugged on his jacket, tucking his left hand into the pocket. "Take your medicine, and don't forget to feed the cat."

"At least that's not a no." Tiny half-moons dimpled her cheeks.

"I'll send you a link that explains what we're doing." She kissed his cheek. "No Blackbirds," she said.

"I hope not," he replied, chucking her under the chin.

Lila's cell phone chirped. She was reading the text before he closed the door.

Silas made his way to the old freight elevator, the sound of his shoes against the polished oak planks a sharp echo in the empty hall. He glanced toward the stairwell. Faster. But there was no hurry. The victim couldn't get any deader. He slammed the elevator gate open, stepped inside, and slammed it closed again. He pushed the lever to release the brake and braced himself. The counterweight flew by, freeing the wooden cage to follow the weight's downward plunge. His stomach dropped as the carnival-ride effect took over his body. The numbered floors passed as the speed increased. Three, two...at the last moment he pulled back on the lever, slowing the plummeting elevator to a screeching stop. "Good job, old gal," he said. "You still got what it takes to give me a thrill."

He stepped into the hallway. A door opened a few feet away. A woman greeted him with a smile that didn't disguise her sunken cheeks. Olive skin stretched over protruding collar bones. The Blackbirds had saved her from a stalker a few weeks earlier. "Good morning, Detective," she said.

He returned her smile. "Morning." He could see the unmarked police car parked at the curb. The clouds from the thunderstorm of the early morning parted. Through the front door an egg blue sky greeted him. Good. Rain was not a policeman's friend.

Silas joined the detective in the black Dodge Charger. Hadley dropped his hand to the gear shift. "Wait." Silas said. The woman he'd greeted in the hall exited the front door. A red light gleamed from the face of the alarm, indicating the door was secure. "Been having trouble with that alarm. Seems okay today. Let's move." The black car rolled away from the curb.

"How's Lila? Did you take her keys?"

"Lila is just fine."

"Ha! You didn't take her keys. I knew you wouldn't. That girl's got you wrapped so tight around her little finger that it's deformed."

Silas glanced at his friend, taking in the tall lean body toned by hours in the gym. Unlike Silas, Hadley liked to chase ladies who appreciated his muscles and oohed and ahhed over the jagged scar across his forehead. Partners for years, Hadley now reported to Silas. They were still more a team than boss and subordinate.

"She wants to go on some crazy float trip on the White River. I told her no, but now she says she won't float, she only wants to pick up trash with some other kids."

"That sounds like Lila. Always out to save the world. I've heard of those groups that pick up the old tires, bottles, and whatever else the river deposits after it goes back inside its banks. I read somewhere a thousand old tires had been found in one summer. Once a St. Louis group found a body."

"I feel so much better now."

"It's in my job description to keep your spirits up." Hadley guided the Charger through the West Bottoms, passing Hy-Vee Arena where the Kansas City Stock Yards had once stood. Turning on to 12th Street, packed with cars, buses, and delivery vehicles, the detective lit up the emergency lights and siren. The masses parted. "The power of fear," he said, turning right on Broadway.

The shiny space-age sculptures atop Bartle Hall came into view. Iconic to the skyline of Kansas City, a person either loved them or hated them. Silas thought they looked like hair curlers his grandma had used.

"Tell me about our latest victim," Silas said.

Hadley snapped off the red lights and quieted the siren. "Caucasian female, dark hair, about twenty-five. Body wrapped in a quilt. No blood at the scene. First report indicated she was nude. The quilt didn't cover her bare shoulders. No cuts or abrasions on the hands or fingers. The photo guru might be finished by the time we get there."

"If there's no defense wounds, someone knew her well enough to catch her off guard or drugged her."

"So it would seem."

"Just like the first victim. Any note?"

"Yep. Enclosed in a plastic bag and pinned to the blanket. Guess the killer didn't want his words to be obliterated by that thunderstorm we had this morning."

"Killers should always be so thoughtful. Maybe we'll get lucky with a fingerprint this time," Silas said hopefully. "Who secured the scene?"

"Woody Mendez."

"Good," Silas said. "I like that young man. He's tough and smart, not afraid to put in the time to solve the crime."

"Aren't you the poet this morning." Hadley grinned. "Is this his first murder? He sounded really shook up."

"Might be. Don't worry, he'll toughen up. A little more experience under his belt and he'll make a nice addition to the homicide unit."

"He is sharp."

"I hope he doesn't let his good looks and charm get him in trouble."

"What?" Hadley smirked. "Has he been giving Lila the eye again? He's a little old for her, but you can't blame the guy. Our Lila is a pretty one."

"She's seventeen."

"Did she look back? Give him that under the lashes appraisal of the man in uniform?"

Silas stiffened. "She has a boyfriend."

"Who? She told you boys are too dependent or demanding."

"Jeremy, Jarod... I can't remember."

Hadley shook his head. "If she isn't talking to and about him incessantly, he's not a boyfriend. Besides, Mendez is too much of a professional." Hadley cranked the steering wheel, making a left on to thirteenth street.

Passing Municipal Auditorium, Silas remembered taking an eight-year-old Lila to see *The Greatest Show on Earth* there. Her mother had succumbed to breast cancer a week earlier. Silas was drowning in grief and struggling to fill his new parenting role. Stuffed with hot dogs, cotton candy, and ice cream, the smell of elephant poop had made Lila throw up in his lap. Nine, almost ten years later, parenting his sister's child, was no less dramatic.

"So, who found the body?" Silas changed the subject.

"Trash truck driver. The park is his first stop of the day."

"Another park, but the killer chose a white woman this time."

Hadley glanced at Silas, raising his eyebrows. "Want me to tell you more?"

Silas shook his head.

"Thinking the victim will whisper in your ear?"

Silas shot Hadley a disgusted look. "Don't start. I pay attention to the details, that's all. Didn't they teach you to do that in Denver?"

"What you do can't be taught."

A few minutes later they rolled past an ambulance and a cluster of cruisers. The street was blocked off, uniformed cops keeping the news media and onlookers at bay. One officer nodded at

Hadley and moved the barrier. The bars that prevented vehicles from entering the park gaped wide. Silas felt the familiar quickening of his pulse at the sight of the yellow crime tape flapping in the breeze. He noted the chain that would have held the gates in place dangled in two pieces. Unlocked or cut?

Nestled in a small five-acre island in the middle of the city, the park was secluded from the street by an eight-foot tall hedge. Oaks and elms provided additional privacy for joggers, bicyclists, and now, a corpse. Twenty yards ahead, a city trash truck blocked the narrow lane. The rear of the truck was clearly exposed. Silas lurched forward. The seatbelt cut into his chest. Barely inside the opening where a worker would dump a container of trash, lay the body.

"What the hell? How did she get there?"

"You didn't want me to give you details," Hadley said, bringing the Charger to a stop.

"Don't see the coroner. Better move the car so she can get her van close." Keeping his eyes on the body, Silas stepped from the cruiser. Murky water splashed over his shoes and darkened the hem of his slacks. "Damn it, Hadley. You parked by that mud puddle on purpose." Now his feet would be wet all day. A chuckle followed him as he stepped away from the car, toes squishing in the cold dampness. The Charger slid past him and backed through the gate.

A woman stood near the body. She wore a navy-blue suit, tailored in all the right places, a white shirt, and shiny pumps. Her black hair cut in a short bob, gleamed in the sunlight. Shoulders square and head high, she embodied authority.

Silas felt his stomach tighten. Chief of Police, Elizabeth Cartwright, didn't usually make an appearance at a murder scene.

4

CHAPTER FOUR

The slim smart phone snapped into Lila's hand like a magnet to metal. She tapped the screen, bringing up a message from Hunter, the cutest street racer in Kansas City.

"Going to White River?"

"For sure!" She typed. Hunter didn't need to know she wasn't going to float. And maybe if the weather cooperated, Silas might relent. She hesitated, thinking of the best emoji to post. She settled for a face wearing a big smile and sunglasses.

Hunter's reply lit up her screen. "Still have your keys?"

"Of course, why would I not?" She added an angel emoji.

"An unmarked followed u home last night."

Heat raced up Lila's neck and across her cheeks. *Darn you, Silas. You make me look like such a baby.* "Friend of my uncle," she keyed a reply, brushing off Hunter's observation. "Where were u? u see me beat Jason?"

"Did."

Lila's heart bumped. Why hadn't he found her before the race? It would have been fun if he'd ridden with her. She sighed. There relationship was different. They weren't dating but Lila felt drawn to Hunter in a way she couldn't explain. Her phone chirped.

"U riding with your friend to the campsite?"

"Susan?"

"No. Jason."

Lila's shoulders slumped. She wanted Hunter to ask her to ride with him. "Don't know yet. R u driving?" *Hint. Hint.*

"May have to go on Sat. Mom's having a rough spell." Sad-faced emoji.

Sweet of Hunter to take care of his mother. No doubt, her rough spell had to do with a hangover. She should offer encouragement, be there for him to talk to. Thinking fast on her feet was part of being a Blackbird, and Lila took pride in her skill. But when it came to Hunter her brain turned to jelly. She released pent-up air from her lungs.

"Bummer," she typed. Then added, "Can I help?" Heart emoji.

One minute. Two. Was he angry? Had she stepped into a personal space where she didn't belong? Maybe the heart emoji was scaring him off.

* * *

She and Hunter met at a street race right before Thanksgiving. His serious expression added appeal to his tall, dark handsomeness. He drove a 2017 Mustang. No competition for Lila's own rocket ship disguised as a Studebaker. She wasted no time proving this to him. Hunter took the loss to a female in stride, suggesting he buy pizza for the winner. He attended a private school, so their paths didn't cross every day. Through Christmas and New Year's, she learned he fluctuated between a quiet cuteness and an irritating tendency to hide his feelings by changing the subject. She thought he would never share his family's tragedy, so she didn't share her story either.

In March, they chose Starbucks to celebrate his eighteenth birthday. The day blew in windy and cold. She ordered a smoked butterscotch latte for him and a mocha Frappuccino with a shot of strawberry for herself.

"Happy birthday," she said, setting the drinks on the table.

Hunter hunched his shoulders deeper inside his jacket, a paper napkin turning to shreds between his fingers.

"What's with the long face? It's your birthday. You should be happy. I'll bet your folks are planning a big party for you."

He raised his head, brown eyes dark, verging on black burned into her own. "Why haven't you asked me about my family?" Bits of the disintegrating paper littered the table.

Lila sat on her hands, fighting an urge to yank away the remainder of the napkin and throw it in the trash. At the same time, she resisted telling him she already knew. A few minutes in front of Big Bertha, Silas' computer, and Hunter Morgan's family history had fallen from its storage place in the Cloud.

"You haven't asked about mine either."

"Didn't want to make you sad."

She bit down on her straw. Did he mean sad from hearing his story, or sad about telling her own?

"Being sad is okay, sometimes," she replied. "It would be nice to meet your family."

"No, it wouldn't. Unless you like drunks and domineering workaholics." He laughed a mirthless laugh. "They're both obsessed with forgetting what happened to my sister. Fear for them is what's consuming *me*."

The words burst from him with so much bitterness, Lila drew back. He made a scary face and pretended to stab an invisible victim. She recovered, reached across the table, and took his hand. "What happened to her?"

He glanced around the crowded Starbucks. "Let's get out of here."

They climbed into his Mustang. He twisted the ignition and the car roared to life. He gunned the engine and the car shot out of the parking lot. Lila breathed deep and silently vowed to not say a word about speeding tickets. She took mental notes of street signs in case she had to call 911 to tell them where to send an ambulance.

Twenty minutes later, Hunter parked in a shady picnic area, overlooking a lake. A three-story brick house commanded a position of dominance over the pristine landscape. From her earlier Google search, Lila recognized the Morgan estate.

"That's home," he said, waving a hand in the direction of the mammoth house. "Did you know my dad is a successful surgeon?"

"I heard he's famous."

"Dad's the domineering workaholic. Not so successful as a family man."

"I don't know about that. You don't seem so bad, except you're a lousy street racer."

"I let you win."

"Liar. You let me win about as much as Jason let me win."

A grin slid across Hunter's face, but it didn't linger. "My dad's given up on my mother." The accusation vibrated with resentment.

She placed her hand next to his. "I'm glad you haven't."

He laced his fingers with hers. "I heard that your mother died of cancer. I'll bet you never gave up on her."

"I was only eight. I don't remember much," Lila lied, but then wondered why she had. The force of her nightmares still robbed her of sleep time and time again, leaving her bathed in perspiration, and missing her mother.

"Where's your dad?"

"Don't know. He disappeared before I was born." The explanation was the truth in a condensed version.

"His loss."

She squeezed his hand. "Tell me about your sister."

"Tricia was older than me." He stared straight ahead. The muscle along his jaw tap-danced. "She was only seventeen when she died. I was eleven. My parents didn't really want more than one child. I was sort of a surprise. They loved me I guess, but Tricia spoiled me. She took me everywhere with her. Right before she died, she taught me how to water ski, and how to drive the boat. She was a good person." He turned his head, meeting her eyes. "Like you."

A flutter, light as a butterfly's wings, touched her heart. "How did she die?"

"A swimming accident. I tried to save her—thought I had." He hung his head. "But she died at the hospital."

* * *

The memories of their talk that day whirled through Lila's mind. One hand absently massaged her throat. The circular motion of her fingers followed the curve of her jaw, behind her ear, and over her glands. First one side then the other—searching—always searching. The sound of an incoming text stopped her probing habit before her hand followed its usual path to her breast. Her jaw clenched. Would she ever be over her fear of finding a lump?

She tapped the screen. Hunter's message popped up.

"I don't want u to feel sorry for me."

She keyed. "I won't if u won't."

An eternity of silence ticked by.

"My mom drinks. How could u help her?"

An electric current jolted down her spine. What should she say now? She hadn't thought about the actual how. What could she offer, and if he accepted, what was she getting into? A dozen more questions raced through her brain.

"Kindness." Her fingers in mid-stroke, Lila hesitated. "And, a woman's understanding." She finished the text. She visualized him pacing. What was going through his mind? Was he too protective to accept help? Embarrassed, maybe?

"What about school?"

What? Why would he care about her school? She was tutored anyway. Her fingers flew. "Got it covered."

"What if your uncle finds out?"

"He won't."

Lila watched the clock on her phone change from 7:00 AM to 7:01. It seemed like an hour. *Chirp.*

"I'd like it if you'd come."

"C U in forty-five" She added a Nurse emoji and pressed send.

She picked up Camelia, the one-eyed cat, and danced around the kitchen. After four months, Hunter was taking a big step. She rubbed her face against the cat's velvety ears. "I won't let him down," she whispered.

Lowering the cat to the floor she hurried into Silas's office. Located in the southwest corner of the loft, the exterior walls were constructed of old barn siding and decorated with antique advertising memorabilia. The inside showed a different side of Silas. Very few were privy to the existence of his sophisticated crime solving center, Big Bertha. Twirling in the brown leather executive chair, Lila positioned herself in front of the computer.

"Wake up, Bertha," she said.

"Good morning, Lila." The computer's soft warm voice reminded Lila of ME Sydney Franco. She grinned, thinking of Silas's not so secret romance with the stunning medical examiner.

Lila entered her uncle's password, searched through his contacts for her tutor, and clicked the message icon. Her fingers flew over the keys, and she wondered why she didn't just tell Silas about Hunter.

She stopped typing and read over the message—Mrs. Anderson, Lila will need to reschedule her session today. She will contact you to make up her work. Thank you, Silas Albert.

Her conscience pricked, but she shook it off. Silas would understand her need to help a friend. *He always did.* Besides, there really wasn't anything to tell him about Hunter, yet. With the assets at her uncle's disposal, he probably already knew about him. She tapped 'send' on the keyboard. The message flew into cyberspace.

Camelia limped across the floor and jumped into Lila's lap. One missing foot and a bad eye didn't slow Camelia. Lila stroked the black and white cat. This room was Lila's favorite spot in the apartment. Four computer screens blended perfectly into the wall's décor. Two bar stools were pushed against the desk. Holsters attached to the stool legs held remote control units. One for her and one for Silas. Silas had helped her with homework here. Now, she helped with his.

"Bertha, take me for my morning walk."

"Surveillance initiated," Bertha responded. One screen emerged. "Basement," the computer announced the first stage of Lila's morning duties.

Lila's Studebaker, parked next to the freight elevator, came into view. Silas's department issued SUV lurked, a few yards away. A survival-equipped four-wheeler was parked near the basement door. Perched in the middle of a utility trailer sat a shiny black Harley Davidson. A far corner held Grandpa's dark green four-wheeled drive truck.

"First floor," Bertha said. The basement remained in view while another screen ghosted into place on the wall, revealing the computer's visual of the ground floor. The surveillance paused a few seconds in the empty hallway, moved down a row of closed doors, before finally showing the gym. A solitary figure dressed in a black bathing suit, leaned into a leg stretch next to an Olympic sized pool. Pulled into a ponytail, her long black hair was streaked with silver.

"Pause scan. Audio please," Lila commanded.

"Audio on," the computer responded.

"Hey Grams," Lila said. "You're rockin' those exercises this morning."

"Hello, sweetie. Got to keep in shape. Have to be ready for what the day may bring."

"You're always ready, Grandma. Anything going on I should know about?"

"Nothing unusual. I left Carla asleep half-hour ago. Your Grandpa just came back from a drive."

"Cool beans. I'm glad Grandpa is getting out more. He spends too much time in front of that computer. I'm on my way to check on our new guest. Just wanted to say hey. Got to go. Love you. Bye."

Lila's grandma waved.

"Audio off. Continue."

A third screen appeared next to the first two. Again, an empty hall. The scan paused at each of the eight apartment doors, including the one Lila knew protected their newest arrival, Carla. Lila's grandparents also lived on this floor. They had moved in when Lila's mother required round the clock care. Grampa hadn't been much help. Unable to cope with his daughter's illness, he'd dove into deep depression that had lasted for years, seldom stepping outside his and Gram's apartment. Although recently, Lila had noticed him coming and going more.

The surveillance exposed a new angle of the hallway. Lila leaned closer to the screen. "Bertha, has the scan pattern changed?"

"Yes."

Only Silas or Lila had clearance to make surveillance changes. Unless the computer had been hacked. And that was highly unlikely. Bertha's firewall was cyberwarfare strong. What was Silas checking for? Grandpa did have authorization to test the systems, but he never made a security change.

"Was the change authorized?"

"Yes."

"When?"

"5:00 a.m. today."

Strange. Silas usually made her aware of those changes. Something had Silas worried. Was it The Blackbird's new rescue, or his new case? Maybe that was the real reason he didn't want Lila to go on the float trip. There was something about these crimes that had him nervous.

"Third floor." Bertha announced.

Lila took in the unoccupied arms training room. There were no windows. Against one wall, artificial lighting showed cabinets guarded with high-tech security alarms. Inside the storage units, guns, knives, archery equipment, and the latest small defense equipment awaited assignment. Opposite the cabinets, targets specially designed to eliminate the ricochet of bullets, arrows, or blades stood ready for a practice session. A woman spent weeks training in this room before being ready to join The House of Audrey as a Blackbird. Lila had taken the training. It wasn't easy.

"Bertha, please check the drone schedule. What day and time is my next drill?"

"Lila is scheduled on Wednesday of next week at 6:00 p.m. Your electronic calendar is updated."

"Bertha, continue my morning walk."

The computer exposed the roof and the exterior perimeter of the building. Nothing seemed out of place.

"Morning walk completed." Bertha announced.

Lila tapped a few keys, erasing computer evidence of the skipped session with her tutor. Her stomach fluttered. She was doing this for a good reason, wasn't she?

Then why did she feel the need to hide her actions?

5

CHAPTER FIVE

Lila unzipped her backpack and tossed a blue first-aid kit inside. A cylinder of her favorite tea and ice packs went in next. She then mixed the ingredients of Grandpa Clifford's hangover remedy, filled a thermos, and added it to her emergency gear. In her mind, the combination of lemon juice, water, dandelion extract, ginger, and the main ingredient active charcoal sounded horrible, but Grandpa swore by it.

Lila threw on her Taekwondo jacket. A few moments later, she stood in front of the safe room. She knocked softly. "Carla," she called. "My name is Lila." She put her ear to the door. "I'm here to help you." The sound of something being dragged across the floor filtered through the oak panel. "Open up, I brought medicine."

A one-inch crack in the doorway appeared.

Lila didn't have time to mess around. Hunter needed her. Why didn't Carla just open the door? Huffing to herself, she pushed on the oak panel and stepped into the semi-dark apartment. Slivers of light slid around the edges of closed blinds. "Carla, where are you?" She strained her senses. Air stirred. Above and to her right, a shadow separated from the gloom. Instinctively Lila twisted her body. A hard object glanced off her shoulder. She staggered. Pain exploded through her neck and arm.

"I'll kill you," the woman threatened.

Lila scrambled for the light switch, driving darkness from the room. Carla ran at her, swinging an iron skillet. Lila dodged and caught the woman around the waist. Carla folded, thrashing and kicking.

"Stop. Carla, look at me. You're safe. I won't hurt you." Lila gently turned Carla's body until they faced each other. The battered woman tilted her head and focused the one eye that wasn't swollen shut. Multi-colored layers of aging bruises marred Carla's face and arms. Her lip was split in two places. Bloodied pink scalp gleamed where patches of her hair had been yanked out. Lila flinched. Even having seen dozens of assaults, the cruelty still made Lila ache inside.

A clang broke the silence as the skillet dropped from Carla's fingers. She covered her face with her hands. Sobs wracked her thin shoulders. "What have I done? What have I done?"

"Nothing," Lila said, nudging the door shut with the toe of her shoe. "Except make a dent in the wood floor with that skillet." She put an arm around the woman's shoulders and gently guided her toward the kitchen.

"I didn't mean to hurt you." Carla's voice shook. "I thought one of Russell's thugs had found me."

"It's okay. You're safe here. There's an alarm system and a guard." She helped the trembling woman into a chair. "Now, sit." She found the triple antibiotic ointment in the first-aid kit. "Give me your finger." She squeezed a generous amount onto the tip of Carla's finger. "This will make your lips feel better." She turned to heat water in the tea kettle. This method took longer than the microwave, but Grandpa believed the complete process soothed the soul. Lila wasn't sure who needed comfort more, her or Carla.

The woman dabbed cautiously at her lips. "Thank God I didn't split your skull."

Lila hefted the skillet. "This thing weighs a ton. You were swinging it like a ping pong paddle."

"I was scared. He almost killed me this time." Carla applied a bit more ointment. "What happened seems like a dream. One moment, he was slinging me across the room by my hair. I closed my eyes, praying to die. When I opened them, I thought I saw—I don't know—warriors. The next thing I knew, I was here."

Lila rummaged in the backpack, hiding her smile. She held out an ice pack. Carla winced when she moved, but she took the ice and placed it against her forehead.

"Where am I?"

"Kansas City. The House of Audrey."

Carla one-eyed the wide-open space, as though seeing the bare brick walls for the first time. "The House of Audrey?"

"A private shelter for abused women."

"How did I get here from Jefferson City?"

"My uncle is Detective Silas Albert. He's in charge of the homicide unit here in Kansas City and part of a team helping women in danger. He arranged everything."

"Are there others like me here?"

"Sometimes." Lila's answer was purposefully evasive. Silas insisted on learning more about a new guest before the others were exposed to her. Lila filled a glass with water and held out her palm with the meds she'd gathered as they talked. "These are for pain. The doctor sent them with Silas."

Carla eyed the pills. "I think I can make it," she said. "My husband forced me to take drugs. I don't want to feel that numb again. Maybe a couple of aspirin if you have them or a shot of whiskey."

Lila smiled and returned to the first aid kit. She held up a small bottle of white tablets. "Here's half-a-dozen or so." In the other hand she held a tube of topical pain reliever. "I use this after a workout. Great for sore muscles."

The teakettle whistled. Carla jerked backward so hard her chair tipped. The few inches of her face that weren't bruised, turned pink. "Sorry. I guess I'll be jumpy for a while."

"No problem." Lila said. She dropped a tea bag into a cup and added hot water. "Drink this. I promise it will help."

"Won't you have a cup with me?"

"Wish I could, but my friend's mother's in a bad way. I promised to see what I could do."

"Don't you go to school?" Carla blew on her tea.

"I'm tutored. This is a special request."

"Is she beat up, too?

Lila pondered the question. "Maybe, but not with fists."

"Hurt to the heart is bad too." Carla said. "Will you bring her here?"

"No. I'm just lending a woman's sympathetic ear." Lila reloaded her backpack. "Remember, my uncle has made this a safe place. Sleep if you can."

"What does your uncle expect in return? I'm short on funds and looking like this..." She studied the depths of her cup. "It'll be hard to get a job."

"Silas only wants to get you through a rough patch. He expects nothing in return."

Carla stared at Lila. "Hard to believe."

"I have to go, but we'll talk more later. Remember Nancy?"

Carla nodded. "She sat with me last night."

"She'll be by later. When she comes, don't try to kill her." Lila rubbed the spot where the skillet had bounced off her shoulder. "She's my grandma."

"I'm so sorry I did that." Carla's swollen lips trembled.

"No worries." Lila zipped her bag, poked her arms threw the straps, and hurried toward the door. "See you later." She raced down the stairs to the basement. Inside the Studebaker, she pulled the phone from her pocket and tapped the screen. *Silas.*

She opened his message. "Check on Carla."

"Done," she replied, turning the key in the ignition. The engine roared to life.

She noted the time. She had fifteen minutes. It was a twenty-minute drive...at normal speed.

6

CHAPTER SIX

Eighteen minutes later, Lila turned into the gated drive. The ornate black wrought iron folded inward. She studied her surroundings. It was obvious that the Morgans wanted the public to know they were successful. Driving toward the three-story brick house, Lila wasn't impressed. If success was a magic super-glue designed to hold a broken family together, according to Hunter it wasn't working for this one.

Parking in a circle drive the size of a soccer field, Lila grabbed her backpack and climbed from the car. Hunter waited on the porch for her cute in cargo pants and a Def Leppard t-shirt.

"Hey," Lila said.

"Hey," Hunter replied. "Thanks for coming." A frown crinkled his forehead. "This must seem weird. It's cool if you want to change your mind."

Her heart went out to him. "I'm good."

"Promise?"

"Promise."

"I knew you'd say that. But I think you mean it, too."

Lila followed him into an immense entryway. She'd visited homes of the wealthy, but this was different. This was artistic genius. Pale blue marble covered the floor. Ballerina shapes pressed into copper panels danced across the fifteen-foot ceiling. A white marble fireplace broke the expanse of the wall to her right. Her gaze naturally followed the gleaming black hearth to where the chimney melded into the copper. Such movement. She wanted to taste the beauty with her fingers. Press her cheeks against the coolness. Stare at it forever.

"My mom's work," Hunter said.

"Gorgeous," she breathed.

"The house wasn't finished when my sister died." He waved his hand to encompass the room. "Mom became obsessed with creating the perfect home after my sister died. It replaced... my sister—for a while. Now, scotch fills in for Tricia. Not much room for anything else." A shadow passed over his face. "Want to see the rest of the house?"

"Maybe later," Lila said. "Is your mom awake?"

"Awake might be a stretch. I haven't seen her yet. Dad checks on her before he goes to the hospital." He glanced at an antique clock on the mantle. "Still early. Hopefully, she's still sober." He shot Lila a nervous glance. "Sounds cold, huh?"

"I'm not here to judge."

He moved on to the dining room.

Lila followed "She won't come downstairs?"

"Not much."

French doors separated the dining room from the next part of the house. Hunter pushed one open and held it for her to pass through.

"Careful," he said.

She stepped down to the kitchen. The room conveyed a sense of warmth. This was where a family would live, having breakfast, reading a book, or talking about the day's events. Through tall windows, she watched the whitecaps bobbing across the lake below the picnic spot where she and Hunter had parked.

But something was missing. There were no pictures, no record of the Morgans' family life anywhere. It was as though the room had been built by a person who loved living, and then life stopped. Lila searched for words to break the heavy silence. "I could live in this room," she said.

Hunter trudged to a window and stared across the lake. "Never live in one room."

"Is that what your mom does?"

He turned toward her. "How did you know?"

"I did the same thing. When my mom died, I was scared I would get cancer, like she did. I wouldn't go to school. My uncle arranged for me to be tutored. I still worry."

"I wondered why you touch your neck so often. Are you checking for a lump?"

Oh, God. Had he seen her touch her breast the same way? Heat exploded across her cheeks. She wanted to melt into the floor.

"Sorry, I didn't mean to embarrass you," Hunter said.

Darn, he'd noticed that, too. "It's—uh—o.k. One of my many bad habits. I've had therapy, and I'm better. I slip sometimes."

"I've been to shrinks, too. I don't think they helped much."

"You seem pretty okay to me. But that's from the outside looking in. I know the inside can be a very different place." She turned toward the kitchen counter. "I smell coffee so, let's take some to your mom."

Cups clinked in Hunter's hands as he placed them on a hand-carved wooden tray that held sugar packets, milk, and a coffee carafe. "You need to know," he said. "Mom doesn't take good care of herself." He added spoons and a handful of napkins. "She's thin and well,...not fixed up." He kept his eyes focused on the tray.

Lila resisted touching him. "It's okay. In my uncle's line of work, I've seen *bad* up close." Her mind flew to The Blackbirds, and Carla's battered face.

"I brought a hangover remedy." She patted her backpack. "Grandpa swears by it."

Hunter's shoulders relaxed a fraction. He hefted the tray. "This way."

7

CHAPTER SEVEN

My viewpoint provides a clear view of the crime scene. I watch as the Chief Detective talks with a uniformed cop. I can't see the trash truck, but I know what was transported. The detective turns in a tight circle, scanning the surroundings. For a moment his gaze seems to rest on the spot where I stand. He points toward the upper floors of a nearby hotel.

I turn away. My task for today is complete. After years of preparation, I'm making progress. No one saw me load the body on the truck. No one saw anything, except another step in the cleansing process.

8

CHAPTER EIGHT

Silas recognized the photo technician. His black shirt screamed POLICE in shattering white across his chest. A camera bag was slung from his shoulder.

"Morning, Detective."

"Morning," Silas replied.

"I expected to see you sooner. I'm finished, so you can do your thing, but beware, Leader Lizzy is on her high horse. A ghost slipped a *serial killer* news flash to the media."

"Do I need riot gear?"

The technician chuckled. "Maybe not quite that bad, but you know Lizzy. She doesn't like it when the department is on the six-o'clock news, and she doesn't have the right answers."

"Goes with the job."

"Maybe, but you guys best get a handle on this one soon, or we're all going to have less backside."

Silas leaned closer to the photographer, his voice a whisper. "Best not let Chief hear you call her Leader Lizzy. She might shoot you."

The technician's laugh trailed Silas. He focused on the trash truck. A tidal wave of emotions rolled toward him from a man dressed in blue coveralls, standing a few yards from the body. The trash man stared at the spot where he'd made the unfortunate discovery. His right hand swept through his scant hair over and over. He shook his head as though he could not believe what he'd found. Most people couldn't. Silas still struggled with the atrocities one human could bring to bear on another. His gaze swept the park, to the hedge, and beyond. The windows of a hotel south of the park reflected the sunshine, seeming to blink like a lazy cat in the morning. A curtain snapped shut. Silas counted the floors and mentally noted the fifth.

Mendez, the uniformed cop, approached. His face was ashen. The morning was cool, but sweat circles appeared under his arms. "We've put a man on each exit and stopped the checkout process," he said, as though noting Silas's concentration. "Our team is going door to door. Wasted effort. The murder didn't happen here."

"Don't jump to conclusions," Silas said. "Criminals love to watch the chaos they create," He jerked his chin toward the hotel. "Check the fifth floor. Someone up there didn't want to be seen watching."

Mendez communicated the instructions to the team then turned back to Silas. "The other technicians are working outward from the body toward the hedge. That will take the remainder of the day. The coroner will be here any minute."

"Good. Was the lock missing from the gate's security chain, or did someone bag it already?"

"It's missing. Truck driver said the gate was open when he got here at 6:00. This was his first stop. It's still dark out then. He drove through to the first receptacle. That's where the truck is now. Discovered the body when he went around back. When he picked up the container to dump the garbage—there she was.

Scared him so bad, he dropped the can and hightailed it into the truck's cab. Scattered trash everywhere. According to him, he didn't unlock the door until the first responders arrived."

Silas closed the distance to the trash truck, Mendez at his elbow. Chief of Police, Elizabeth Cartwright, blocked his path. There was fire in her eyes. Silas had once appreciated a different kind of fire in this beautiful woman. But that was before Audrey had died and his niece needed him more.

"Detective Albert, glad you could grace us with your presence." Elizabeth's sharp tone kindled a slow burn in Silas's stomach. Her gaze settled on his coffee-stained tie.

"Thank you," he said in a sugar-coated tone. "I didn't want to step on the photo tech's toes. If you have already solved the crime, I'll just move on."

Mendez stiffened beside Silas, but wisely remained silent. Silas knew time was a critical element in an investigation. The landscape of a scene changed by the second. Weather disturbed the body. Trace evidence vanished. Elizabeth knew as well as Silas that no one could do anything until the photo tech finished. He braced himself, already regretting the way he'd let her get under his skin.

"Get serious, Detective." Elizabeth's glare could melt the hide of a rhino. "I had a call from a reporter this morning. The media's getting their teeth into this one. They have christened the killer, The Surgeon."

"Catchy," Silas said, but he wasn't finding it funny. Not much of a leap from the first victim being found with a scalpel to the title. According to Hadley, a surgeon's scalpel would be at this scene as well. How had a reporter gotten that information? Leaking evidence was a dirty thing to do. Could be for money this time, or someone had a grudge. The stupid move could end a career, or at a minimum, warrant a demotion. He glanced toward the trash truck. Unless there was no leak at all—only the killer wanting attention.

"For God's sake, we're not talking about a beer commercial here. Two women have been murdered."

"I'm quite familiar with the facts, Chief. If you don't mind, I would like to get started."

Elizabeth's chest heaved. "It's about time," she said, her lips twisting. She stepped aside, allowing Silas and Mendez passage. "Don't you want to know why I'm here?"

Silas stopped in his tracks. He swung around, facing his former lover. He was right, Elizabeth's arrival was no accident. He waited.

"Her name's Peterson."

The name rang a bell, but Silas couldn't remember why. "Do I know her?"

"Remember JoAnn Peterson?" Elizabeth's voice softened.

The bell in his head clanged. "Your best friend? The victim is JoAnn?"

"No. The victim is Savannah, JoAnn's daughter." Elizabeth's face crumpled. "The killer called the media. I had to find that out from a damn reporter. Nice way to start the day."

Silas wanted to wrap his arms around this woman, hard as nails on the outside but soft and vulnerable on the inside. Or at least, she once was. He didn't move.

"Need your best work here, Detective."

Silas nodded. "You've got it." He joined two cops positioned to secure the scene at the rear of the trash truck. The air felt thick. The burden of solving this crime had taken on a different meaning. He remembered Savannah. She wasn't that much older than Lila. From the corner of his eye, he saw Elizabeth reach the gate. Head held high, shoulders back. If he were a betting man, there were tears in her eyes. But not one of her officers would ever see that chink in her armor.

He swung around, noting Hadley guiding the truck driver away from the scene. No one spoke. Silas tried to see the woman as the killer would have. Young, attractive, blonde hair, long and tightly braided. Where was the loose thread in the killer's embroidery? What was the thing that connected these women to each other? Mendez could barely stand still. He looked everywhere but at the victim. He had to get over this problem, or he'd never fit into the homicide unit.

"Mendez, see anything unusual here?"

The uniformed cop squared his shoulders. "No visible wounds. No bruising except around the nose and mouth." His voice shook, but he continued. "The killer appears to have taken exceptional care to not disfigure his victim. The quilt may be a symbol of protection. The placement is unique, but I don't have a clue why."

"Very good." Silas nodded. The sweet spring air remained unspoiled by the metallic smell of blood or the putrid odor of feces. "Wonder how far she traveled, and what kept her on the truck," he said. "Kansas City's streets aren't exactly pot-hole free." A sharp wind blew across the park. The quilt fluttered. "Look at that," he said, pointing to the cotton rope binding the body to a steel plate. "Our perp leaves nothing to chance." The left-over chill of winter plucked at Silas's bones, or was it his own reaction to the coldness of insanity?

"Excuse me, guys." A woman in a white jacket and black jeans elbowed her way between Silas and Mendez. Her black medical bag banged Silas' leg. "Can a lady get in here to do her job?"

Silas stepped aside. "Hello Sydney." His pulse hummed.

"Dr. Franco." Mendez nodded to the coroner.

"Officer," she said to the uniformed cop.

"Silas, we meet again so soon." Eyes as dark and warm as melted chocolate met his. The tease was hard to ignore. He controlled the heat threatening to climb his neck and expose his feelings.

She glanced over her shoulder. "I heard the Chief knew the victim, but I didn't expect to see her here."

"Me either," Silas said.

Sydney Franco raised an eyebrow. When she got nothing from Silas, she turned to Mendez expectantly. She shrugged, snapped latex gloves in place, and began her examination. She palmed her phone. "Recording," she said. She moved the phone like an MRI machine over the body, pausing at each exposed knot of the cotton rope. She verbally noted her observations. Unpinning a plastic bag from the quilt, she used tweezers to remove a white piece of paper.

Silas leaned close, wanting Hadley to be wrong, the words to be different. For this to not be a play written by a sick mind.

I saved her from rejection.

Silas straightened. "The same message as last time," he said.

Mendez removed his gloves and snapped on a fresh pair. He studied the note, labeled an evidence bag, and held it while the doctor slid the paper inside. Using the tweezers again, Sydney reached forward and displayed the plastic bag that had held the note. The sun reflected the shiny edges of a surgeon's scalpel.

"I'm betting that's blood on the blade," the ME offered.

"Convenient." Silas said. "I'm betting it's not his. He's either setting someone up, or this is a red herring."

Sydney opened her bag, removing a rectal thermometer and other tools used to estimate the time of death. She cut the rope and pulled the quilt away from the body. Silas ached to protect the victim's naked innocence. But that time was past. Instead he followed the ME's smooth methodical movements. Again, she carefully recorded every inch of Savannah Peterson, and registered her comments. She motioned for her assistant to roll a gurney into position behind the truck. A soft thud, and the human shell lay face down on an unzipped body bag, waiting for further examination. There were no visible wounds.

Ten minutes later the black bag was zipped shut, the zipper teeth rasping together in a cold matter-of-fact way. Technicians loaded the body into the ME's van. Mendez had moved on to get updates from the team.

"Approximate time of death 4:00 a.m.," Sydney reported. "Exposure to the rain and the airy ride from the death scene throws that off a few minutes. I'll get back to you on the official cause of death, but experience tells me your guy caught her off guard, probably asleep. Gave her a whiff of chloroform, blocked her nose and mouth, and waited. No fuss, no muss. So far, no physical purpose for the scalpel. Sound familiar?"

"Unfortunately," Silas said.

The ME climbed in the van and drove off.

Hadley had finished his interview with the truck driver. Silas brought him up to date on Sydney Franco's examination.

"Ever figure out why Chief Cartwright was here?"

"She knew the victim."

Hadley's body jerked taught. "What? Who is it?"

Silas told him. "Chief found out from a blasted reporter. Two murders to investigate, and now we've got a dirty rat feeding the media. Anything of interest from the truck driver?"

"We've locked down the yard where he picked up his truck this morning. I've sent a team to go over the area, and Mendez is backtracking the driver's every move. He took Hopkins with him."

"Nothing more we can do here," Silas said. "Let's head back to the office." The two men walked side by side through the gate, where Elizabeth Cartwright leaned against her dark blue SUV.

"Sorry to hear about your friend," Hadley said.

"Thank you," Elizabeth replied. Dark sunglasses hid her eyes. Her jawline might have been formed from cut glass.

"I'll get the car," Hadley said.

"I'm very sorry, Elizabeth." Silas stepped in close enough to smell her light floral scent. "I remember Savannah as a little girl. Is there anything I can do?"

She swiped a finger under the lens of her sunglasses. "Life isn't fair, is it?"

Her vulnerability smashed his heart. "No Liz, it isn't." His own voice sounded husky. "Do you want me to talk to Savannah's parents?"

Her lower lip trembled. "No, I need to be there for JoAnn." She put a hand on his left arm above the prosthetic. "But would you go with me?"

Under the warmth of her palm, his skin tingled. He flinched.

She tensed minutely, a hint of anger present. "I'm sorry, it was wrong of me to ask." She turned away.

"Liz, wait. Of course, I'll go with you. Get in the car." The words tumbled from his lips. "I'll radio Hadley. He can organize the war room." He reached behind her, opened the door, and gently shoved her inside. She would never let him drive, and he wouldn't be surprised to see her drive off, leaving him standing there like a fool. His feet flew as he raced around the car and jumped into the passenger seat.

She leveled a stare at him across the seat, her cheeks unnatu-

45

rally pink. "Don't get used to bossing the boss."

9

CHAPTER NINE

There were oak stairs to the right of the French doors and Lila followed Hunter to the second floor. "Dad still sleeps in the master bedroom down there." He pointed to the hall leading off to the right. "Mom moved in...that one, down there. He motioned to the left. "This is my room." He nodded at the closed door in front of them.

The tragedy of separated parents with their child caught in the middle wasn't lost on Lila. Hunter's parents were as far apart as two people could be and still live in the same house. Maybe it wasn't really living. They co-existed, and according to Hunter not very well.

Hunter turned toward his mother's room but stopped at the first door he came to. "We'll check here first. Most mornings she ends up in here." He bumped his knuckles against the oak. The soft sound could barely be considered a knock. Lila strained her ears. A clock chimed somewhere on the third floor.

"You didn't tell me her name," Lila said in a hushed voice.

"Oh, sorry. It's Sophie." He twisted the knob. "That's funny, the door's locked."

A chill sprang across Lila's skin.

Hunter fished a ring of keys from his pocket, inserted one, unlocked the door, and pushed it inward. "Mom, it's me," he said, stepping inside. "I brought a visitor."

Pulled along by an invisible string, Lila followed Hunter, heart pounding. Sharing another person's pain changed the relationship. She hoped helping his mom brought them closer, but it could become a wall. Families like the Morgans' rarely wanted the world to know their secrets.

The room was dimly lit and decorated with white furniture, frilly curtains, and a purple bedspread. Old rock star posters hung from one wall. Every other wall was covered from floor to ceiling with snapshots. No one had to tell her they were of Tricia Morgan. Other family photos sat on every available space. The history of this family's life had moved to this room.

"Mom, are you... awake?" Hunter hesitated. "I brought you coffee."

Lila poised on the balls of her feet, prepared to react. To defend. Sophie Morgan might decide she was an intruder, the way Carla had. But one look at the figure curled in the fetal position on the lime green love seat changed Lila's mind. This woman's eyes were closed. A few strands of lank, dirty-blonde hair striped her face. The once beautiful face was ashen and gaunt.

"Momma, wake up." Hunter leaned over his mother, touching her shoulder.

Lila inched forward. Hunter made room. Beneath the loveseat lay four empty scotch bottles. Her nose twitched. Stale liquor and—body odor. She shrugged out of her backpack, grasped Sophie's wrist, knelt, and counted. A pulse throbbed against Lila's fingertips, rapid and strong. She touched the woman's forehead. No fever, but fingers came away sticky from the clamminess of her skin. "Sophie, open your eyes."

The woman stirred, eyelids slitting.

Lila pointed to a door a few feet away. "The bathroom?"

Hunter nodded. "I didn't know she was this bad. I've been gone. Flew in from New York yesterday. I didn't even come home. I went straight to the street race."

Lila recognized guilt talking and she let him get it off his chest.

"I sent Dad a text. He said everything was alright here. He was supposed to take care of her." He growled the last words.

Lila gave him a sharp look. Sophie Morgan had not been taken care of. Had Tyler Morgan, famous surgeon, checked on his wife at all? "Can you get me a damp washcloth?"

He disappeared into the attached bathroom.

When he returned, she gently wiped the woman's face. "We need ice chips," she said.

"Why?"

"Dehydration."

He blinked. The sound of his feet pounding down the oak stairs let her know he understood the urgency.

Sophie squinted up at Lila. "Who are you?"

"A friend."

Sophie scowled. "Go away. I have no friends."

"You have one now." She picked up the woman's hand and wiped the cloth across her palm, between her fingers, and over her knuckles. She did the same to the other hand. "I'm going to help you sit up."

"I don't want to sit up," Sophie whined. "Leave me alone."

Lila got to her feet. She slipped one arm behind Sophie's shoulders and the other under her thighs. She swung the woman's legs over the edge of the loveseat. The edges of her backbone poked Lila through rumpled pajamas. How many days had Hunter's mother worn these same night clothes? Lila sat down beside the woman, capturing the swaying figure before she tumbled to the floor. "Do you know what day it is?"

"Who cares?" Mild belligerence pushed aside Sophie's whine.

Lila needed to freshen the washcloth, but she was afraid to leave the woman for even a moment.

"How is she?" Hunter stood in the door, holding a bowl. His gaze darted around the room, like he'd prefer to be somewhere else.

"Better. I'll take the ice. Rinse this or bring me a fresh one." She handed him the cloth. Filling a spoon with ice chips, she held it to Sophie's cracked lips. "Suck on these. The ice will make your mouth feel better." Sophie opened up like a bird, and Lila tilted the spoon. The woman's throat bobbed. Lila filled the spoon with chips a second time. Sophie's tongue flicked across her dry lips.

Hunter returned with the washcloth and a small glass of water. "Perfect," Lila said. "If she keeps the ice chips down, we'll give her a sip or two." She pushed up Sophie's sleeves and massaged her arms with the cool cloth. No visible needle tracks or bruises from a man's fists. *At least not so far.* Lila breathed easier.

Sophie narrowed her eyes, the same mahogany brown as Hunter's. "Why are you doing this?"

"Because you need a friend."

"Are you from some church? If you are, you can just leave. God gave up on me a long time ago."

"My name is Lila. I'm Hunter's friend."

Hunter held the glass of water to his mother's lips. Without coaxing, she swallowed.

"Thank you, son." She lifted a shaking hand to his cheek.

Lila stood, dropping the washcloth to the floor. "Time for Grandpa's special concoction." The loveseat dipped as Hunter lowered himself beside his mother. Sophie's uneasy gaze followed Lila's every move. She retrieved the hangover remedy from her backpack and filled the thermos cup.

"What is that? Something to drug me, so your father can send me away? He'd like to move on and get rid of the drunk wife and unfit mother."

Hunter gasped, while Lila hurried to answer. "This is something my grandpa recommends—for someone who's been—not feeling so good. It's safe. Smell."

Sophie tilted her head forward and sniffed. "Lemon," Sophie murmured. "I love that smell."

Score one for Lila. "Me too," she said. "This will make you feel better. Want to try a taste?"

Sophie's nod was hesitant.

"Mom, have you seen Dad today?" Hunter's voice was strained.

Sophie's brows knitted together. "I never see your father. Why would I want to?" A coy smile replaced the frown. "Sally brings me everything I need."

Hunter's neck and face blazed scarlet. He throat vibrated like he'd swallowed a bumble bee.

Lila's training kicked in. She held up her hands to stop the impending explosion. "Hey! Chill out. I don't know who Sally is, but you have to deal with her later."

"I'm not mad at Sally." Hunter folded his arms across his chest.

"Are you mad at me, Son?"

"No, Mom." He released a heavy sigh. "I'm not mad at you."

Well, he was sure mad at somebody, and this conversation was headed nowhere. Lila used a diversion tactic. "Can you make chicken noodle soup?"

Hunter stared, and then burst out laughing. "Are you serious?"

"Soup is good for the soul."

"Where is Sally? Is she sick today?" Sophie sent the conversation spiraling back to the danger zone.

"No Mom, Sally isn't sick!"

Hunter started to say more, but Lila made the zip your lip motion. "Go make the soup or—something."

He stomped from the room.

"I think I like you," Sophie said, the hint of a gleam in her eyes. "You take charge."

Lila smiled. "Want me to show you my secret?"

"I'll try a sip of that lemon drink first."

"See, you're already doing it. Am I good teacher, or *what?*" Lila flipped the ends of her hair smartly, but her mind scrambled to understand why Hunter was upset by the mention of Sally. Lila placed a cup of hangover remedy into Sophie's trembling hands.

After first breathing in the aroma, Hunter's mom took a healthy swallow. "Mmmm. Delicious." Sophie emptied the cup. Her ashen cheeks brightened.

I owe you one, Grandpa. Lila tipped the thermos and added a little more to Sophie's cup.

The tension in the room lightened as Sophie continued to sip the drink, but the unpleasant body odor lingered. Hunter's mother needed a bath in the worst way. Lila's gut tightened. She'd helped abused women bathe, women who were hurt or sick when Silas brought them to the warehouse, but this was different. A seventeen-year-old girl wasn't supposed to ask a potential boyfriend if she could give his mother a bath.

"Hunter does make delicious soup." Sophie said, confusion in her eyes. "But he doesn't usually get mad about it."

"Chicken noodle soup after a bath is always nice." Lila prayed for the power of suggestion to work its magic. And it did.

A few minutes later, Sophie was submerged up to her neck in citrus-scented bubbles. Lila bent over the frail woman, working shampoo into her hair. The bathroom was steamy, and Lila pulled her own shirt loose from her neck.

"How did you get that scar?" Sophie asked.

A black hole gaped wide inside Lila. She jerked her shirt back in place, glancing down to be sure the scar was hidden. Conflicting emotions filled her. Her surgery was a taboo subject. Being the focus of morbid fascination and unwarranted sympathy was not her thing. Yet she felt the urge to open up to this woman.

"I had a heart transplant," she said.

10

CHAPTER TEN

Sophie's eyes widened. Her short rapid breaths burst the bath-water bubbles by the dozens. "You had a—transplant!"

"Sorry," Lila said. "Didn't mean to shock you."

Water streaming from her arm, Sophie patted Lila's hand, searching her face. "You don't like to talk about it do you? I shouldn't have asked."

Lila shook her head. "It's okay." Her eyes misted over. "It's just that—no one understands—the guilt, and the responsibility to be deserving." She clapped a hand over her mouth. This conversation was not going in the right direction. Yet, for some reason, sharing with this woman released a pressure valve deep within her chest.

"It's alright," Sophie said. "Guilt is a terrible thing. I should know. I've let it ruin my life."

Finding the sleeve of her shirt, Lila wiped her eyes. "Life gets us mixed up sometimes. I'm glad to be alive, don't get me wrong. But—a person had to die—for me to live."

"Do you know your donor's family?"

Burying her fingers in Sophie's hair, Lila massaged the woman's scalp thinking how to answer. She felt strange, mouth dry. "I don't think I'm ready. Maybe when I'm older." She picked up a sophisticated, spa-type, shower nozzle. "Going to rinse now," she said, squeezing a lever. The warm water spurted from the nozzle in slow circles. Suds slid down Sophie's neck, and she rolled her shoulders in pleasure. Seconds of silence passed.

"I wrote once," Lila said. "Never heard back."

"That's too bad. I ached to reach out to Tricia's recipients, but Tyler wouldn't hear of it. Said she was gone, and we just needed let her go." She tried to laugh, but the sound was more the croak of a broken bird. "He didn't want me to embarrass him."

Tricia's recipients. Blood rushed to Lila's head. *Sophie's daughter had been a donor.* Groping for the right words, time and sound and light merged together. "Making that decision must've been hard."

"My husband hated the idea, but I insisted. I convinced him to do what Trisha would have wanted. She was beautiful and sweet with a heart as big as all outdoors." A tear escaped from the corner of Sophie's eye. "I couldn't let that goodness slip away." She raised a damp hand and touched Lila's cheek. "A recipient like you is what a donor family prays for. Someone to give a future."

"But wouldn't it be weird? I mean—if you met."

"Others tell me it can be awkward. Families are desperate to see a sign of their loved one in the recipient. A sign some part of them is still alive." Sophie's eyes narrowed. "Is that what you're worried about?"

"A little. I need this heart." Lila tapped her chest. "But I can't be two people."

The bubbles were mostly gone. "Out you come," Lila said, helping Sophie from the tub. She averted her eyes from the too thin body. Grabbing a white terry cloth robe from the back of the bathroom door, she guided Sophie's arms into the sleeves.

"I feel better," Sophie said, taking a few steps to lower herself to a dressing bench. "Thank you."

A tortuous lump formed in Lila's throat. "Can I ask a favor?"

Sophie nodded. "By all means."

"Don't tell Hunter about this." Lila patted the scar with two fingers.

"I won't say a word. I am honored you shared something so personal with me."

Lila turned to the linen closet, blinking rapidly. She pulled two plush towels from a shelf. The sound of clinking glass made her peer deeper inside. *Holy Moly! Sophie's stash.* For a person who didn't go out of the house, a plentiful stock of booze was at her fingertips. Lila stared at the bottles of Scotch. How many days would it take for Hunter's mom to drink that much. Sophie had a supplier. Sally? Her husband? Maybe he didn't care if she drank herself to death. A knock on the bathroom door interrupted her thoughts.

"The soup's almost ready," Hunter said. "Everything alright in there?"

"Your mom decided to take a bath. Now she needs a change of clothes. Will you find some soft leggings and a sweater of some kind? She'll need socks and underwear, too."

"Not pajamas?" Hunter sounded confused.

"No. Not pajamas!" She imagined him, leaning his head against the door. It wasn't every day that a girl asked a guy to bring them their mother's underwear.

"I'll see what I can find." Hunter muttered so low she barely understood the words.

Lila located the hair dryer, a brush, and styling gel. "We're going to make you beautiful." She worked the gel into Sophie's hair.

"I still don't understand why you are going to all this trouble."

"Stop it." Lila scolded. "You're Hunter's mother. He's my—friend. He was worried about you, and I never let my friends down. Besides, I live with my uncle and I never got a chance to do this with my mom." Her voice came out stronger than she felt.

"Hunter asked you to help me?" Sophie's eyebrows arched.

"Your son loves you. He doesn't want to lose you too."

"I'm back," Hunter called through the bathroom door. "I'll just—uh—leave Mom's clothes on the bed."

Lila flipped the hair dryer's switch. She turned under the ends of Sophie's hair, framing her face. The booze had not ruined the woman's skin, yet. Lila dug through a drawer, finding moisturizer and mascara. She applied a liberal amount of the lotion to Sophie's face then dragged the black brush loaded with mascara through Sophie's lashes. Luminous in her thin face, her brown eyes glowed.

"When was the last time you looked in the mirror?" Lila asked. She knew from working with guests of The House of Audrey, abused women didn't like their own reflections. It hurt too much. She assumed this was true even if part of the abuse was at the person's own hand.

"A long time ago." Sophie fixed her gaze on her hands.

"Sit tight." Lila hurried into the bedroom. Across the bed lay a pair of cream-colored leggings, a soft pink sweater, and mismatched bra and panties. Poor Hunter. He must have grabbed the first items in the drawer. A pair of moccasins rested atop the pile. Her stomach churned. A son shouldn't have to do this for his mother. She gathered the clothes and carried them into the bathroom.

A few minutes later, Sophie was dressed. She stood in front of the mirror.

"Who's that pretty lady?" Lila asked.

"I don't know. I haven't seen her in so long I don't recognize her." Sophie tilted her head, first one way and then the other. A ghost of a smile crossed her face.

Lila squeezed the woman's shoulder. "When was the last time you left this room?"

The smile faded. "The last time my husband dragged me into the hall and locked the door."

"He locked you out?" Lila recalled Hunter having to unlock the door. She glanced at the door. The inside knob was missing. If there had been a fire, Sophie would have been trapped.

"Back then, he didn't like me to stay in here with Tricia's things." There was a catch in Sophie's voice.

The sound hurt Lila's heart. "Sophie, when Hunter and I came up here, the bedroom was locked from the outside. Do you know who did that?"

Sophie sank to the dressing bench. A pathetic shrug ruffled her shoulders. "Tyler. He changed his mind about me staying in here. Said it was just what I deserved. I wasn't fit to be with others—especially Hunter." She hung her head.

Lila knelt at Sophie's feet and reached out. Sophie cowered, shielding her body with her arms. Bursts of panicked breathing snapped her chest up and down. Lila relaxed, remembering her training—no fast movements. "It's just me, Lila," she soothed. She was getting an image of Sophie's husband, and it wasn't one she liked. When Sophie's breathing slowed, Lila extended her hands palms up. After a moment, Hunter's mother rested her own in Lila's.

She voiced a hunch, "Does Hunter know his father hits you?"

Sophie blinked. "You're a smart girl." The woman fixed her

gaze on a spot across the room. "My husband wasn't always mean. Trisha's death changed him. I've tried to keep our son from knowing, and Tyler was an expert at how to hit where no one would see the bruises." Her eyes darkened. "Most of the time." She took a deep breath. "He put me in the hospital with broken ribs once and a fractured clavicle another time. I lied to Hunter about what happened." Sophie lifted her chin. "And it's hit past tense now. My husband doesn't care enough for even that."

"Is that when you started drinking? When he beat you?"

"I only drank a little at first. I needed something to get me through those rough days. Tyler handled his grief in another way. He said he couldn't do his work if he was sad all the time. He entertained. It was as though he'd forgotten Trisha had ever lived. I had to drink more to survive the happy people." She bit her lip. "He hit me when I couldn't keep up the front. He claimed I was no longer good for his career."

Lila rubbed Sophie's hands between her own. This wasn't the first time she'd heard a story like Sophie's. Hunter's father appeared to be a chameleon. Successful businessman to the public. Manipulating wife beater behind closed doors.

"Don't tell Hunter," Sophie said, her voice quivering. "I don't know what he might do."

Lila nodded, thinking how full of secrets her life was. "How about making Hunter happy by going downstairs and having a bowl of Hunter's chicken noodle soup. Can you make the trip?"

"If we take the elevator." Sophie slanted her eyes.

An elevator? Lila clapped her hands. "I like a woman who knows how to solve a problem. Lead the way." She placed a hand on Sophie's elbow. "I'll help you."

Sophie shook her head. "I can walk by myself."

59

A few minutes later the elevator door swooshed open to the sight of Hunter at the kitchen stove guiding a long-handled spoon around a steaming stainless-steel pot. The aroma of celery, parsley, and hints of garlic and sage made Lila's mouth water. She announced, "Look who decided to come downstairs."

11

CHAPTER ELEVEN

Silas radioed Hadley. "Chief and I are on our way to notify the deceased's family. Set up the war room. Start the review process with the team. You can bring me up to date when I return." The answering void of silence wasn't lost on Silas.

"You're with the chief?" Surprise, edging on shock, dripped from Hadley's voice.

"That's what I said. Do you have a problem taking care of those details?"

A cough and the sound of Hadley clearing his throat rattled through the speakers. "No problem." He said. "No problem at all."

Silas broke the connection. "Guess Hadley didn't expect the two of us to be in the same car unless I'm in handcuffs."

Elizabeth remained quiet.

Silas studied her profile. "I like the new haircut," he said. The short bob showed off her ears. He'd always liked her ears. A dainty snail shape, they clung close to her head. His blood warmed at the memory of pressing his lips to her ear lobe.

"Quit staring at my ears." Elizabeth's voice jarred him back to reality. She turned to glare at him. Guess she had her own memories.

"Keep your eyes on the road," he shot back. The SUV barreled down the freeway, zigging and zagging between cars. "Nice to see you still wear earrings." His skin burned hot enough to fry an egg. The diamond edged dragonflies were a Christmas gift from Silas. He had planned to ask Elizabeth to marry him the following June. By May, his niece needed a transplant. Burdening Liz with that responsibility was something Silas refused to consider. He had buried the needs of his own heart and focused on Lila's health.

"I've had them a long time," she said. "They were a gift."

"The person had exquisite taste," he said.

"Not like you. Can you wipe those spots off your tie before we get to JoAnn's house?"

Silas gritted his teeth. *Okay, she's asking for it.* "Sure, I can try, but it's coffee from this morning and catsup from yesterday. Might be chili from the day before that. May not come off very easy." He stuck out his tongue, lifted his tie and pretended to lick. He mocked her by imitating the sound of a dog lapping gravy.

Elizabeth jerked her head toward him, murder in her eyes. "If you want me to strangle you with that damn thing, just keep it up."

"Well I wouldn't want that." He loosened the offending item and pulled it over his head. One hand dove into his pocket. "I brought an extra just in case I ran into you. I really want to be as classy as the guy who gave you those dragonflies." He dangled his best tie in Elizabeth's line of vision then slipped it around his neck. As the car exited the freeway, turned east, and rolled to a stop at the intersection, he tied a perfect Windsor knot.

A dimple appeared in Elizabeth's cheek. At last a crack in her armor. Her lips trembled. A giggle escaped. She put a hand over her mouth, fighting for composure. The giggle turned into laughter, spilling between her fingers.

He smiled. "I've missed your laugh," he said.

She quieted. "I've missed you too, Silas, but I shouldn't be laughing. My best friend's daughter has been murdered, and I'm about to deliver the news that will break her heart." She drove through the intersection. "Do you have *anything* I can give her? Any of those *gut feels* you're famous for? Like why Savannah was selected?"

Silas sucked in a breath. "Elizabeth, you know we don't have much to go on. A ghost of a profile is taking shape. The killer studies his victims, learning their habits. They may know him, or at a minimum, trust him for some reason. My gut tells me, this killer is motivated by loss, guilt, or a sense of duty—and, he's counting. The notes and the scalpel are symbols. They may represent a mind-shattering event that ignited his mission."

She glanced at him with an odd expression in her eyes. "Most of that I can't share with JoAnn and David."

"The best way to help them, is by asking them to work with us. They know Savannah's contacts better than anyone. You know we can't do the questioning. We need to call in another team member. You and I are too close to the family. We'll be there for them but not in a professional capacity."

"Just call Woody."

Silas nodded, a little surprised at Elizabeth's informal use of the officer's first name. "Mendez took Hopkins with him to develop a timeline with the trash truck driver. Hopkins is a good man. I'll have Mendez hand off his assignment and meet us there. What's the address?"

Elizabeth rattled off the street and house number. "I don't want to arrive before Mendez, but I pray to God, we get there before the news media."

Silas had dispatch get Mendez on the radio. "Call me on my cell," he said.

A moment later he was relaying instructions. "Don't want any eavesdropping," he said to the young officer. "We're trying to beat the reporters."

"We haven't left VETERANS Park yet," Mendez replied. "I'll get my own car and meet you there in ten minutes."

"Shut down the lights and siren two blocks from the address I gave you."

"Yes sir."

Silas broke the connection.

"We're five minutes from JoAnn's house. If I drive slowly, we should arrive about the same time as Mendez," Elizabeth said.

"Do you ever drive slow?"

"Most of the time I don't get to drive at all. Being Chief isn't all it's cracked up to be. I hug a desk more than I like."

"Why did you take the job? I thought you were happy in St. Louis." After his decision to give up what they had, Elizabeth had relocated to St. Louis to accept the job of Assistant Police Chief. At the time Silas thought it was to advance her career. She hadn't shared her plans, but of course, he hadn't been available. Every moment of his time was consumed with the problems of Lila's failing heart.

Elizabeth gave him a sharp look. "This is home. Everyone I care about is here. The job came up, and I threw my hat in the ring. Kansas City needed a woman in a leading role in the police department. My timing was good."

Silas felt his heart thud against his rib cage. Elizabeth's parents were gone. Who did Elizabeth care about? It certainly wasn't him. She'd made his life difficult since she'd taken over as chief. She embarrassed him in front of the press, constantly checked on his team, and criticized his every move. Now she seemed to be reaching out to him. "I heard you had stiff competition. Don't fool yourself, being a woman was not a priority on the Mayor's list of qualifications."

"It's a good fit, but I do miss the action of the street."

"I'll call you sometime, and you can ride along." The car grew silent, not even the squawk of the radio to interrupt the invisible wall of ice sliding between them. Silas's gut twisted. He'd said the wrong thing.

Elizabeth guided the SUV around a corner. "JoAnn's house is up ahead, second on the right. I hope David's home. He's JoAnn's pillar. She'll need him." A rawness clung to her words.

Silas caught movement in the vehicles side mirror. A police cruiser swung in behind them. He turned to Elizabeth. "Mendez is here. Your timing is perfect." The attempt to restore their connection proved futile. Her face exemplified the police professional's emotionless mask. Their earlier feeling of closeness had been sucked out of the car like air from a punctured balloon.

The vehicle rolled to a stop in front of a neat two-story gray house. Cheerful burgundy shutters bordered the windows. The yard was freshly mowed. Silas had lost touch with the Petersons, but he remembered Savannah was their only child. He steeled himself for the destruction about to be delivered.

Silas and Elizabeth stepped from the car. Mendez joined them on the sidewalk. "The parents are JoAnn and David Peterson." Elizabeth stated. "Detective Albert and I are friends of the family. We will advise them of the situation. You will conduct the preliminary interview."

"No problem." The uniformed officer stepped aside to let them pass.

Side by side, Silas and Elizabeth strode up the drive toward the house. Mendez fell in behind. Tension rolled off their bodies in waves. An overwhelming urge to take Elizabeth by the elbow and give physical and emotional support swept over Silas. He thrust the feeling away. Respect of her position would help her more. They stepped onto the porch. A swing creaked in the breeze. A magazine lay on a pillow in the seat, as though the reader had been called away.

Elizabeth rang the doorbell. From somewhere inside, a dog barked. A moment later, a man peered through the glass side panel of the front door. David Peterson was home. A smile burst across David's face. He flung open the door.

"Liz, what a surprise!" Over his shoulder he called to his wife. "JoAnn come see who's here. You won't believe your eyes. It's Liz and Silas." Then his eyes registered the grim set to their jaws and lack of returned smiles. As David's gaze found Officer Mendez, his welcoming expression faltered.

"David. Can we come in?" Silas said. "We need to talk to you and JoAnn."

The man's knuckles whitened as he tightened his grip on the doorknob.

Silas understood. Fear of the unknown would make a man want to slam the door, board up the windows, and hide his family in the basement. Death was never easy, but murder left a different mark. One that tested the metal of a relationship and assaulted a human's mental equilibrium.

"What's wrong? What's happened?" David's voice rose an octave. "Is it JoAnn's mother?"

JoAnn peeked over David's shoulder. "What about Mother?" She squeezed her body between her husband and the door frame. "It's so good to see…" Her smile dissolved as fear skated across her face.

"JoAnn, we need to talk to you inside. Something has happened to Savannah." Elizabeth stepped close to her friend, attempting to place an arm around her shoulders.

JoAnn jerked away. Her legs pumped frantically, carrying her backward, past her husband, and deeper into the house. The open door forgotten in the moment's panic. David raced to his wife's side, capturing her reeling body in his arms.

Entering the Peterson's living room, Silas felt the weight of his job crushing his shoulders. Officer Mendez pulled the door shut, blocking the view of curious neighbors.

"There is no easy way to tell you this." Elizabeth gulped. "Savannah is dead."

"Nooo," JoAnn wailed. "Not Savannah. Not my baby."

David's face emptied of color, but he didn't release his wife. "Dead," he said as though he couldn't comprehend the word's meaning. "I talked to her last night. She was fine."

"JoAnn, David, please sit down." Silas used a gentle but firm tone. The couple stared at him with an expression that said, *how much worse can this get?* Silas knew the horror was just beginning. He wished he could spare them, but death showed sympathy for no one. Murder had even less compassion.

Wavering on his feet, David managed to guide his wife to the sofa. He gathered the hysterical woman against his side. *To protect, or be protected?* It was hard to tell. Great heaving sounds that only soul breaking grief can produce wracked the room.

"Tell us," David said.

"Savannah's body was found near the Memorial Fountain in Vietnam Veterans Park this morning about six-o'clock. We believe she was murdered." Silas delivered the news as humanely possible.

David's eyes bulged. JoAnn sobbed openly.

"Murdered!" David's voice held a hollow sound. "Who would do such a thing? Everyone loves her."

"Had she been..." Unable to speak the unspeakable, JoAnn shoved her fist into her mouth.

Elizabeth sat down on the other side of JoAnn. "There is no evidence of rape." She entwined her fingers with her friend's. "An examination will be done."

"When you're ready, the coroner will need one of you to make an identification," Silas stated. The words sounded cold and hard enough to shatter what was left of the Peterson's hearts.

David's chin quivered. "I'll do it." He appeared close to breaking down. "What in the world was she doing in the park? In the rain?"

"We hope to have answers soon." Silas pointed at Woody Mendez. "This is Officer Mendez. He will ask you a few questions."

Mendez stepped forward. Silas noted the officer's ashen color was gone. Now he carried a determined set to his jaw. Silas took the Mendez's place at the door.

"Mr. and Mrs. Peterson, I am very sorry for your loss." He spoke in a voice sincere and compassionate. He held out his smart phone. "I am required to record our interview. I will be asking questions to establish a timeline of your daughter's activities and identify her circle of contacts. May I have your permission to record?"

"Anything we can do to help," David replied. "And please call me David. My wife, JoAnn."

JoAnn dragged her fist from her mouth. "Of course," she whispered, blood oozing from teeth marks across her knuckles.

"Thank you," Mendez said. "Where did Savannah live? We need to send a team to check the residence."

David startled. His jaw tightened as though he was on the verge of telling them they couldn't invade his daughter's privacy.

"I'm sorry, sir," Mendez said. "Your daughter's home may provide critical evidence."

"I know, I know. I just can't think straight right now."

Mendez waited.

David straightened his shoulders and sat a bit taller, his arm still encircling his wife. "Savannah recently moved a couple of miles away in a rented house." He recited the address.

"I'll notify the team," Silas said. He edged deeper into the house. He glanced right and left, passing an office then a dining room. Pictures of Savannah hung from the walls and sat on various pieces of furniture. Nothing unusual caught his attention. The kitchen lay straight ahead and connected to the dining room. Silas brought up his contact list. A moment later he'd relayed Savannah's address to his team. A unit would be dispatched. "Secure the residence. Don't enter. I'll be there to walk through with you. Start your door to door. And, send one more unit here to help Mendez keep the press away from Mr. and Mrs. Peterson." He disconnected.

In the kitchen, Silas roamed the room, absorbing vibes, searching for one that didn't fit. The décor had changed since he and Elizabeth had been here last. He remembered a chicken theme. Now, there were owls everywhere. The effect was cheerful and warm. Normal.

He returned to the living room.

Mendez continued to question the heartbroken couple. "David, you mentioned talking to your daughter last night. What time was that?"

Silas listened, approving of the young officer's sensitive—yet thorough technique. He beckoned to Elizabeth.

"I'll be back in a minute," she whispered to JoAnn. It was doubtful the words even registered.

Outside on the porch, Silas admired the fluffy white clouds free of rain floating overhead. He savored the smell of the world bursting to life after hiding beneath the weight of winter. If only for a moment, the harsh realities of his job faded into the background.

Elizabeth joined him, her diamond earrings no longer showing. He guessed she'd pocketed the troublesome reminder of another time. Silas brought her up to date. "Take the SUV," she said. "I'll stay here with JoAnn until her sister arrives. I just called her while you were talking to your team."

Turning toward the street, he sensed Elizabeth stiffen. A Channel Nine News van spun around the corner and skidded to a stop across the driveway. "The least they could do is keep the drive open," Elizabeth said in disgust.

"We need to go inside." Silas placed a hand in the middle of Elizabeth's back. "We have to tell David and JoAnn, their daughter died at the hands of a serial killer. We can't let them hear that on the news." As he spoke, a patrol car stopped in front of the van. The officer bailed from his vehicle.

A camera man slung his camera over his shoulder and followed the female reporter already running toward the house.

"Stop right there," the officer commanded. "You are on private property. I have orders to keep this area clear."

"Chief Cartwright," the reporter shouted. "Chief Cartwright, is it true the mother of the victim is your best friend?" Skin taut, eyes hungry, lips a slash of red, Silas expected this blood sucker to bare her teeth at any moment. What do you have to say to our community about the serial killer on the loose?"

Anger vibrated through the fabric of Elizabeth's tailored jacket.

"Damn vultures. Why can't they show some respect?" She turned and stomped into the house. Silas followed.

"What is all that yelling?" JoAnn twisted toward the front windows.

Mendez blocked the view. Silas liked the way the officer thought. Protect the innocent but uphold the law.

"There is a reporter from Channel Nine outside," Silas said. "There will be more here shortly. We have posted an officer to keep them away from you."

David glanced from Silas to the window, and then to Elizabeth. "Why would we need protection? The reporters are just doing their jobs. I might even ask the public for their help. Maybe someone saw something."

"Silas, what haven't you told us?" JoAnn slid to the edge of her seat. Fragile control dragged her lips into a frozen slash. The next bomb dropped would likely shatter even that.

He sensed Elizabeth wanted him to explain, but years had passed since he'd interpreted her feelings. Out of respect for her position he waited for a signal. Her chin dipped his direction in a barely noticeable nod.

"There are reporters outside," Silas said. "We believe this will become a highly sensationalized story." He hesitated, but there was nothing to be gained by delaying the truth. "We are certain Savannah's death was at the hands of a serial killer."

He might have said Martians were on the front porch. David gasped, and JoAnn's mouth flapped like a fish gasping for air.

"The killer left a note and a significant piece of evidence with your daughter's body," Silas continued. "Savannah is the second victim with the same signature."

"A serial killer," JoAnn moaned. "Dear God, help us." She hugged herself, her fingers cutting into the soft flesh of her forearms. The weight of this new knowledge so unbearably heavy, she hunched her shoulders. "I must know, Silas," she said. "Was she tortured? What did this son-of-a-bitch do to my daughter?"

"Her body showed no signs of... abuse." He stopped short, avoiding the danger of divulging facts about the case. "I'm sorry, but until the medical examiner completes her examination, I can't say anything more."

"We understand," David said.

"If you have a key to Savannah's house, I'll need that."

"Of course." David stood, pulled a key ring from his pocket. He removed a single key and handed it to Silas.

"Take the SUV. I'll stay with Jo Ann." Elizabeth put her arm around her friend.

Silas headed for the door.

"Silas. I need a word." David struggled to his feet. "Outside."

Through the window Silas could see three news vans, but the reporters waited by the curb. He motioned for David to follow.

On the back porch, David looked him in the eye. "Do I need to worry about keeping JoAnn safe? Are we in danger?"

"I can't give you a good answer. You will have police protection until we know more." He flexed his prosthetic fist. "We will catch this guy."

12

CHAPTER TWELVE

Hunter twisted toward them. "Mom! Is that you?" His eyes widened. "Wow! You look nice." He hurried to his mother and guided her to a place at the table.

Lila turned off the stove's burner, smiling at the suspicious empty cans sitting on the counter. She should have known. Hunter wouldn't make soup from scratch. She filled the three bowls he'd set out with steaming chicken noodle soup. She considered Sophie's alcohol tortured stomach and restricted her serving. She set a bowl in front of Sophie and one in front of Hunter.

Sophie inhaled deeply. "I think I'm actually hungry," she said, picking up a spoon.

A mile-wide grin spread across Hunter's face. Lila felt a bit giddy herself. She grabbed the third bowl and sat down. Hunter watched his mother take a few bites. His eyes sparkled. Lila took a second to appreciate the affection she saw there.

"Are you afraid of my cooking?" Hunter's eyes danced, challenging Lila to take a bite.

"Of course not," Lila said, digging in. "This is wonderful." She smiled mischievously across the table at Hunter. "Will you share your recipe? My uncle would love this." She glanced at Sophie, realizing the woman didn't know her family. She hesitated, having already shared more than she intended.

But for some reason she trusted this woman to not feel sorry for her. "I live with my uncle," she said. "My dad's not part of my life." She swallowed hard. "My mother was sick for a long time with cancer. Uncle Silas moved us in with him when Mom needed special care." She held Sophie's gaze. "When my mother died, I stayed with Silas."

Sophie stared at Lila for a long moment. "Your uncle is a special person."

"I know. Besides being a police detective..."

"Silas Albert," Sophie interrupted, her fine eyebrows arching high on her forehead. "Your uncle is Detective Silas Albert?"

"Chief Detective," Lila corrected. She tasted another spoonful of soup.

"I met him once, years ago. He gave my husband a black eye."

Lila's intake of breath sucked bits of chicken into her windpipe. She coughed and slapped a napkin over her mouth to keep from spewing noodles across the table. Sputtering, she gulped a slug of water. Hunter raced around the table and proceeded to pound her on the back. "Stop," she gasped, knowing she looked like the biggest idiot west of the Mississippi. "And don't you dare give me the Heimlich." The weak threat sent her into another fit of coughing.

"Your face is so red." He gave her a worried look.

"Can you breathe?" Sophie asked.

Lila bobbed her head. Several swallows of water later, she was able to speak. "Sorry," she said, wiping tears from her eyes. "Silas gave your husband a black eye. Why?"

"Tyler has an eye for beautiful women. And Elizabeth

Cartwright took pleasure in making her date, your uncle, jealous. She made fools of both men in front of the mayor and a room full of city officials."

Lila imagined how the incident must have hurt Sophie. But her description made Elizabeth seem mean and Silas a hothead. Nothing like the two people Lila knew. "Did your husband hit Silas back?"

"I'll bet he didn't." Hunter returned to his seat across from Lila. "Surgeons never do anything that would damage their precious hands."

"It doesn't matter now," Sophie said. "Before I interrupted, you were about to tell us more about your family. And, we can't let this wonderful soup go to waste." As though to prove her point, she lifted a spoon filled with noodles to her mouth. A drop of broth spotted the table's top, but no one wiped it away.

Uncertain now if she should continue, Lila stirred her soup. She felt the need to replace the image of a man in a jealous rage with one more familiar. "Silas is a caring person," she said, finally. "He started a shelter. He helps abused women get a fresh start."

Sophie swallowed. "What made him do that?"

"A promise," Lila said. She shared the story of the warehouse and the blackbird with the broken wing. "We call our guests Blackbirds."

"You help your uncle." Sophie stated. "That's why you knew exactly how to make me feel better."

Lila chose her words carefully. "Yes, I guess I do. We work mostly with women who fear for their lives and, having a safe place to recover is a big thing. I try to make them feel comfortable. My grandparents us too. My grandmother is a self-defense instructor. When a Blackbird is healed on the outside, Grams helps restore her self-confidence and heal on the inside. We don't teach violence, but we teach each woman to protect herself. That is, if she chooses. Most of these women are now dedicated to helping others."

Sophie shifted, sat up straighter. "That is different from any shelter I've ever heard of." Her brown eyes brightened. "Those women are very lucky to have found a place like that." Spoons clinked against bowls in the comfortable silence.

"I can't remember the last time you ate that much." Hunter picked up the empty dishes and put them in the dishwasher. "Must be the company." He smiled at Lila. Her heart warmed.

"I need to get home," she said. She reached across the table and took Sophie's hand. "You look ready for a nap."

"I am sleepy. But I wish you could stay. I enjoyed your company."

"If you want, I'll visit you again tomorrow." Lila glanced at Hunter. "That is, if Hunter doesn't mind."

"Sure," Hunter said, smiling from ear to ear.

"I've got to get my bag. I'll be right back." Lila raced up the stairs, gathered her backpack, hurried into the bathroom, grabbed two towels, wrapped and loaded the three bottles of scotch inside.

Back in the kitchen, she hugged Sophie's thin shoulders. "I'll see you tomorrow. Can I count on you to meet me here?" The motion of her hand encircled the room. "In the kitchen, at 9:00?"

Sophie glanced from Hunter to Lila, a battle of emotions marched across her face. She bit her lip. In the end, her chin raised a defiant inch. "I'll be here."

Lila's heart swelled. There was a chance for Sophie. Especially since she didn't have any booze, at least not now. *She hoped.* She turned toward the front door.

"Hunter, where are your manners? Walk your friend to her

car."

A red blush crept up Hunter's neck. "I'll be right back, Mom."

Lila paused in the living room for a last view of the marble fireplace. Hunter stopped beside her. Outside, a car door slammed.

Hunter rushed to the window. "Dad." He spit the word into the air. Fisting his hands, he bolted for the door.

"Wait! Hunter what's wrong?"

He jerked the door open and charged outside.

Lila raced after him. Her training made her hit record on her phone. A silver Mercedes was parked next to Lila's Studebaker. The car looked familiar, but she couldn't say why. A tall man dressed in a designer suit, tailored to fit an athletic body, strode toward the house. He slung his arms wide and hard as he walked. From her Google search, Lila recognized Hunter's father.

Hunter met his father at the bottom of the steps. "It's the middle of the day, did you finally decide to unlock the door and check on Mom? It's been two days since you fired Sally for bringing Mom booze."

Dr. Morgan's eyes widened. "How did you know that?"

"Don't act so surprised. Sally sent me a text while I was in New York. Our housekeeper cares more about Mom than you do," Hunter shouted. "You knew I was gone. Did you even check on her once? Or did you hope she would die?"

Lila's brain clicked. Sally was the housekeeper and the supplier of the scotch. Now, Hunter's earlier anger made sense.

"Don't use that tone with me, boy. Why aren't you in school?" A skimpy inch separated the chests of the two men. "I know who that car belongs to. What is Lila Girard doing here?"

A chill touched her spine. How did Dr. Morgan know who she was? She stepped from beneath the shade of the porch. "I'm visiting your wife. She's not feeling well. Hope you don't mind."

Hunter's father stared daggers at Lila. His voice was cold steel when he said, "I do mind."

He shifted his attention back to his son. "How many times do I have to tell you? We keep family problems private. Your mother needs my—our—protection."

"You're only trying to protect your precious image." Hunter jabbed his father in the chest with his forefinger. "At least she doesn't hide her obsession, like you do. And I don't mean your work. You think I don't know what you keep in that room on the third floor. You're pitiful."

"Shut up." The sound of a flat-handed face slap cracked the air.

Hunter's head snapped sideways. A roar of rage burst from deep in his chest. He shoved his father and drew back his fist. The doctor dodged to the side. He avoided Hunter's blow but stumbled and fell backward into a flower bed. Hunter dove after him.

Seeing only flailing arms and legs, Lila plunged down the steps. She circled the two men like a referee in a boxing ring. "Stop it," she shouted. Hunter was astride his father, punching him in the face. A stream of cuss words colored the air blue.

Then she heard the sound. An unmistakable click. She whirled. Sophie stood on the top step of the porch a Colt 45 gripped in her trembling hands.

"Sophie. No!"

The weakened woman wove her way down the steps. A drunken sailor's path would have been straighter. "I will not let him hurt Hunter."

Lila laid a hand on Sophie's arm. With remarkable strength, the older woman shoved Lila away and stumbled toward the flowerbed. Sophie's husband rolled on top of his son, pressing an arm across the boy's throat. Hunter bucked and clawed at his father's face, gasping for breath.

Sophie pressed the metal bore of the gun against her husband's temple. "Get off my son. Bastard. Now!"

"You don't have the nerve to pull that trigger." The man smirked.

"No. But I can do this!" She pulled her arm back and slammed the gun into the side of her husband's head.

The smirk changed to shock, blood gushed, and Hunter's father dropped like an anchor.

Surprise spread across Sophie's face. Her arm dropped to her side, and the gun clattered to the ground. She turned to Lila with an uncertain smile. "Blackbirds have choices. I chose to protect my son." Her voice faded to a whisper, her knees buckled, and she crumpled to the ground.

Lila ran for the gun, scooped it from the pavement, and tossed it into a nearby bush. She clicked on her phone's connection to Big Bertha. "Bertha, send the closest Blackbird with medical experience to this address. Urgent." She reeled off the Morgan's street and number.

"ER Nurse, arriving in five minutes." The sound of Bertha's voice normally calmed Lila. But five minutes was a long time. Her gaze shot between Sophie and her husband. He lay still across his son's chest. Sophie wasn't moving either.

With a mighty grunt, Hunter rolled his father's body to the side and crawled from the flower bed, coughing and rubbing his throat. Dirt and leaves clung to his clothes and hair. Blood splattered his Def Leopard tee-shirt. His eyes seethed as he stared at his unconscious father. "I hope he's dead," he panted.

"No, you don't." Lila shrugged out of her backpack and ran to peer at the man sprawled in last year's mulch. She checked his pulse. Steady.

Hunter knelt at his mother's side.

"Go open the gate," Lila said. "Help's coming. I called a Blackbird."

He stared at her. "You called a what?"

"I told you about The Blackbirds. Some have special skills. The one coming is a nurse." Lila bit her tongue. She didn't want to give away, too much. "Your father may have a concussion. She can get him to a hospital—discreetly."

Hunter smoothed the hair away from his mother's face. "It would be just like him to have Mom charged with attempted murder."

"Let him try!" Lila's voice was firm. "My friend is the police chief, and my uncle's in charge of the homicide unit." She cringed inwardly at the idea of explaining this situation to Silas. She'd be kissing her Studebaker goodbye for sure. Or maybe not. She was, after all, doing what he'd taught.

Hunter struggled to his feet and hurried into the house. Shortly, he returned, holding two short lengths of cotton rope. "The gate's open. Now I'm tying the jerk up." He trailed his fingers down his throat. "I thought I was a goner."

Sophie moaned and opened her eyes. Lila helped her to a sitting position. Wide-eyed, the woman took in her husband's legs dangling over the edge of the flower bed. "Did I kill him?"

"No. But he's sure going to have a whopping headache. A nurse is on the way to check him out."

"Ohhh, he won't like that." Sophie struggled to her feet, wobbling left, then right, as though buffeted by a stiff wind.

Lila steadied her with a hand under her elbow. Sophie shook Lila off.

"He hates negative publicity," Sophie muttered. "And he gets very angry when another person gains the upper hand." She backed toward the house. "Where's my gun?"

A Jeep Cherokee turned in the drive. Good. It was Amy who bailed from the vehicle already dressed in nurse's scrubs and carrying a medical kit. "Hello Lila," she said. "Got some excitement going on here, I see." She hurried to the man in the flower bed, checked his pulse, and peeled back his eyelids. With a small flashlight she examined his pupils. "Possible concussion," she said. "Anybody else need checked out?" Her eyes rested momentarily on the red mark on Hunter's throat. She scanned their faces, pausing for a long moment to study Sophie. "I'm guessing he made the first move and anybody who defended themselves felt they were in danger of losing their lives." When there was no answer, she added. "Lila?

Lila nodded.

"I want him to go to jail," Hunter said.

"Hospital first, then we'll see. I'll take him there for his protection, and yours. Help me load him in the Jeep. Those are good knots. They should hold him." The nurse spun to Sophie. "I will see he gets an overnight stay at the hospital. Use this time to file a restraining order. Change the codes on the alarm systems and the driveway gate. Consider changing the door locks as well. He's going to be upset when he wakes up." She flung instructions as though there was little doubt the unconscious man in the flower bed was dangerous.

Lila wanted to hug the nurse. There would be a lot of explaining to do once Big Bertha updated Silas, but Sophie and Hunter would be safe.

"I—I don't know how to file a restraining order." Sophie said.

"A lawyer does," the nurse said.

"And this is video proof your lives are in danger." Lila held up her smart phone.

13

CHAPTER THIRTEEN

Silas left David Peterson standing on the back porch. As he rounded the corner of the house, the reporters jumped into action, their camera crews swarming behind them.

"Detective, is Savannah Peterson the latest victim of The Surgeon?" A woman shouted.

Waiting had made them wolfish and Silas was their tasty morsel. He angled across the driveway.

"Do you have a profile for the killer?"

"You have a reputation for solving a crime by getting in the killer's mind. Our audience thinks that's creepy. How do you respond to that opinion?"

The questions bounced off Silas like rubber bullets. They didn't make him bleed, but they sure as hell made him burn. He knew better than to give even one reporter satisfaction. His face would be on the news, but no statement. That was Elizabeth's job. He only had to get to the SUV. Another reporter headed in for the kill. The officer posted at the end of the drive blocked his path.

Silas took the opportunity and scrambled into the SUV.

"Is David Peterson a suspect?"

The SUV's door slammed on the last question. Silas fought

the urge to jump out and punch the reporter in the mouth. Why couldn't they show a little respect? This family had just received the worst news of their lives. He adjusted the seat, started the engine, and pulled away from the curb. He wanted more than anything to give the reporters the finger. But in his heart, Silas knew David and JoAnn were both suspects. Neither he nor Elizabeth could protect their friends from the process of the law. For the couple's sake, he hoped his team cleared them quickly.

The sun's glare on the windshield had warmed the interior of the car. Silas switched the air conditioner on low. The fan stirred a hint of Elizabeth's perfume. He breathed deeply, holding the smell of her close.

As Silas pulled away from the curb, a dark green truck passed through the intersection ahead. For a second, he thought the Ford F150 belonged to his dad. He shook his head. Couldn't be. His dad didn't go out much since the loss of his daughter. The last time Silas was aware of Clifford Albert venturing this far from The House of Audrey was when Silas took him to the Chiefs football game last October. Silas sighed. He needed to make more of an effort to get his dad active.

Five minutes later Silas arrived at the address David Peterson had provided. Three squad cars hugged the curb. A crime lab van idled in the drive. David had described Savannah's car as a dark blue, 2011 Toyota Corolla. The car was not parked in the drive.

Two uniformed officers moved door to door, notebooks in hand. Neighbors were huddled in their yards in small groups. Some hugged each other. Others wrapped their arms around themselves. The news was spreading—a murderer was on the loose. Tonight, doors would be locked, and shades drawn. Some might sleep with a gun under their pillow. Silas didn't blame them.

Stepping from the SUV, he approached the cheerful yellow bungalow built on a concrete slab. Pansies dipped their purple heads from white pots sitting on a small concrete stoop. He recognized the two technicians dressed in department issued crime scene bunny suits and fashionably accessorized with bodycams. "Be sure those cameras are on when we enter the house," he said. "That's the best protection a cop has against a smart defense attorney."

They nodded, handing him his own bunny suit. He tugged it on. "This may or may not be a murder scene. I'm glad to see no one wants to make a mistake." He pulled on booties, a head cap, and slid his right hand inside a glove.

"Before you arrived, we lifted prints from the exterior doors." A technician spoke.

"Good. I don't expect to find anyone inside, but I'll clear the house as a precaution." Silas pulled his weapon and then tested the doorknob with his prosthesis. If this was where Savannah was killed, someone had locked up afterward. Using David Peterson's key, he unlocked the door. The two technicians tracked his movements with their body cams. Rustling like a collection of Walmart bags, the group proceeded into the house.

In the living room, textbooks lay on the sofa. A light-weight jacket was flung across the arm of a chair. The tiny kitchen held a small drop-leaf table and two chairs. No dishes in the sink. No take-out cartons on the counter. On the floor, bowls marked *Cat's Food*, and *Cat's Water* held a small quantity of each. Splotches of red stained the floor. "We've got blood." Silas pointed. "Watch your step." The click of evidence markers being placed on the tile floor followed him across the room.

Silas opened a door. The garage was on the other side, empty. Inside the bunny suit, the temperature climbed. Moisture dampened his armpits. "Clear," he said. "Note. The victim's car, a blue Toyota Corolla, is not in the driveway or the garage."

Next, a tiny bathroom held only a shower, a toilet, and a small vanity. A towel hung across the open door. He fingered the terry cloth fabric. Dry. No stains. His pulse thumped. First bedroom, unfurnished, but held a pet bed and a litter box. No fresh droppings. No cat.

The technicians waited in the hallway as he entered the last bedroom. He took a deep breath, freeing his senses to absorb the briefest of scents, notice the smallest object out of place, or recognize a clue beyond the obvious. The room appeared neat. Decorated in a light-hearted tropical theme, odd-shaped containers held shells, starfish, and muted pieces of broken sea glass. Whimsical watercolors of the ocean at sunset and of beaches dotted with bright umbrellas hung on the walls. Did the brush strokes belong to Savannah?

Scattered across the top of the dresser were a dozen colors of nail polish, sunglasses, and more hair ties than he cared to count. Photos of a smiling Savannah with friends and family were scattered about the room. No picture identified a significant other. One side of the bed appeared in disarray. Silas's chest constricted.

According to Sydney Franco, estimated time of death was 4:00 in the morning. The body had been located by the driver at 6:00 a.m., leaving roughly two hours to move it to the parking lot and tie it to the back of a trash truck. The one whose first stop was Vietnam Veterans Park. All happening before the driver started his routes. Not much time, and little room for errors.

Turning slowly, Silas recorded. He panned his smart phone across the walls, the ceiling, and the floor. One obscure item could solve the most complex crime. He moved to the bed. Leaning over the rumpled sheets he checked for blood and other body fluids. A faint scent grabbed him, taking him back to his high school biology labs, then dragged him forward to the coroner's words. *Chloroform. No muss, no fuss.* He bent at the waist and scanned the floor under the bed.

"We've found the crime scene," he called to the technicians. "Notify the officers to put up the tape." He pointed to a small white wad of cloth. "That's the murder weapon."

One technician entered the room. The other hurried toward the front of the house. Silas continued to move around the room, careful to not touch any surface. There were no wounds on Savannah Peterson's body. Whose blood was in the kitchen?

He retraced his steps.

In the corner by the garage door, he spotted a small stainless-steel trash can. A dribble of brown marred the shiny exterior. The moment stretched, cracking the air. He crossed the room and using the tip of an ink pen, pried at the lid. The cover gapped the width of a paper napkin. Crouching, he poked harder. The lid flew open.

He dodged backward, fighting for balance. His artificial hand found the wall. He steadied, shined the light from his phone into the can, and peered inside. The unmoving glassy- eyed stare sent a shudder through Silas's chest. Blood smeared the inside of the container. He leaned closer. The same red darkened the gray cat's fur.

"Shit!" Bile boiled in Silas's throat. Resting on its back, four bloody stumps remained where paws should have been. Savannah's cat had used up its ninth life. Silas hoped the hint of Chloroform coming from the can meant the cat hadn't suffered.

Silas located one of the technicians. "You'll find a cat in the trash can in the kitchen. It's not a pretty sight. Someone removed its paws. I don't think they are in the can, but don't disturb the contents. Send everything to the lab. Our killer is a cat hater, that's for sure."

The technician paled. "Seriously? My little girl has a cat."

"You don't have to look inside. I took a video."

"Don't worry, I can handle it. But you know, sometimes I just want to be a parking meter attendant."

"I understand," Silas said. "You know what to do?" The man nodded, and Silas returned to the front door. He exited the house, glad to see an officer posted on the concrete stoop. Silas strode on to the SUV. Removing his bunny suit, glove, and hat, he opened the door and tossed the bundle into the backseat. Inside, he called in the APB for Savannah's Toyota then checked his messages. A Blackbird flapped across his screen. His skin tingled. Bertha had sent two messages. The first fifteen minutes ago. The second ten minutes later. He tapped the first.

"Blackbird requested by Lila," the computer announced. Bertha continued, identifying the location and the time of arrival.

Silas stiffened in the seat. Lila should be with her tutor. Why would she be needing a Blackbird, especially a nurse? And he didn't recognize the location. He scrolled to the second message.

"Blackbird transferring injured male to St. Luke's Hospital. Possible concussion. Does not need assistance."

A breath escaped Silas's lungs. Lila wasn't hurt. "Bertha, identify the injured party."

"Injured party is Dr. Tyler Morgan."

The name stirred an ugly memory. A party held by the Mayor, the society couple with the husband who paid too much attention to another woman. Specifically, Liz. Caught up in the man's charisma, Liz had flirted back. A jealous Silas had told the guy to back off. A look had passed between the two offenders, and then

Liz had laughed. Silas had wiped the smug look off the man's face with his fist. He recalled arguing with Liz and later apologizing. Liz had never explained what had been so funny, and Dr. Morgan had never pressed charges.

"Bertha, who is the owner of the property?"

Seconds passed. "Property owners are Dr. Tyler and Sophie Morgan, husband and wife."

"Are there other members of the household?" Another second.

"A son. Hunter Morgan, eighteen years of age."

Silas gripped the wheel. Lila hadn't asked for his help. She was a fully trained Blackbird. However reckless she might be, she knew how to take care of herself. He swallowed hard. A bit more reassurance wouldn't hurt. She was still only seventeen.

"Bertha, does Hunter Morgan or Sophie Morgan have a police record?" Time dragged.

"Hunter Morgan has several speeding tickets. Arrested in 2016 for street racing. Charges dropped. Sophie Morgan has no police record."

Silas ran his finger around the inside of his shirt collar. What would his sister do with Lila? A heaviness filled his chest. His sister wasn't here. He started the SUV. April's cool weather had disappeared inside the vehicle. He blasted the air conditioner. Lila had some explaining to do. But she deserved an opportunity to have her say.

"Thank you, Bertha." He broke the connection. First, he'd ask Liz's opinion about how to handle Lila. On second thought, that was not a good idea. He and Liz were barely talking, and Savannah's parents needed Liz more.

Sydney—Lila trusted Sydney.

14

CHAPTER FOURTEEN

Silas pulled away from the curb. Grouped like students at a bus stop, the neighbors whispered behind their hands, staring, and not quite turning away. No one wanted to bring attention to themselves. He studied their postures. Who was talking? Who was standing apart? Was there a person who didn't fit?

He made a right at the corner. A Channel Four news van waited in the opposite intersection. The victim's next of kin had been notified, Savannah's name and address common knowledge by now. The reporters were on the trail. There was some satisfaction in knowing the uniformed men and women behind him would give them nothing.

A nagging thought crept into his mind. Personal agendas in homicide cracked the department's wall of trust. The leaked evidence to the reporters was the first tremor. The department had a spy, or the killer wanted to see the police squirm. If this guy enjoyed his self-assigned task, more news coverage meant greater gratification.

Silas passed cars parked along the shaded street, where children played, and mothers pushed strollers. This block's residents had no idea what had happened around the corner. He called

Hadley.

A moment later, the detective's voice entered the SUV, "Hadley here."

"Anything I need to know?"

"Are you with the Chief?"

Silas's defenses jumped to attention. "What difference does that make?"

"I've had a heart attack."

"Funny."

"No, not funny. The fact that you were in the same car with Elizabeth Cartwright almost sent me to the emergency room."

"Too bad it didn't kill you. Now, tell me something good."

"We have an identification of the first victim. Name's Abbey Bryant."

A jolt of energy slid under Silas's skin. "How did we make that happen?"

"Sydney Franco matched a missing person's photo to the victim's morgue-shot. Husband identified the body. Said she didn't come home from a walk. Claims he didn't think much of it at the time. They'd had an argument. He thought she'd spent the night with a girlfriend. According to him, she'd done that before."

A red streak pierced the corner of Silas's vision. Sunlight splintered from chrome. He swerved and stomped the brakes. Tires squealed. A flash of blue, a bump. The SUV came to a stop slightly sideways in the street. "Shit!"

"Did you hit something?" Hadley shouted. "Are you alright?"

"I'll call you back." He flipped on his emergency lights and hurled himself from the vehicle. Heart in his throat, he raced to the front of the car. The upended tricycle lay inches from the front of the vehicle, wheels spinning. A blue cape hung from the seat. He spun left, then right, scanning the pavement for a tiny body.

A man sprinted between the parked cars. A moment later, he hoisted a screaming boy aloft like a trophy. Air shot from Silas's lungs. The boy waved chubby arms, pointing to the street.

By some miracle, the tricycle was undamaged. Silas picked up the three-wheeled toy and carried it to the little boy. "Hey buddy," he said. "Did this get away from you?"

A worried brown-eyed gaze landed on the tricycle. The boy nodded, fisting his eyes.

Silas turned to the man. "Are you his father?"

"Yes."

"You want to explain how this got in the street." He gestured to the trike. "And your kid almost with it." Silas's voice was sharp. The fear of what had almost happened, justified his tone.

"Oh crap, that was a close one," the man said. "He got the tricycle today for his birthday. Before I knew what happened, he rode the darn thing right off the curb. Lucky, he fell off, and didn't roll into the street."

"Scared me spitless." Silas scraped a palm across his forehead. "Some would say the Lord was with us today."

"Amen."

"Tansfomah." The little boy pointed.

"No, son. Your transformers are inside."

Blond curls swung side to side as the boy shook his head. "Tansfomah. Tansfomah hand." The boy wiggled in his father's arms, pointing at Silas's left hand.

The man's eyes narrowed. His focus switched to Silas's left side. Silas prepared for the common signs of revulsion, for the man to correct his son. "Want to touch my super-hand?" Silas asked the little guy. The boy tucked his face into his father's neck.

"I know you," the man said. "Detective Silas Albert isn't it?" The man stuck out his hand. "I'm James Torey. I'm a big fan."

Silas shook the man's hand. "You're my one and only, unless you count my mother."

"You might be surprised," James chuckled. "You've got backbone, Mister. When Fox 4 news interviewed you about your mechanical hand, I was hooked. It was great how City Hall wanted to put you behind a desk, but you fought those suckers."

"I did my best," Silas replied.

"Tansfomah, like Daddy," The little boy interrupted in a sing-song voice.

"That's right, son." James grinned at Silas. "Lost mine in Afghanistan." He pulled up a pant leg, showing a state-of-the-art prosthesis. "The government made me a good soldier. It's a damn shame I've got to prove I still am."

James bore a granite-like jut to his jaw. Silas sensed a determination to break those military barriers into dust. "Keep fighting," Silas said. "You'll be glad you did."

"Come this far, not quittin' now, but what are you doing in the neighborhood? Aren't you in Homicide now?"

Silas glanced at the little boy. His attention was glued to Silas's mechanical hand. "I am afraid there's been one around the corner."

"Damn!" The man's lips parted as he dragged in a sharp breath.

"Daddy say bad word!" The little boy shook his finger. "Momma say no, no!"

"And Momma's right." The father ruffled his son's hair. "I'll do better."

"The victim is Savannah Peterson." Silas said. "You know her?"

James studied Silas for a second. "I'm guessin' you know a

little about PTSD. Might even have trouble sleeping yourself."

Where was James going with this strange response? Silas did understand PTSD. His own nightmares made sleep a cherished commodity. He decided to see where the conversation led. "I do," he said.

"I used to sleep like a baby, until the Army put me in Special Ops. Now, I'm in hyper-vigilant mode twenty-four seven. When I can't sleep, I walk the neighborhood and try to focus my brain. Ask me where some kid riding his skateboard lives, I can tell you. Ask me who's fussn' and fight'n, I might know that too. But names..." James shrugged his shoulders. "Savannah Peterson doesn't ring a bell. A picture would help."

"The victim drove a dark blue 2011 Toyota Corolla."

"Now you're speakin' my language." He cocked his head. "I do remember the car. Now let's see." He pursed his lips "Missouri X0Z P9L. The girl lived in the yellow bungalow in the middle of the block, next street over?"

Silas's heart thumped. "How can you be sure?"

"Need to keep the mind sharp—for when I get back to my guys. I memorize stuff."

"Do you remember seeing any strange cars or other unusual activity in the area recently?"

"Hmmm." James shifted his son to the other arm. "A week or so ago, some guy was cruising the neighborhood in a high-end, silver Mercedes. He passed by once; I admired the car. Second time figured he was lost. Third time, special ops kicked in."

"What'd you do?"

"Went on recon."

"And?"

"He parked on the block where your Savannah Peterson lives—I mean, lived." James looked at the ground for an instant, then continued. "I circled the block twice. Took a ten-minute break each round, about twenty yards behind the Mercedes. Never saw him get out of the car."

James Torey was a prosecuting attorney's dream come true. "Could you identify him?"

"I think so." James grinned. "And...." He paused for effect.

Silas raised an eyebrow. "You memorized his license plate too?"

"Missouri..." As if by magic, the combination of letters and figures rolled right off the man's tongue.

"I want to hug you," Silas said, "but it doesn't fit my tough detective reputation." A silver Mercedes and a license number? Maybe the near accident was meant to bring him to James Torey. "What about other traffic at the yellow bungalow?"

"Not much. An older green truck has been travelling the neighborhood. Never seen it parked though and the license plate was bent over."

A nerve pinged in Silas's brain. "Did it have a big dent in the door?

"Not that I noticed. Why?"

Silas released a breath of relief. Crazy to think the truck might have been his dad's. James Torey would have zeroed in on a dent the size of a watermelon. "Someone else mentioned seeing a truck like that. How about boyfriends. Did you see any at Savannah's house?"

No boyfriend that I could tell. A couple came and went. Thought they were the girl's parents." James described the couple. "The three seemed close." His eyes settled on his son. "I'm sorry for them."

"Me too." Silas said. He handed James a card. "Thanks for the information. Another officer will be by to get a more detailed report and show you a photo of Savannah. Getting that plate number is a big help."

James glanced at the department issued SUV and back at Silas. He seemed about to say more.

"Was there something else?"

The man hesitated, then shook his head. "Sorry."

Silas pointed to the card. "Call me if you think of anything else."

"Will do."

"You're setting a fine example for your son." Silas said. "Good luck with the government." He extended his good right hand to the little boy.

"Nope!" The boy's blond curls shook. "Shake tansfomah hand."

Silas's heart strings plunked. "Gimme five," he said.

The boy grinned and slapped the artificial hand.

15

CHAPTER FIFTEEN

Back at the SUV, Silas surveyed the front of the vehicle. Not a scratch. At least Elizabeth wouldn't have that reason to chew on his backside. He climbed inside the SUV and switched off the red lights.

He tapped the handsfree calling icon. "Call Hadley."

"Hadley here."

"I'm back," he said, explaining the recent tense moments.

"Close call," Hadley replied. "I was about to send back-up."

"Some days, the good Lord carries a person in the palm of his hand. The little boy's father did give me a lead." Silas told Hadley about James Torrey's mental exercises. "The license number will help, but I got the feeling he's holding something back."

"What do you think? Scared to get involved or covering for someone?"

"More like unsure. He doesn't want to make a mistake. I'll have another visit with him. Let's get back to the missing person report. What took so long?"

"The Northeast precinct has a victim, or three, every night. Personnel over there is stretched tight. Unfortunately, they didn't get the picture filed until a couple of days ago. Sydney

Franco matched it right away."

"Damn budget cuts!"

"Agreed."

"What did the Bryants argue about?"

"Money."

"Any children?"

"One little girl together, three years old. Each had a ten-year-old boy from previous relationships. The husband is pretty torn up. Seems genuine, but you never know."

Silas's chest pinched. More children without their mother. He remembered how hard it had been for Lila after Audrey' death. Cancer, the invisible killer had crept into their lives uninvited, much like this killer had done to the Bryants and the Petersons. Hiding in the dark until it was too late for a person to survive the attack. He shook his head. He couldn't cure cancer. The only relief he could offer these families from the killer was to find him. "Anything from the war room yet?"

"Having the first victim's name gives us something to sink our teeth into. No connections so far. Finding the owner of the Mercedes will give us our first big break." A breath of silence. "Will you be coming back with the Chief, or do I need to come and get you?"

"The Petersons need to identify the body. We'll see who Elizabeth wants to take them to the morgue."

"Elizabeth is it?" Hadley mocked him. "You haven't called her anything but Chief since she came back from St. Louis."

"She asked for my help."

"Riiiight. Elizabeth Cartwright hasn't needed anyone's help since she started in the Police Academy. She may want to bury the hatchet. Be careful she doesn't bury it in your chest."

"She's entitled."

"Oh yeah, you told me. You told her to get lost, because you didn't want to burden her with Lila's illness. In case I haven't told you this *already*, that was a heartless thing to do."

"You've reminded me a dozen times." He sighed, all too aware of what he'd done in the interest of protecting Liz. "Thanks for the psychiatric counselling session, Dr. Hadley. Now, can we get back to the case?"

"If you insist." Hadley snickered. "Let's see, where to begin? The Bryants live in that low-income complex on the north side. A team interviewed a neighbor who claims a lot of yelling often came from the couple's apartment."

Silas knew the area. A rough part of the city, poverty a silent predator to those who lived there. "Wives rarely press charges. Alibi?"

"Larry Bryant works the midnight shift at the Water Department. When his wife didn't come home, he called his mother to stay with the kids and went to work. According to the team, he arrived on time and didn't leave work until 7:00 AM. The coroner's estimated time of death is 4:00 AM."

"Similar to Savannah Peterson."

"True, but that and a dollar will get you a taco, not a suspect."

"It's the little things, my friend. You know as well as I do, it's about putting together all the little things. Team find anything at the trash company parking lot?"

"A big hole in the fence. We can't be sure when the hole was cut. The security cameras don't scan to that depth, and the trucks back into the slots. The routes are assigned by seniority. The trucks are numbered and parked in the matching numbered slot every day. It would be easy for an interested party to figure out what truck went where. Anything new on your end?"

"We found Savannah's cat." Silas described the sick scene.

"Damn, serials pick the strangest trophies."

"I have to take the SUV back to Elizabeth. Find out if the Bryants have a missing cat." Despite the serious nature of the request, Silas smirked. Hadley hated cats. "It may be nothing," he said. "But I'd like to know. A sick mind clings to symbolism. We need to find out what The Surgeon is hung up on."

"The lowly depths to which I have sunk. While you sit in the lovely presence of Elizabeth Cartwright, I have cat detail."

"I keep telling you, solving crime is in the details." Silas broke the connection.

He turned onto the Petersons' street. Two news vans remained. Mothers had swept their children into their homes and hidden them behind closed doors. Curtains fluttered, nudged aside by nervous residents.

A Chevy Tahoe he didn't recognize was parked in the Peterson's drive. He hoped it was JoAnn's sister. He remembered they were close. But his years in homicide told him no one could make this day easier. He held up his badge to the two officers blocking the drive. They tipped their caps and stepped aside. He parked behind the Tahoe.

Mendez met him on the front porch. "The Petersons provided a list of contacts, but not one person to focus on," he said. "I'll be knocking on doors and making calls the rest of the afternoon."

Silas shared what he'd found at Savannah Peterson's house.

Mendez paled. "The son of a bitch killed the cat too." The muscle in his jaw knotted. "They mentioned a tabby Savannah had adopted." He jerked his head toward the house. "These folks are torn up. I'll be putting in extra hours, Sir."

Silas gripped the young officer's shoulder. "I appreciate that. If you come up with anything or need to bounce an idea off me, call."

Mendez jogged down the drive and Silas entered the Peterson house. The living room was empty. "Hello."

"We're in the kitchen, Silas." Elizabeth answered.

Emotions in a bear trap of control, he joined Elizabeth and Savannah's parents. Another woman Silas recognized as the department's grief counselor spoke softly into her cell phone.

The rich aroma of coffee greeted him. A normal setting. Sandwiches rested on white plates trimmed in pink flowers. The mouse-like nibbles breaking the edges of the bread's crust destroyed the affect. The sight of JoAnn blindly hacking hunks from an angel food cake shattered it completely. Eyelids swollen to narrow slits; she could have passed for the loser in a prize fight.

David was no better. He stared blankly at the opposite wall. Surviving the trip to the Medical Examiner's office without collapsing, seemed doubtful.

Elizabeth placed a cup of coffee in his hands. Their fingers touched. She froze...turned away. That touch, that look, and those earlier moments in the car showed she had feelings. And damn it, he was going to thaw them out. For a second the face of Sydney Franco, the woman who welcomed his attentions, flashed through his brain.

He shook his head. What was he thinking? He was over Liz Cartwright.

16

CHAPTER SIXTEEN

Lila hesitated as the Jeep Cherokee drove away. "I should go," she said. "If you have any trouble getting the restraining order, call me. My uncle can help."

"Thank you," Sophie said. She glanced at Hunter, her lower lip trembling.

"It's okay, Mom," Hunter said. "We'll do what it takes to be safe." He moved close to his mother, putting his arm around her shoulders. "I'm proud of you."

Sophie's brown eyes widened. "You are?"

"You're here when I need you."

A smile brightened Sophie's face. "Do you know where my cell phone is? Your dad took it from me."

Hunter blinked. "We'll find it later. Use mine to call a lawyer." He dug the device from his pocket and handed it to his mother. "Let's get started." He took her by the elbow and guided her up the stairs.

"Did you say your father fired Sally?" Sophie asked.

"Yes."

"I'm calling her first. She needs this job."

"We need to talk about that, Mom."

Lila scanned the bushes for the gun. Her eye caught the sun's reflection off the barrel. She dropped to her hands and knees. Pebbles poked through her jeans, and branches scratched her arms. The handle was cool to her touch as she plucked the gun from the ground. She rocked back on her heels and ejected the magazine. She stared, laughing a little. The gun couldn't fire. There were no bullets.

Lila tucked the gun into her backpack. One more item and the zipper wouldn't close. She hefted the load, a ton heavier than when she arrived. At the rear of the Studebaker, she popped the trunk, and placed the bag inside. Bertha would have notified Silas when Lila's requested Blackbird flew. She didn't want her uncle to worry. She rolled up his contact icon.

"Hi," she typed. "You already know I requested a Blackbird today. Everyone is safe. Will explain at first opportunity. Hope you solved the case. Can't wait to hear the details. Love you." She pressed send.

Lila leaned against the car, staring at the brick mansion. A cool breeze spun across her skin. Dr. Morgan might be a famous surgeon, but he wasn't a nice person. Had the loss of his daughter hardened his heart, driving a wedge between him and his grieving wife? Five years wasn't long, and no click of a stopwatch could make the pain stop. Lila's mother had been gone nine years, and Lila still missed her every day.

She slammed the car's trunk lid shut, climbed inside her Studebaker, and started the engine. The vibration warmed her blood. She drove through the Morgan's open gate. The car's rearview mirror showed the gate closing behind her. Hunter's father would be in for a surprise the next time he used his remote control.

Lila's thoughts were jumbled. She needed to drive. Cruising

down the street, she kept well under the speed limit. It wasn't enough. She needed speed to clear her head. Ten minutes later she reached the outskirts of town, shifted gears, and punched the Studebaker. Sixty, seventy, eighty, ninety. The car sped by pastures dotted with cattle. Focused on the car's control, the tension in her shoulders eased.

At one hundred, she backed off. The handbook for life highly discouraged swerving at high speeds. She continued through the countryside. As the powerful engine purred, Lila's thoughts returned to the loss of her mother. Back then, Grandma Nancy had tried to prepare her. But Elizabeth Cartwright had shown her the path to face her fears and live beyond her grief.

A slightly weird feeling stirred in Lila's chest at the memory of her mother's last days.

* * *

"Your mother is going to a better place," Grandma had said. "A place where she will not hurt anymore."

"Stop saying that," Lila shouted, clamping her hands over her ears. "Momma will get better. Lisa's mom had her boobie cut off too. She loved Lisa too much to leave her. Momma loves me, too."

Lila clung to her hope. But in the back of her mind she saw her friend Tommy sitting at his school desk, sobbing. His daddy had gone to Heaven. Lila didn't know what to do about the thing that tore her insides to shreds and left a black hole bubbling over with fear.

She refused to go to school and avoided the room her mother occupied. The awful cancer might get Lila, too. By not looking, her mother would always be there, waiting to brush Lila's hair or read her favorite book.

One day, Grandma found her boxing up her favorite dolls and teddy bears. "Baby, what are you doing?"

"I don't like them anymore." Lila replied. But the truth was, she was afraid they'd get sick, too.

Grandma squinted her eyes like she did when she didn't want to cry. Her chest pumped up and down real fast. "Not even Smelley Elley?"

Lila smiled at the memory of Smelley Elley. The doll had earned the nickname when Lila, as a toddler, doused her in her mother's favorite perfume. Smelley Elley occupied a privileged spot on Lila's dresser.

But that day, Lila shook her head. "I'm too old for dolls and silly bears."

Grandma watched her shove the last box into the closet, then gathered Lila in her arms and rocked her to sleep. Each day Lila secretly checked those boxes to be sure her favorite toys hadn't grown thin or lost their hair.

A lady from the hospital also talked to Lila about her mother going to a better place. Lila blocked her words. She'd heard it all before. How could a place be better for Momma without Lila? Unless Momma didn't love her after all. Unless Momma wanted to forget about Lila, the way her father had forgotten.

One day, Uncle Silas's girlfriend, Liz, took her to the park. The sun was warm. Squirrels chattered and chased one another up and down the trees. Liz and Lila sat on a bench throwing bread to the ducks. It had been fun to watch them stretch their necks and waddle back and forth.

"Your mother misses you," Liz said. "She understands that you're frightened." Liz put an arm around Lila. "You know, you can't get the cancer from your mother."

The words caught Lila off guard. She looked at her shoes, the red high-tops she'd wanted so badly. Grandma had said no, but Momma had Silas buy them. Her mother always understood. But if she went to that other place, who would understand Lila then? She bit her lip. Who would know how scared she was?

"How do you know?" Lila asked, through teary lashes.

"Your mother told me."

"Did she ask you to tell me?"

"Yes."

"Do you believe her?"

"Yes."

Lila's throat went dry when she asked Liz the next question. "Why doesn't Momma love me enough to stay here?"

Liz dropped to her knees in front of Lila, sadness in her blue eyes. "Lila," she'd said. "Do you believe your mother is in pain?"

The memories of those awful noises coming from her mother's room late at night made it difficult for Lila to breathe. Not exactly crying, but a chilling moan that brought Silas or Granny to Momma's bedside, while Lila sat outside the door hugging her knees.

She squeezed her eyes tight, answering Liz's question with a nod.

"My momma had to go away when I was about your age," Liz said. "She loved me very much. Like your mother loves you. My daddy wouldn't let me be with her. He didn't think it was good for me." Liz took Lila's hands in her own, squeezing them tight. "I would give anything if I could have spent a few minutes making her feel better. I never got to say goodbye. I never let her know how much I loved her." Lila would never forget the intensity in Liz's eyes. "Be brave. Don't miss the chance to show your mother how much you love her."

Lila nodded and hugged Liz's neck, and they cried together for a few minutes.

That night, Lila crept into her mother's bed. "Momma," she said, "I'll always love you. Even when you go to that other place. Can we still make memories for you to take with you?"

Her mother pulled her close, caressing her hair. "I love you too, baby. Of course we can still make memories." Tears leaked down the pale sunken cheeks. Lila brushed them away.

"Happy memories, Momma. Only happy memories."

Lila unboxed her dolls and teddy bears and carried them to her mother's room. She placed Smelly Elley in the crook of her mother's arm. The smile that the perfume tainted doll brought to her mother's face was Lila's to treasure. She read to her mother every day, colored with her, sang to her, cuddled under the covers, and created memories for both of them. When her mother was feeling good, she shared stories about her family history and funny tricks she'd played on Silas when they were kids.

One day, Lila asked about her own father. "I don't know who he is," her mother said. She turned her face toward the wall, but not before Lila saw something else—something frightening to an eight-year-old.

Lila lay her head on her mother's chest. "Don't be afraid, Momma. I don't want to talk about him anyway. I'll read you a story."

As the days passed, they both tried hard not to cry. Most of the time they succeeded.

* * *

Lila guided the Studebaker in a sharp U-turn to head back to the city. Liz had helped Silas and her grandparents understand that

Lila was coping with her mother's illness in her own way. She missed the beautiful, intelligent woman who had been so in love with her uncle.

And for the first time in ten years, Lila wanted to know about her father.

17

CHAPTER SEVENTEEN

Margaret Culver leaned back in Charlie's old recliner. Tommy, the cat, formed a big 'C' as he snuggled in her lap. Her gnarled fingers absently stroked his soft fur. Abbey Bryant was dead, and guilt burned in Margaret's heart. She should've warned her friend, called the police, or done something. But she'd been selfish, afraid Abbey wouldn't visit her at night anymore. And night was when Margaret needed her most. Abbey kept the voice in Margaret's head quiet. The way her granddaughter had, until she married a man just like Charlie. "At least I did the right thing for my granddaughter, didn't I Tommy?"

The cat flicked an ear.

"That woman from the hotline told me she was in a safe place now. My call saved her life."

She should have done the same for Abbey the first time evil followed her friend. But Margaret had blamed the incident on an old woman's imagination. The second occurrence frightened her, but still she had done nothing. Then she found the black ski mask. Solid proof her mind was not playing tricks.

The mask lay on the floor mocking her. She'd meant to call the police about Abbey. Like she should have rescued her granddaughter the first time the telltale bruises appeared. Margaret had a bad habit of waiting until it was too late. A lonely tear slipped into a deep crevice in her face. Now she was alone—again.

Alone, alone, alone. Charlie's taunts rang in her head. *No friends to help you.*

"Shut up," Margaret shouted to the empty room. "You don't live here anymore."

Tommy crouched, prepared to jump from her lap to safety. She soothed him with an age- spotted hand. After a moment the cat resumed his comfortable curl. Margaret raised the receiver of the old black desk set. Closing her eyes, she searched her murky memory for the officer's name.

"Tommy? What was that nice policeman's name?"

The cat blinked. "Didn't he say to call if I needed help?" Margaret shook her head. "No. That's not right. He said to call if I remembered anything." Tommy opened his mouth, showing his pink tongue and white teeth. Margaret bent closer. The cat's whiskers tickled her cheeks.

"Silas, you say? Oh dear, Tommy, how could I have forgotten Silas Albert? He needs to know about the man who followed Abbey. The man dressed in black." She stiffened. No, no, no. Silas Albert belonged in a different memory. One from years ago.

Then who had knocked at her door today? Or was it yesterday? Mendy, Monday, Mendez. Yes! Mendez. She needed to call Officer Mendez. She patted her sweater pocket. The card the policeman had placed in her hand was there. She traced the small rectangle with her index finger. What if she got her stories mixed up—again? What if she confused the devil who followed Abbey with the one from Margaret's own past? Her foggy brain couldn't be trusted. She was eighty-seven. No one would listen to an old woman. Abbey might have, but Margaret hadn't given her a chance. Guilt was a heavy burden, and for a moment the old woman's breathing was labored. How would she ever face the Bryant children?

Margaret longed to move to her porch swing and make-believe Abbey was there with her, sharing problems and hopes amid the sounds of the night. Officer Mendez had warned her to stay inside, but if the killer was coming back, he would have by now. She gathered her courage. She'd darn well go out if she wanted. Margaret's head ached. She hadn't used her brain this much since Charlie had gone.

Tommy jumped to the floor, arched his back, and stretched. He batted the ski mask across the floor, and then strolled to the door. "Meow." He looked over his shoulder. "Meow."

"I guess you need to go out." Margaret lurched from the recliner. She opened the backdoor. The cat disappeared into the night. April's evening breeze carried a chill, and the old woman tugged her sweater closer. A bad smell drifted through the night air. She wrinkled her nose. "Poison must've worked," she muttered.

From a shelf near the door, she fumbled for the black flashlight and a key on a leather shoestring. She hobbled toward the house's detached garage, the yellow beam parting the darkness. Her old bones ached, but she forced herself forward. She didn't need a neighbor investigating the smell. A dead rat or two she could handle.

She raised the light exposing the lock. The door hung half-open. *I know I locked it. I don't want anyone in here.*

Hesitating at the opening, she played the light across the floor, walls, and ceiling. Gardening tools and tomato stakes hung from one wall. A wheelbarrow loaded with flowerpots, a length of water hose, and a sack of mulch leaned drunkenly against a post. A rickety picnic table sat opposite the overhead door. Same as the last time she'd been out here. Nothing had changed—except the smell.

The yellow beam exposed a neatly folded pile of clothing. A gasp froze in her throat. She shuffled forward eyes fixed on the white picnic table. One step followed another. Her slipper caught. She stumbled. The flashlight spilled from her hand. Darkness thick as velvet soup filled the building. Stink rose from the ground in waves.

She dropped to her knees, scraping the ground with her fingers. First left, then right, finally her knuckles bumped the rubber casing. Her hand found the grip and—something soft—like fur. She recoiled but managed to come away with the light. She frantically flicked the switch. A light ray jittered then steadied. She struggled to stand. "Please God," she said. "Let my imagination be playing tricks." She played the beam across the picnic table and her heart crumbled. The pale blue windbreaker, red sneakers with candy cane laces, blue jeans, and a red tee-shirt was the last thing she'd seen Abbey Bryant wear.

Margaret's arms fell slack. She bowed her head low, chin against her chest. "Forgive me, dear friend," she prayed. Then her gaze found what had caused her to stumble. The Bryants' cat lay dead at her feet.

"Oh no!" The significance of what she'd found struck Margaret with the force of a sledgehammer. The dirt floor tilted. Poor Abbey murdered right here in the garage.

Had the killer used the cat as a decoy, dragged Abbey in here, murdered her, and Lord only knows what else? Perhaps the cat fought to escape. She hoped there were claw marks an inch deep on the man's face. Abbey had died fifteen yards from Margaret's front porch where she'd waited night after night, thinking her friend was angry. A sob built in Margaret's throat. If only she'd told Abbey someone was following her.

Margaret pressed a cool hand to her sweating forehead. "Stupid old woman," she muttered. "You've faced worse than this. Just like before. Live with what you've done. Those children's hearts are broken. You can't possibly tell them their cat was murdered, too."

She shuffled to the door and pushed it shut. The windows had been boarded over years earlier. No need to attract the attention of a curious neighbor. She returned to the picnic table. A shiny object caught Margaret's eye. Must belong to Abbey. She picked up the item and dropped it into her sweater pocket. She'd keep this one memento of her friend. Quickly scanning the ground under the table, she breathed easier. The old dirt there was undisturbed.

"Too late to protect their mother." Margaret removed a shovel from the garden tools hanging on the wall and drove it into the dirt floor of the garage. "No one will ever know what happened here."

18

CHAPTER EIGHTEEN

The grief counselor cleared her throat. "The medical examiner is waiting for us. As I mentioned earlier, I will be with you during the entire identification process. My goal is to make this as gentle as possible."

From three feet away, Silas heard David exhale. The grieving father raised himself from the chair. Nothing about him resembled the man who had been happy to greet Elizabeth and Silas at the door such a short time ago.

JoAnn embraced her husband. "We will both come," she said, biting her swollen lower lip. The couple leaned into each other. For now, they weren't throwing blame at each other. Even nice people lost their grip at a time like this.

The counselor waited. No doubt, analyzing the couple's stability amidst a hurricane of emotions. "When we get there, you take as much time as you need," she said. "Nothing will be done until you are ready."

David managed a weak nod. "We'll be ready," he said.

Silas knew they would never be ready. No one ever was.

"My Tahoe is parked right outside. I will drive you there and bring you back." The grief counselor's shoulder angled in such a way as to include Elizabeth. "I know the Chief is a close friend. Would you like her to come with you?"

"Would you?" JoAnn didn't mask the plea for her friend's support.

"Of course."

No one glanced his way, and Silas backed through the door guilty relief washing over him. "I'll move the SUV. Lila can give me a ride. That way your vehicle will be available when you're ready to leave."

"She isn't in school?" Liz frowned her disapproval.

"Not today." He escaped into the living room tapping his phone a few times to send a voice to text message to Lila. His niece's whereabouts was none of Liz's business. "Hey Sweetie, in a bit of a bind. Can you pick me up at this address?" He recited the Peterson's street and number. After a few brief words, he clicked off.

Through the front window, he saw the reporters engaged in interviews a half-dozen houses down the block. "Liz?" He whirled to call out a second time. Her name died on his lips. She was there, close enough to touch, wearing a wistful expression that sent a shiver through his body. Had she been about to reach out to him? Was she about to...

Seconds passed. His mind reeled, memories stirred—satiny skin, silky hair, scintillating smell. He held his breath fighting his reaction. He spun to the window scrambling for words and actions to cover his thoughts. "If JoAnn and David load from this side of the Tahoe, they'll be hidden before the wolves catch the scent." He pointed toward the street.

Liz's gaze followed his gesture. "I'll take it from here, Silas." The cool and in control police professional had returned.

"Sure," he said, keeping his face neutral.

Moments later, the two officers blocking the drive stepped aside. The grief counselor drove away, Liz sitting tall in the passenger seat, while JoAnn huddled in a rear corner of the back seat, supporting David's head against her shoulder.

Silas approached the uniformed cops. He squinted in the bright sunshine. "My niece, Lila Girard will be here to pick me up in a few minutes," he said. "She's driving a 1953 Studebaker. Let her through."

"Yes sir," one cop replied. "Is she blonde, about seventeen, and likes to drive fast?"

"Why? You give her a ticket?" Silas held the officer's gaze.

"No. I stopped someone...else—as a precaution."

"Precaution? I don't understand."

The officer shifted from one foot to the other. "Sergeant told everyone on our shift that Chief wanted those street races shut down. Word is, your niece likes to race. Her car is easy to spot, so I had been following her. Thought she might lead me to the racing site." He glanced at his fellow officer as if for support. The cop strolled to the other side of the drive, making it clear he wanted no part of poking a hornet's nest. "I personally don't think it's a bad thing. Kids block off the street and let off some steam. It's better than doing drugs in the basement of someone's house. But it is against the law."

Silas hid his impatience waiting for the young officer got to the point.

"As I followed her, I noticed I wasn't the only car staying on her tail. Every time your niece made a turn, another car did the same. This went on for a mile or more. Too far to be a coincidence and the neighborhood wasn't right for a quality car with a white male in the driver's seat."

A band of steel tightened around Silas's chest. "What did you do?"

"I pulled him over. A regular wise guy, too. Turned out to be a doctor. Threatened me with all kinds of nonsense. I told him I was giving him a routine warning, because he'd made an improper lane change. He calmed right down. I checked him out," the officer continued. "Doesn't have a record, but the incident didn't sit right with me."

"When did this happen?"

"Two weeks ago. I remember, because it was the same day the woman's body was found in Loose Park. Asked what he was doing out. Gave me a weird answer. Said he liked to take photographs at night. Had a fancy high-powered camera on the seat beside him too."

Silas swallowed. "Do you think he was interested in the car, or my niece?"

"He actually mentioned he'd been following a sharp old Studebaker, trying to get a photo. I told him he'd better be careful. A person might think he was a stalker. The good doctor's face turned three shades of pale. Light as his silver Mercedes. His name was..."

"Dr. Tyler Morgan." Silas spoke the name before the officer could finish.

19

CHAPTER NINETEEN

The Studebaker glided around the corner and pulled to a stop in front of the Peterson house where Silas waited. Lila waved. Silas gathered his mental list of questions, stomped to the car, and climbed inside. A long conversation lay ahead.

"Hi," she said. "What's up with the guards on the driveway?"

"Do you remember Savannah Peterson?"

"Vaguely."

"She was the victim found in the park this morning. Her parents live here. The department is providing security."

"From the media, or the killer?"

"Too soon to say for sure. Right now, both. We're not taking any chances for a day or two. You hungry?" Silas wasn't, but public places encouraged his self-control.

She shot him a raised eyebrow look. "I had a bit of chicken noodle soup earlier, but I could eat. Burger Nest okay?"

He nodded. The restaurant was a dive, but it had booths where they could talk and eat mouth-watering, artery-clogging food. He studied Lila's profile as she backed from the drive. No bruises, but he could see her arms were scratched, and her jeans had dirt on the knees. He glanced into the rear seat.

"Where's your backpack?" he said.

"In the trunk. Not a good idea to have a gun and three bottles of scotch under the front seat." She turned a corner as calmly as if she'd announced she had a dozen eggs in the rear of the car.

A throbbing pulse slammed his temple. He imagined his blood pressure reaching stroke level. He reined in his temper, refusing to succumb to her challenge. "Strange cargo for an underage girl who is on the radar of every cop in town."

"I didn't want it in the hands of the wrong person."

"And who is the wrong person?"

"Could be one of three. Dr. Tyler Morgan, his wife Sophie, or Hunter."

Silas held up his hand. "I need to call Hadley."

"Has something else happened?"

"You'll understand in a second," Silas replied. In a moment Hadley's voice entered the Studebaker via Silas's phone.

"Yes, Boss."

"Hadley, we need to find Dr. Tyler Morgan. He should be at St. Luke's hospital. He's a patient. Get to him and make sure he doesn't disappear. If he's conscious, question him about his whereabouts at the time of the murders. Ask him why the young women he follows taking pictures of at night end up dead?" Silas shared more of the young officer's claims. Beside Silas, Lila drew a sharp breath.

"Dr. Tyler Morgan, the surgeon?" Hadley said. "I know that sorry SOB, he's the one that operated on my brother." Hadley's tone turned chilly. "I'll be glad to ask him a few questions."

Silas remembered his friend's brother had died when a low-risk surgery went terribly wrong. Silas was surprised that Dr. Morgan was the operating surgeon. The procedure had taken place in Denver. "Are you going to be all right doing this? Don't let *personal* screw this up."

"I'll take Mendez with me. He knows the case, so he can do the questioning. If Morgan is our guy, I'm the last person who wants him blowing in the breeze on a technicality. Dare I ask why the doctor is in a hospital?"

A layer of tension faded from Silas's shoulders. "I'm getting to the bottom of that in a few minutes. I'll let you know what I find out. Keep yourself parked at his bedside. I'll call you back. If Morgan tries to check himself out, haul him in as a person of interest in the murders."

"Shit! That's big." Hadley's voice cracked in his surprise. "Didn't see that coming."

"I hope to have more information before his lawyer can intervene."

"Are you with the Chief?"

Silas grimaced. "Why all this concern about whether I'm with her or not?"

"Don't be so testy. I was only going to ask how Leader Liz was handling the situation with her friend. Geeze, a person would think you were hiding something."

"The grief counselor took the family to the ME's office. JoAnn Peterson asked Liz to go along." Silas bit his tongue as soon as that single incriminating word slipped out.

"There it is. Liz again. Sounds like the ice between you and the Chief is thawing. Good luck, Buddy. You need someone. Just don't end up losing two good women."

Silas felt Lila's stare. "That, my friend, is none of your business."

"Maybe not, but someone has to give you advice. You're dangerous on your own. By the way, I checked with the first victim's family. They did have a cat and it's missing. I'm betting we find what's left of that cat, and we find the murder scene."

"After two weeks, that's not likely."

"Maybe not, but these cats smell like a connection. Anyway, the husband says his wife thought someone was following her. And some guy asked to take her picture. Drove a fancy car and she told her husband she thought it was a Mercedes. Sound familiar?"

An electric current sizzled through Silas's blood. He breathed deep through his nose and glanced over at Lila. Her eyes were on the road ahead, but the tension in her body said she'd missed nothing. "One step at a time. If Morgan has an alibi, this theory all goes up in smoke. Be careful. Let me know if he gives us anything."

"Will do. Keep an eye on my favorite girl." Hadley disconnected.

"Why? Am I a target?" Lila's gray eyes met his. Steady, no fear.

"That's the million-dollar question. The doctor claimed he wanted to take a picture of your Studebaker. Now he's connected to the first victim for a similar reason." Saying the words aloud changed the sizzle of his blood to an icy chill.

"What are we...."

Silas held up his hand again. "We'll talk about everything at the diner."

Lila tapped her fingers against the steering wheel, her jaw tightening. He'd seen the indicators from her before. His niece wanted to get her teeth into the case and use her skills as a Blackbird.

But this was different—personal. This time her life might be at stake. The thumb and forefinger of his right hand worried the crease in his pants. He almost hoped the doctor had an alibi. Taking pictures wasn't a crime, and more importantly, Lila wouldn't be some psycho's target.

The Burger Nest sign flashed a block ahead. Silas glanced out the window, the scenery a blur. The situation was tricky. In his bones, he felt the killer wanted to be caught, but not until he finished his list of misguided tasks. Then there was his timeline - if he even had one. Dr. Morgan had the right qualifications for The Surgeon moniker and was the man under Silas's investigative microscope, but what about hard evidence? At this point, he didn't even have enough to get a warrant to search the doctor's house. But he did have The Blackbirds. And if he decided to use their skills to stop a serial killer, he was pretty sure his FBI allies would approve.

Silas stepped from the Studebaker in The Burger Nest parking lot. He silently thanked his grandpa for giving him The House of Audrey, and for his own ability to find those who gave it heart.

Opening the door to the diner set off a jangle of bells, as he let Lila enter first. Smells of coffee, grilled hamburger, and greasy French fries struck him in the nose like manna from heaven. Silas nodded to a wino he'd given a few bucks, an attorney he'd bailed out of jail, and a white-haired lady who had been his third-grade teacher. "Somewhere in the back," he said to the hostess.

"Hope none of your enemies cause a problem today," she replied in a conspirator's whisper. "The boss is in a bad mood."

"You know I try to avoid trouble," he whispered back. "I just can't control who holds a grudge."

She led them to a booth near the kitchen's swinging doors. He slid across the seat, having to raise himself over a duct-taped repair in the cushion. Lila plopped onto the opposite bench.

A thick waisted waitress appeared, apron rustling, pen and pad poised. She took their usual orders for cheeseburgers with the works, fries, and chocolate shakes, and disappeared behind the swinging doors.

"I see you changed your tie."

"It was that or be hung by the other one."

"Chief wants her man...I mean her men, looking sharp." Lila grinned.

"Don't think you're going to sidetrack me. How do you know the Morgans? Why did you need a Blackbird, and why do you have three bottles of scotch and a gun in your trunk?"

The grin evaporated from Lila's face. She clasped her hands, intertwining her fingers as tight as a woven basket. "I told you about Hunter, remember?"

Silas didn't. "Refresh my memory."

"His Mustang is the one I beat in a street race, about four months ago. He bought pizza after. We've been friends ever since. He's a good guy, but his family's a mess. Dr. Morgan is Hunter's father." Lila's explanation spewed from her lips as though she was anxious to bring to light a dark secret.

"Continue." Silas pushed his shoulders into the booth's backrest and stretched his legs. Her story of Sophie's situation poured out, and his insides wound tighter. Even if the doctor wasn't the killer, he was one egotistical, sick bastard. "Would he have killed Hunter?"

"I wouldn't have let that happen," she said coolly. "But he had a crazy look in his eyes. He was out of control."

"Did you see anything that would give us grounds for a search warrant?"

"I don't think so." she said. Then her eyes narrowed. "Maybe."

20

CHAPTER TWENTY

The waitress arrived and slid plates of food across the table. "Thanks," Silas said. He shoved salty fries into his mouth, needing time to process Lila's story. Her intertwined fingers and tightened lips reminded him of her toughness. She'd shown incredible strength during her mother's illness, her own failing heart, and the loss of Silas's hand. But teenage friendships could be treacherous. She hadn't touched her food.

"I need to call Hunter," Lila said.

The air shifted. She had mentioned this boy's name twenty times in five minutes. Which direction would her loyalty take her?

"You know you can't do that. His father is a person of interest in two murders. There may be critical evidence in that house."

"Hunter would never do anything to protect his father. He hates him."

"Tell me what you saw. Then we'll decide how to handle this."

"It might be nothing." Her eyes implored him not to ask her to make it something.

"If it's nothing, you wouldn't be concerned."

Lila dropped her gaze and picked at the lettuce peeking from the edges of her burger. "It wasn't what I saw, but what I heard." Her voice came out small. "Hunter accused his father of being obsessed. Said he knew what he had on the third floor. Called him pitiful. That's what made his dad blow up."

"Not enough for a search warrant," Silas replied.

"Send a Blackbird. We all know how to disable alarms and pick locks." She tilted her head, rubbing the skin below her ear in a circular pattern. "Here's a better idea. I promised Sophie I'd be back tomorrow. She'll turn the alarms off to let me in. Sophie and Hunter will be distracted. Our Blackbird goes in, checks things out, and no one is the wiser."

Silas cleared his throat. "You failed to mention *those* plans." He took her hand, gently pulling it away from her throat. "Lila, you doubt me too much. I would have approved. Although, I may have suggested sending a Blackbird with you."

"Suggested? Insisted is more like it."

He picked a fry from her plate. "Eat." He poked the greasy morsel into her mouth. "And would my insisting on protection have been so bad? Lila. Don't allow your emotions to jeopardize your safety. Your friend sounds like a decent guy. When were you going to introduce me?" He bit into his sandwich.

"He's not... I mean, he's nice... it was just...." Her shoulders slumped. "We like hanging out together. After what I saw and heard, he'll never talk to me again."

Silas took a long draw from his chocolate shake. "You stumbled into a dangerous situation. Now there are other people who need protection. Hunter, for example." He tapped her plate with his prosthetic. "Don't let your food get cold."

Lila pulled a fry from the heap on her plate and chewed slowly.

Silas continued. "What Hunter referred to may or may not have anything to do with the murders. We know Dr. Morgan is out of control, and until we know how far that goes, we have to assume the worst."

"Will you send a Blackbird tomorrow?" Lila's straw rattled as she slurped the thick shake through the narrow tube.

"Yes, and I'll be nearby. I trust your instincts, but Sophie Morgan may be a very good actress."

Lila shoved the shake away and crossed her arms. "That would mean Hunter is an accomplice. What I saw was not an act. Sophie is a victim."

"Victims rise up. She could've asked her son to help set up the husband. Her bedroom door was locked. Unwilling restraint is a crime."

"You're suggesting Hunter and his mom staged the whole thing. No way!"

"It's happened before. Traumatized family. Abused wife. Loving son. Didn't you say the gun wasn't loaded? Doesn't that seem a little convenient?"

A shadow flickered in the depths of her eyes. He hated that he'd put it there.

"Send the Blackbird." She jutted her chin. "I'm meeting Sophie at nine tomorrow morning. You'll see. Hunter was only trying to help his mom." She chomped into her cheeseburger.

He almost smiled. A pit bull chewed with more finesse.

Across the room, coins clattered against a tabletop. A chair screeched. Heads turned. A man fixed Silas with a piercing stare, stood, and threaded his way through the crowded diner. Richard Maeken. Thin pale arms covered by tattoos identified his gang affiliation. Silas swallowed, remembering the first time he'd met Richard.

That day, Silas was inside the run-down house in East Kansas City. A meth-lab smell like cat urine guided him forward. Hand on the doorknob, gun ready, the door exploded from its hinges and slammed his body backward. A scream pounded his ears. His own.

"Detective Albert, we meet again." Richard Maeken's voice dragged Silas from the memory.

Silas flexed the fingers of his prosthesis and slid his gun hand inside his jacket. Prison changed a person, sometimes for the better...sometime for the worse, but the person never stayed the same. "Richard. Heard you were out."

The ex-con towered over them, sliding his arm along the top of the booth's vinyl backrest. Vibrations from the man's drumming fingers stirred the hair on Silas' neck. The stink of old alcohol and rotten teeth blew across his face. Quiet fell over the diner like a bar before a brawl.

"Heard you got a new hand," Richard said. "I'm sorry you had to do that."

"No hard feelings," Silas said.

The swinging doors to the kitchen flung wide and the diner's owner stomped through. A white apron stretched over a bulging belly. "Is there a problem here?" he said, waving a pipe wrench. "I've got a deep fryer on the blitz, and I don't have no time for trouble."

"Nope." Silas grinned. "Richard's an old acquaintance. We're just catching up."

"I know all about your *acquaintances*, Silas." The proprietor glanced from one to the other. "I'm still not recovered from the last brawl you stirred up in here." His gaze swept to Lila, the tough man expression softening. "And don't you be putting this little sweetheart in danger. I've been servin' her tapioca pudding in here since she was eight. You gonna have trouble, keep her out of it." He slapped the wrench into the palm of a hand as big as a plate.

"Hey man, everything's cool." Richard's lips pealed back in a meth-blackened grin.

"You better not be lyin'," the owner threatened. He turned and stomped back into the kitchen.

"Kinda touchy, ain't he," Richard said. "Didn't mean no trouble. Been gonna look you up. And then, by damn, here you are. Must be God's work." He dragged a chair from a nearby table, turned it backwards, and straddling the seat, draped his burn-scarred hands across the backrest.

"Lila," Silas said, "Richard Maeken."

Lila's eyelids flicked, then she extended her hand. "Nice to meet you. I'm Silas's niece. He's told me the story. You gave up your chance for freedom to carry him from a burning house." A gracious sweetness softened her voice. "You could have run, but you stayed and tied a tourniquet around his arm. Your scars show how brave you were. Thank you."

Richard gripped Lila's hand for a moment, blinking rapidly. "The first thing I ever did right was save a cop. Go figure. But really, your uncle saved me. Five years in the slammer got my head straight."

"So, why'd you want to see me?" Silas asked.

"I want to help you, man."

"How?"

"Do you remember that I was on parole from a two-year stretch when you and I met?" Richard's head drooped. He studied his hands. When he raised his head again, his eyes were damp. "Without your help I would've done fifteen to twenty—if I'd lived. What I'm sayin' is, I owe you."

"You don't owe me anything. Make the payment to yourself. Stay straight."

"I plan to do that," Richard said. "I got something to tell you."
He glanced at Lila, hesitating.

"Go ahead," Silas encouraged. "She's not like most teenagers."

Lila smiled.

Richard hesitated then continued. "I met some strange dudes
in prison. One of the strangest was seven years ago. I shared a cell
with Norman Shields for a while. Then Mike Rojas arrived, and
I was transferred to another block. After Shields was murdered,
Rojas told me a story about Norman. The recent news reports
have made me think of that day. Norman Shields knew your killer.
Might even be related to him."

Silas's temple throbbed. "Really?" He searched the ex-con's
face. "Richard? How long you been out?"

"Couple months, why?"

"The guy we're chasing has only been active for a few weeks."

The ex-con's eyes narrowed. He leaned back and crossed his
arms.

"That's what you think."

21

CHAPTER TWENTY-ONE

Silas shook hands with Richard Maeken, paid the cashier, and followed Lila to the Studebaker. Wind twisted an empty Burger Nest bag across the parking lot in front of him. The thoughts in his brain were about the same, whirling to comprehend the destruction blowing through his life. Richard's story was hard to believe, but the man didn't have anything to prove by coming forward.

"Do you believe him?" Lila asked.

"I have no reason not to," Silas replied. There was no doubt in his mind where Lila's thoughts were parked. "Whether I trust Richard's source is another question. Allowing a convicted felon to be an organ donor is highly unusual. I'll have the story checked out."

Still as stone, she stared through the windshield. "If what Richard said is true, the case you're working on is connected to a killer who donated his organs seven years ago. And someone hates him enough to hunt down the transplant survivors and eliminate them one by one"

A blanket of silence hung thick between them. Silas pushed back his anxiety. Lila couldn't have received the heart of a sadistic killer—could she?

"Lila. Look at me," he said firmly.

She turned to him, a stricken expression on her face.

"I wish I could tell you what you want to hear, but I can't. I don't know who your donor was, but it's unlikely that your heart would be from an adult. Doctors rarely use organs from an older person. Especially the heart." Silas wasn't lying. Doctors preferred younger hearts, but he also knew that the donor age limit had expanded to sixty. A donor as old as fifty was not unheard of when Lila received her transplant.

"I know," she said bitterly. "But our family has a history of rotten luck."

"Not always. We're alive, aren't we?"

"For now," she said. "But I'm at the top of a serial killer's list. What if the reason I'm living is thanks to a murderer? And don't forget, my good friend's father has a major screw lose. How much better can life get?"

"Not much until we stop this killer. Dr. Morgan has access to surgical instruments, and chloroform, but a judge won't give us the time of day. We need facts—hard evidence. Sophie Morgan could help. Filing charges against her husband for unlawful restraint would give us a solid reason to place him under arrest. That would gain us time to investigate and establish a clear motive. Do you think she could do it?"

"I'm not sure, and if she did, that jerk will have her arrested for attempted murder." Lila rolled her window down a few inches, allowing a brisk breeze to blow across the car's seat.

"He might anyway."

"Well it won't stick. Not if Hunter uses this video I took with my cell phone." She waved her device. "This live action clearly shows Sophie defending her son."

"One more thing you didn't mention."

A dimple flicked at the corner of Lila's mouth. "Do you have an update from Hadley yet?"

Silas opened his messages—two from Sydney Franco—one from Hadley. He opened the latter and listened.

"Hadley found Dr. Morgan in St. Luke's Hospital. Sophie must have whacked her husband a good one. He's still unconscious."

"Hunter said he wished his dad was dead, but he didn't really mean it." Lila swiped her finger across her own screen. "Speaking of Hunter..." She raised her eyebrows, questioningly.

"See what he wants."

She tapped the screen. "Says his mom called her lawyer. He advised her to file charges against her husband, but she didn't." Lila thumped her fist against her leg. "Dang. That would have helped so much." She continued to read. "Her lawyer did get a judge to sign a temporary restraining order." She gave Silas a thumbs up.

"That was fast. Sophie's lawyer must play golf with the judge."

Lila nodded. "According to Hunter, his mom's feeling like Wonder Woman. He convinced her to stay in a hotel tonight. But she's still looking forward to seeing me tomorrow." She read silently for a moment. "I'll just tell him I'll see them at nine." Lila returned her attention to her screen.

"Okay," he said. He hoped the situation with the boy's father didn't end up destroying Lila and Hunter's friendship.

Silas opened the first message from Sydney. "Call me." The second text repeated the first with exclamation marks. He turned to ask Lila a question, but she was absorbed in typing the contents of her message. He waited.

She glanced up, catching his smirk.

"What is wrong with you?" she said.

"Seems like a long text to say I'll see you tomorrow."

She made a face. "How do you know? You can barely text. I was giving Hunter a couple of tips in case his mom gets the detox shakes."

Silas met her steady and unwavering gaze. "Remember what we say about being a Blackbird?"

Lila nodded. "Fight the snake who embodies your greatest fears." She turned the key in the ignition. The power of the Studebaker's engine vibrated through the seats.

"Drop me off at the Precinct. I need an update from the team. I'll have someone give me a lift home. And don't be going back to the Morgan place on your own." He delivered the last sentence with steely authority.

Lila gripped the marble knob of the gearshift. Finding reverse, she backed from between two cars. "What a mess. Hunter will be sorry he ever asked me for help."

A typical teenager, all brave and knowing one minute and a jelly bowl of doubt the next. He could almost see her brain sorting through the facts, second guessing a fragile situation. No girl wanted her friend's father to be a serial killer or herself to be his next victim.

"Are you sure we're not barking up the wrong tree? Hunter didn't seem alarmed at whatever was on the third floor, only disgusted." She pulled into the street. "His father might only have dirty pictures in that room."

"We can only hope, but Dr. Morgan wasn't wanting to take dirty pictures of victim number one. Or you."

"Hunter will think I betrayed him."

"Not if he's the young man you think he is. He'll be all about protecting his mother, and you. Trust your instincts." His common sense told him he was giving her good advice, but his protective nature pulled him in the opposite direction.

The car rolled to a stop at the intersection. She leaned across the seat and kissed his cheek. "I love you, Uncle Silas."

"I'll bet that's what you tell all the guys."

"Not true. They get spooked when I call them uncle."

Laughter bubbled in Silas's throat, blocking a retort.

A car horn blasted behind them. "Geeez," Lila said. She popped the clutch and spun the tires. Plumes of black smoke trailed the Studebaker.

"Do you want a ticket?" Silas fought the urge to grip the edge of his seat.

"Not worried. I know *people.*"

A few minutes later, Lila dropped him off at the Precinct. He waited for her to drive out of sight before he tapped the icon for Bertha. "Lila has left the precinct in her Studebaker. Deploy a Blackbird for discrete, protective surveillance until my niece's arrival at Audrey House. Affirm when she is in sight. Note: She may stop for gas. Advise me immediately of any other detour."

"Request confirmed," Bertha responded.

He strolled to the end of the block, leaned against a light pole, and held his phone where he could see the screen. Two minutes passed then three. He left the pole, paced the length of a football field, and returned. Three times he repeated the distraction. His screen lit up. *Bertha.* He breathed a sigh of relief.

"The Blackbird has advised the Studebaker is in view. Lila is confirmed as the driver. Further updates will be made only if a problem arises. A notification will be given when Lila is inside The House of Audrey. Will that be all?"

"One more thing." He glanced around, waiting as a young couple strolled past. His next request was for Bertha's receptors alone. Moments later Silas ended his instruction.

CHAPTER TWENTY-ONE

"Progress will be reported in two hours." The computer responded.

22

CHAPTER TWENTY-TWO

Silas crossed the intersection. Bradford pear trees bursting with white blossoms adorned the next block. The wind blew softly from the south. Ornate iron benches captured the falling white petals. Silas brushed off an empty seat and lowered himself. He tapped Sydney's icon.

Well, it's about time you called," she scolded. "I left you a message an hour ago. I was beginning to think you didn't love me anymore."

"I'm calling now. What've you got?"

"I haven't completed the autopsy on Savannah Peterson yet. But I heard something interesting I wanted to pass along. Got a call from Roy an old ME friend in Denver."

"That's convenient," Silas said.

"Well, we were an item once. We still talk."

Silas swallowed. He'd never once thought of Sydney having another man in her life. He wondered why she had never mentioned the guy, and why she wanted him to know now? Was it her subtle way of giving him a wake-up shove?

"What's the matter Silas, cat got your tongue?" Sydney teased. "Anyway, I was telling my friend about The Surgeon.

It seems they had a similar murder in Denver two years ago. One Gloria Sweeney, Asian, age 26. The same message, same mementos, and never solved. He's forwarding me the autopsy report and photographs of the woman. Here's the interesting part. Remember me telling you Abbey Bryant was a transplant recipient?

"Yeah, she had a tattoo. *Love my organ donor.*"

"Right. Medical records confirmed a dual cornea transplant."

"And?"

"The Denver victim had received a donor's pancreas. So, I completed a cursory examination of Savannah Peterson's body. She has a scar that's in the right place for a kidney transplant. I'm waiting for her medical history."

Silas sucked air like he'd taken a blow to the mid-section. Dr. Morgan had performed other surgeries in Denver. Hadley had called his brother's surgery routine. But the man had died.

Silas pictured the scars Lila carried from her heart surgery. The months prior to finding a donor match resembled a dense fog in his memory, but he vaguely recalled Liz telling him Savannah was sick, too. He'd been so focused on his niece, that he'd never asked Liz if Savannah was okay. He regretted the selfish person he'd been during that time. He'd lost much.

"Two years since Denver," he said. "There could be a dozen victims located all over the country. If we're lucky, the killer's first selection was in Denver. We have to make sure he doesn't get out of Kansas City."

"If he hasn't already. Will you be notifying the FBI?"

A motorcycle roared past, leaving an echo pulsating through the concrete artery of the city. In front of the precinct, an American flag and a Missouri flag snapped in the breeze. He frowned. Calling in the FBI would make the case a national drama.

Manpower would be sucked up to deal with the freak-groupies. Unless, he worked with Special Agent Archie Hamilton. Archie had the means to offer FBI assistance without creating havoc. They had a secret working arrangement that included The House of Audrey.

"Not today," he said. "I have a lead, but investigating the suspect will be like touching a hot coal with my good hand. Guy's a big shot in the medical world, rubs elbows with the mayor. You know the story. I need one more day. I'll update the team, but I need you to sit on this transplant connection. I don't want the public to go crazy."

"By sitting on it, you mean don't advise Elizabeth Cartwright. Silas, when are you going to stop protecting her?"

"I'm not protecting her." Silas snapped. "I'm trying to protect the investigation. There's an inside leak to the media, and I need to get a handle on it."

"And you're suspicious Elizabeth is on a grandstanding mission."

"Are you serious? She's the Chief, for God's sake. Besides, the reporter called—her." Silas snapped his jaws shut. Even to himself he sounded defensive. And Sydney had hit a nerve. Elizabeth liked an audience.

"How do you know?" Sydney stomped the nerve.

"I just know. What does she have to gain?" He realized too late, he might as well have thrown gasoline on Sydney's fire.

"Your attention," she snapped. "She's never gotten over you, Silas. Dear God, why are men so damn blind?"

A sound like breaking glass crackled through the air. The noise broke the tension and gave him an out. "I love you when you're angry." He chuckled, visualizing a shattered coffee cup. "That's when you do your best work. And that's what we need right now."

He took a breath. "Trust me, Sydney. Elizabeth Cartwright's not over hating me. That's what she's not over." He said the words with a confidence he didn't feel.

Today's murder had thrown he and Elizabeth together in a way they hadn't been in years. Savannah's death had given them a common goal. And, if Silas was honest, Liz seemed different, on the verge of forgiveness. "I'm over Elizabeth and that's all that matters." He realized too late; his words had been overheard.

A woman with snow-white hair was strolling by the bench where Silas sat. She smiled knowingly. He turned away, embarrassed. For a moment Silas thought Sydney had hung up. "You there?"

"I'm here."

"Look, I don't want to have this conversation over the phone. If the Chief calls, tell her what's going on. If she gives you a hard time about communication, tell her you expected me to keep her informed. I'll take the heat.

"Forget it," Sydney said. "I can take care of myself. Besides, Elizabeth Cartwright doesn't have much use for me. She won't call."

"Are you going to blackmail me with this later?" He attempted to lighten the subject.

"Don't ev-en think I'm doing this for free." She paused, as though she was mulling over her extortion fee. "The Denver autopsy report should be here later today, but bodies are lined up in the morgue requiring my immediate attention. I'm guessing I won't lay eyes on the report before noon tomorrow."

"I'll owe you."

"Damn straight! But I'll go easy on you. A night on the town will suffice. And I don't mean a year from now, and I do mean somewhere nice."

"I rather like that idea." Silas grinned. He visualized the soft crinkle at the corners of her dark eyes. "One more thing," he said. "Can determine how much time has passed since each victim's surgery occurred?"

"Always one more thing with you. Sometimes, I think you're Columbo reincarnated." Sydney's sigh huffed through the phone.

"Sydney," Silas said softly. "You're capable of miracles. We're needing one now."

The phone went quiet. At last, Sydney spoke, "The victim's medical records will give us what we need. I'll see if I can come up with a timeline. Wouldn't it be interesting if the victims had the same operating surgeon? But, if you're thinking of getting to the donor families, think again. That would take a court order."

"The best connection we have is the transplants. Find me something concrete. I'll get the court order." His phone announced a message from Bertha. "Hold on a second. I have to take this." He clicked on the computer's icon, scanning the message.

"Lila has arrived and entered The House of Audrey. Protective surveillance ended." He switched back to Sydney. "Sorry. That was important."

"Is Lila okay?"

"How did you know the call was about her?"

"I've taken Silas Albert 101," she said, her tone silky. "You don't go away unless it's Lila, or about her."

"Your intuition is scary," he said, but his heart skipped a beat. He stood.

"She's lucky to have you," Sydney said.

"No. I'm the lucky one."

"And the transplant connection worries you." Her observation was a statement.

"I've believed from the beginning that the killer's selection is not random."

"They rarely are," Sydney agreed. "Have you found anything?"

"There's the possibility The Surgeon is connected to Lila's heart donor." The words left his mouth drenched in a foul aftertaste.

"If you have that information, you know who The Surgeon is."

Silas stared long and hard at his artificial hand. "We're working a lead from Richard Maeken. Remember him?"

"Of course."

Silas told Sydney the ex-con's story.

"Lila must be devastated." Sydney's voice sounded strained. She cared deeply for Silas's niece. After Liz relocated to St. Louis, leaving Lila without her friendship and guidance, Sydney formed her own connection with Lila. She didn't try to be a mother, and she wasn't a sister either. The mix was somewhere between, and Lila responded well. When his niece needed a female's understanding, it was a toss-up between her grandma Nancy or Sydney.

"It's not the best news she ever received," Silas agreed. "The media will tear her to pieces if it's true."

"Now I get it. You're shielding Lila. That's the real reason you're not telling Chief." Sydney's sigh whispered through the phone. "I guess you know, you're getting close to obstructing justice?" She made no reference to the fact that he'd made her an accessory as well. "If you're about to do something crazy, don't tell me what it is."

"Don't worry, I won't drag you down with me. But I am in protection mode. Dr. Morgan's in the hospital. He can't hurt Lila or anyone else. He's confined, at least until he wakes up. By then, I'll either have enough evidence to hold him for questioning, or I won't care if he's released."

"Take care, Silas," Sydney said.

The warmth in her voice settled like sunshine in his heart. No other woman drove away his demons like Sydney.

"Always." He disconnected.

23

CHAPTER TWENTY-THREE

I have memorized the names but am drawn to check the list as an addict might a stash of cocaine. The fold lines of the paper are nearly worn through. My fingers twitch in eagerness.

The sheet of paper lies open across my thighs. Grey pencil marks like rungs of a ladder, identify my progress. The corneas, the kidneys, the pancreas, and other body parts are crossed off. The lungs are next. Two names are listed. *Two.* My heart thumps. Can I do it?

Transfixed by the idea, I snap on plastic gloves. From the desk drawer I retrieve a plastic bag. The stainless-steel surgical knife inside catches the light. I hesitate. The exact number of packets rest next to notes carefully prepared to explain what otherwise will be considered insane. The sooner the final name is crossed from the list the sooner I will exhale in relief.

I take the second bag, and two notes.

24

CHAPTER TWENTY-FOUR

Silas entered the war room. Three screens, the perfect size for watching Kansas City Chief's football hang from the ceiling, strategically located front and center. Soda cans, water bottles, and coffee cups cluttered the desks. The scene resembled a sports bar without the raucous noise of exuberant fans.

The faces of his investigative team bore a fan's similar intensity. Glued to computer screens, they ran with any crime solving lead, prayed for a fumble by the killer, or an interception of his intent. The facts displayed overhead outlined a deadly opponent where murder wasn't a game.

Silas nodded to the skimpy crew. With the murder rate in Kansas City at an all-time high, the Homicide Unit was stretched thin.

Clipped to a large bulletin-board hung an enlarged photo of Abbey Bryant sitting on a porch step. Next to Abbey's hung one of Savannah standing beside her blue Honda. Later today the woman from Denver would be added. Silas wanted his people to take the deaths personal and derive an emotional energy from the photos. The kind of energy needed to slog forward when the leads went nowhere.

Silas scanned the overhead screens. Columns of information displayed a smattering of red and blue lines crisscrossing from one list to the other. An intersection of color represented a confirmed connection between Savannah Peterson and Abbey Bryant. The junctures of red and blue were painfully scarce. He walked to the center of the room. "We have another victim."

"Jesus," Someone muttered. "We can't catch a break."

"Here?" Another investigator asked.

"Denver," Silas replied. "The case is two years old, but there's no doubt it's the same M.O." He outlined Sydney Franco's discovery. "The transplant connection is likely, but not confirmed. We'll be calling in the FBI. The Chief will make a public announcement soon."

"Did he kill her cat this time?" An older officer spoke.

Silas wheeled toward the voice. "Denver didn't mention one. But we'll have a report this afternoon. We'll send someone to Colorado to work with their homicide unit."

"Send Hadley, he's a cat lover."

Laughter rocked the room. Silas smiled. Hadley was terrified of cats.

"Don't be a bunch of smartasses. Cats are important to this case. Don't ignore the facts."

Silas whirled toward the woman's voice, recognizing Janice Sloan, a hardworking cop who had started as a parking meter attendant. He respected her top-notch crime investigation work.

"What are you thinking?" Silas encouraged.

"Dismembering an animal's body indicates an enormous fear, or a raging anger, maybe both. The killer has experienced a trauma, probably as a child. Claws may equal a human's fists. He is rendering them harmless. The trauma may have included cats."

"A cat phobia?" The cop in the corner spoke. "Like Hadley. He thinks the only good cat is the one in a cage."

A buzz spread through the room. Silas nodded, approving of the interest Sloan's comment stirred. "Other observations?"

"So far, we have one dismembered feline. Likely the paws are trophies." A voice offered from the back of the room.

"Killer's hung up on rejection. Identifies his own paranoia in women he selects."

The ideas flowed.

"Revenge motive? The victims represent evil or pain."

"The method," Janice added. "Asphyxiation is the cause of death, but chloroform kept the person from fighting. Chloroform also throws the case into the slot of poisoning."

"Do we have anything on the scalpel?"

"Standard surgical tool. Nothing unique. Joe Blow can order them online."

Silas paced across the front of the room. "Have you been able to trace Abbey Bryant's steps the night she went missing?"

"Neighbors reported she liked to put the kids to bed and take late night walks. She'd been friendly with a neighbor. Hadley or Mendez interviewed the woman. Oh yeah, it was Mendez. He's still out. Said he thought she was screwy in the head."

Silas halted. "Screwy? How so?" He nailed the youngest member of his team with a hard stare. The comment didn't match the professional habits of Mendez.

The man scrambled for his notes. His reddening cheeks indicated he recognized his tactless mistake. "Well, he didn't exactly say, screwy. Confused is more accurate. She talked to Tommy, her cat, and an invisible man named Charlie."

"Does Abbey Bryant's friend have a name?"

"Margaret Culver," the young man replied without referring

to his notes. "Age 87. Lives alone. Abandoned by her husband, years ago. Her only child is deceased."

Silas's gut turned upside down. He knew Margaret Culver. "You got that information from a confused woman."

The younger man held his gaze. "No, Sir. I dug up everything except her name."

Silas nodded. "Good work. Keep digging."

"Margaret Culver can't be a suspect—can she? She's 87 years old."

"Suspect? I doubt it. Witness? Yes. Close friends of a victim often observe more than they realize or want to admit. Margaret Culver would be especially sensitive to domestic abuse. Twenty years ago, her husband nearly killed her. Margaret Culver was the first case of domestic abuse I ever worked. She would recognize the signs and may have tried to help her friend Abbey.

Margaret was also the first abuse victim he'd ever tried to rescue. And not the last to refuse help. Claimed she'd fallen down the stairs. The incident helped him recognize how to keep his promise to his grandfather, and how to give The House of Audrey a heart. Women like Margaret needed a safe place.

Silas faced the enlarged photos of Abbey Bryant and Savannah Peterson. Behind him the voices fell silent. The team trusted him. As Chief Detective, he should give them everything they needed and let them do their job. But for him, this was about Lila. He wouldn't step back.

He whirled to the group. "We have a suspect." He shared Richard Maeken's theory. "He pointed to Janice Sloan. "I'm putting you in charge of this group's work assignment. Dig into Dr. Tyler Morgan's life. Find out if he has any siblings. Check out any connection to Norman Shields. Keep me informed."

Silas abandoned the war room. He wandered the halls, glancing into darkened cubicles. Margaret Culver having entered the investigation had sent a strong sense of a puzzle piece turned the wrong way. He sighed. Years of solving crimes where the only tool he had was his gut, led him to trust the way his brain worked through his instincts.

He entered the office at the end of a corridor, settled into the desk chair, put his feet up, and checked his messages. Bertha's promised text waited in his mailbox. He read the brief message and opened the attachments. For twenty minutes he studied the intricate schematic, aerial photos, and floor plans. He created a file and saved the data in case The Blackbirds needed it later.

His mind's eye went back to the computer screen in the war room. Every way he turned the ghost of Norman Shields appeared. Richard Maeken's story was strange enough to be true, but second hand. Silas needed to go straight to the source. He searched his phone contacts for the Jefferson City Correctional Center and Warden Henry Jasper's private number.

"Well, if it isn't Prince Albert," the familiar voice of Silas's friend cackled from the phone.

"The one and only." Silas chuckled at the reference to his last name. The old man ran the prison with an iron grip. For over thirty years, he faced the worst of the worst, but never lost his sense of humor. He'd once told Silas that life was too short to be taken too seriously.

"With a serial killer on the loose, I know you didn't call for a friendly chat. What's on your mind?"

"You heard about the murders?"

"Who hasn't? Every TV station in the state has the 'breaking news'. Will we have a new guest joining us here soon?"

"We have a suspect. But I need your help. Can you set up an interview with Norman Shields' cellmates?

CHAPTER TWENTY-FOUR

"The Norman Shields who murdered his wife?"

"He's the one."

"You do know the man's dead?"

"I do. It's what he said before he died that I'm interested in."

"Richard Maeken was one of his cellmates. The two of you have a connection. He's been released. Do you want his address?"

"No, I've talked to him."

"Norman only had one other cellmate, Mike Rojas. I'll set up the meeting. When can I expect you?"

His friend's memory never failed to amaze him. "Seven-o'clock in the morning, if you'll have the coffee ready. Oh yeah, there is one more thing."

"Why am I not surprised?"

"Can I get a record of Shields' visitors?"

"He didn't have many."

"Surprised you don't remember their names, too."

A dry laugh rattled in Silas's ear. "Things have changed since you were here last. You'll know what I mean, someday. I'll have the records pulled."

"Appreciate the help. See you in the morning." Silas remained in the dim light long after his conversation with the warden ended. The sickened expression on Lila's face when she learned her organ donor might have been a killer, hung in his mind. He remembered how close to death she'd been, and how desperate he'd been, at the time of her transplant. Agreeing that under the circumstances an adult donor could be used. The idea that in her chest beat the heart of a child abuser, and killer, belied unfairness to the extreme.

A hardy knock broke through his dark thoughts. Hadley stood in the doorway. "Taking a little nap?" He flipped on the light.

Silas's feet hit the floor. "Who's with Morgan?"

"Cool your jets, man." Hadley chuckled. "Mendez is holding our suspect's hand. Figured you needed a ride home." He spread his arms wide. "So, here I am."

"Have you been to the war room?"

"Yep. Heard we have a third victim. The crew gave me a hard time. The Denver connection, they called it. Suggested that since I hate procedure, I might be—The Surgeon, because I hate cats, I'm from Denver, and my brother died from a messed up surgical procedure. What a bunch of jokers." He laughed. "I think they hold it against me for being a Broncos fan. Do you need a ride home or not?"

25

CHAPTER TWENTY-FIVE

"Let's go." Silas followed Hadley, winding through halls and the parking garage to the Dodge Charger. Once inside the car, he said, "I'm worried about Lila." He shared his fears, regarding Norman Shields and the fact that their suspect, Dr. Morgan, might have selected her as his next victim.

Hadley remained silent for two blocks. "See if I've got this right?" he said. "After Shields ended up in prison for killing his wife, the children were placed in the system. Probably adopted. Who knows what those kids witnessed? They're all bound to be damaged. A rational mind would want his mother's killer dead. An irrational person would want even the man's organs dead, too. Sounds like a motive to me. Now, we have to give Lila some answers."

"How?"

"DNA comparison takes too long," Hadley said. "Lila will want to meet this head on. You've got to help her. First step, ask Sydney Franco to compare blood types. You trust her. If Norman Shields is eliminated, great. If not, go for the DNA. We'll help Lila cope. You can bet, her body has already kicked out any bad influences from her donor."

Silas exhaled, already tapping Sydney's icon. "You do have a brain—even if it's madeof straw." When she answered, he put her on speaker and made his request.

"Lila is way ahead of you." Sydney said. "She's been here ten minutes. I was just getting ready to call you."

A fist of steel gripped his heart. "Does she know the answer?"

"No. She wants you here."

The Charger slowed as if the statement weighed more than the engine could move. A coldness enveloped Silas. "Hadley and I are five minutes away."

Designed for speed and balance, the police cruiser roared through downtown. Arriving in four minutes, they pulled into a no parking zone in front of a modern, low-slung stucco building. Lila's Studebaker stuck out amongst the modern models in the parking lot.

Sydney and her crew served four counties in the Kansas City area. Last year, nine autopsy stations as pristine as any operating room handled 700 bodies. The statistics were a statement to Sydney's dedication. Even as he ran toward her office building, a weight the size of a boulder settled on Silas's shoulders. His recent requests, if discovered, could ruin her career. She should have told him no. But she hadn't. He couldn't help thinking, Elizabeth wouldn't have broken the rules for anyone, not even Silas.

The Assistant Medical Examiner met the detectives at the door. "Right this way, gentlemen," she said. "Dr. Franco is expecting you." No warmth lifted the corners of her lips or brightened her pale blue eyes. Silas didn't fault her. If allowed, the ugliness of death stripped life's joy from a person.

"I realize you know the way, Chief Detective Albert, but protocol requires all visitors be accompanied."

"No problem." Silas said.

Sadly, the AME's comment was as close to a personal one as they might ever hear from her. As he and Hadley followed the woman, Silas thought of the Petersons' visit earlier in the day. Thank God this heartbreaking experience no longer took place in a gloomy basement capable of birthing ghost stories. At the end of a long hall lined with autopsy alcoves, the AME knocked on a closed door. "Dr. Franco. Chief Detective Albert and Detective Barker have arrived."

The AME waited for Sydney to open the door then turned aside and returned the way she had come. The two men followed Sydney inside. Silas didn't see any shards of the broken coffee cup, however a substantial dent marred one office wall.

Sydney's desk faced away from high windows where bright office lights pressed back the blue gray of early evening. Half-a dozen diplomas hung on the soft green-colored walls. Ceramic pots contained bird of paradise, black elephant ear, and a three-foot tall jade plant. Amidst the plants, a sign protruded from a plain clay pot. *I choose life* danced across the single piece of barnwood. A tiny sign in a smaller pot said *I do too. Lila had scrawled her name across the bottom.*

Lila sat facing Sydney's desk in the only chair not covered in stacks of books. She jumped to her feet, whirling to face Silas. "I have to know," she said. "I told Grandma everything. Grandpa Clifford was there too. He said to call Sydney for help. After I got here, I wanted you here—in case—well—in case the news is bad."

"I'm not mad at you." He moved close. "I understand." How easily the lines blurred between an adult's strength and the uncertainty of a child. "No matter what we learn." He gently tapped her chest. "This heart is good and pure." He kissed her forehead the way he had since she was a baby in his sister Audrey's arms.

"We're all here for you, sweet girl," Hadley said, his voice husky.

Silas stepped back, feeling like a trial lawyer awaiting a judge's life or death decision.

The skin of Lila's throat expanded and contracted with her quick swallow. "B positive," she said.

Silas fixed his gaze on Sydney's face. Sydney faced horrible situations without flicking an eyelash, but today, the shift of her eyes downward betrayed her.

Lila saw it too. "A match."

"Yes," Sydney said, gently. "I'm sorry. Norman Shields' blood type was also B positive."

For a second Lila's head drooped, then she squared her shoulders. "Nothing to be sorry about. Sure, I wanted the results to be different, but I realized something. In the last days of Norman Shields' life, he chose good. The decision to donate his organs may have been the only time he made that choice. I will not allow myself to dishonor that decision."

"The blood test is not conclusive," Sydney said. "I'll run a complete DNA analysis. Then we'll know for sure." Sydney's gaze again shifted downward.

Silas interpreted her body language. "There's more."

"Yes." Sydney's expression softened as though she were about to speak to a victim's family. "Savannah Peterson's medical records confirmed she had a kidney transplant. She also had B positive blood type, the same as Abbey Bryant. Less than 10% of the population has that type. As soon as the autopsy report from Denver arrived, I checked Gloria Sweeney's blood type. The Surgeon's victims are all B positive and their transplants were all done within hours of each other. I know I don't have to tell you—until there's an arrest, Lila's in grave danger."

26

CHAPTER TWENTY-SIX

A funeral-like atmosphere descended over the group. Silas struggled to find an encouraging word. None seemed appropriate. His helpless gaze found Lila at the window where she stared into the deepening dusk. She appeared fragile in the glass's reflection. He clenched his teeth. Each victim had been selected, having already stared down the face of death. Now, the killer sought to trample out those second chances.

Lila faced them. "It is what it is," she said, rock-solid determination in her eyes. "Gloom and doom's for losers. By tomorrow we won't have to worry, The Surgeon will be under arrest." She stepped around Sydney's desk. "Guess I need an escort to the door. I'm going home to check on Carla. I can be useful there."

"Carla?" Sydney arched a slim black eyebrow.

"Latest domestic abuse rescue," Silas said.

"I'll show you out," Sydney said as she led the way. At the exit, she hugged Lila. "Let Silas keep you safe." She placed a hand on Silas's arm, giving the slightest squeeze of encouragement. Her eyes expressed deep concern. If they had been alone, she would have offered more.

Twenty minutes later, the Studebaker's taillights disappeared down the drive behind The House of Audrey. Hadley stopped the cruiser at the front door. "I know Lila is tough, but that was some seriously bad news. Do you think she'll be okay?"

"I hope so." Silas dragged a hand over his eyes.

"I'll be checking on our doctor friend at St. Luke's," Hadley changed the subject. "Mendez probably needs a break."

Silas and Hadley spent another few minutes discussing Silas's trip to the prison the next day. "Call me when Morgan's conscious," Silas said as he climbed out of the Charger.

"Will do." Hadley touched a hand to his brow in a casual salute.

Silas pressed his thumb to the security device and entered the old warehouse. Creaking and popping like the joints of an old man, the elevator climbed skyward. Sometimes he pulled the brake, pausing between floors...for fun. On those occasions, he never failed to feel the presence of his grandfather's spirit. But not today, he was too tired.

He folded back the elevator gate at the fourth floor. Inside the apartment, Camelia tilted her head giving him a one-eyed appraisal. He picked her up, cradled her in his left arm and stroked her black and white fur. "Need a little lovin', do you?"

The cat answered by rubbing her head against his artificial hand. "I wish you could talk," he said, a smile tugging the corners of his mouth. "We could share stories about our missing paws." The smile spread. "Or—what we want for supper."

He set her on the floor and checked her water and food bowl, adding a bit more of her favorite fish nibbles. Rewarding his thoughtfulness, Camelia wound in and out between his ankles. "You're one loyal female," he said, glancing down at his mud splattered pants. "You don't mind a messy guy." He placed his phone on the counter and removed his prosthesis. He needed to shower, eat, and try to get some sleep.

The hot water pummeled his tense muscles. He closed his eyes. The faces of the dead women passed behind his lids. He leaned his head against the cool tile. What makes a successful doctor turn into a killer? The loss of his daughter maybe?

Silas remembered the family's tragedy. He'd been in the hospital with Lila, waiting, and praying for a heart. A news update showed the Morgans holding a press conference. Silas had been sympathetic, even though he disliked the doctor. And that day Morgan didn't even try to fake grief. His daughter's organ donations served only as an opportunity to be center stage—nothing more. Silas had lost even more respect for the man.

Silas's eyes shot open. What would the Las Vegas odds be on one family having two deaths, and two organ donors—weeks apart? And, according to Richard Maeken, Morgan had visited Shields. Within a few days of that visit Shields was murdered.

The importance of his upcoming trip to Jefferson City rocketed into the stratosphere.

Dressed and back in the kitchen, Silas prepared his stump, fit the sock over the end, and attached the prosthesis. He quickly sent a voice to text message to Janice Sloan. "Assign a person to examine Trisha Morgan's death. I have a hunch it wasn't an accident."

The response came in the simple acceptance of the assignment. No argument, no complaints, no excuses.

Later armed with the makings of a double decker ham and cheese, he hauled the bundle of food to the kitchen table. On the spur of the moment, he slapped two sandwiches together, eyed some leftover cranberry wine, grabbed two sodas instead, dropped everything into a brown paper bag, and headed for the morgue. Sydney was bound to be hungry.

He steered his way through downtown traffic. When had he fallen in love with Sydney Franco? She'd been in his peripheral vision for years, pretty and smart, a constant steadiness he counted on. That had changed to something filled with magnetic energy. Now, the sparkle in her brown eyes attracted him like Haley's Comet.

Then why did he have this lingering boomerang of feelings for Liz? This sense of unfinished business. He knew one thing. Hadley was right. If he wasn't careful, he'd end up the loser all the way around.

He turned on the radio, settled on Keith Urban's, 'Blue Ain't Your Color', and cranked the sound. Pulling into the morgue's parking lot, he noticed Sydney's shades were drawn. He rolled up his list of favorites on his phone and pressed her number. She answered on the first ring.

"I had a feeling you'd be calling," she said. "Having trouble sleeping?"

"Guilty. Have you eaten?"

"No, but I can't leave now. I need to finish a few things and everyone else is gone."

Silas grinned like a silly fool. "No problem, I brought food."

"Here?"

"Just open the door."

"Silas, you're going to get me fired."

"No, I won't. I'm on police business. Open the door or I'll use my super magic powers to pick the lock."

"You don't have super magic powers, and we have an alarm system. I want to see you, pick that!"

Silas laughed. *If only he could tell her about Bertha and the computer's skills at disabling alarms.* He grabbed the brown paper bag and jogged to the entry. "It's going to rain any minute. You'll be sorry when I get wet and catch a cold."

The security panel flashed green. He nearly danced through the open door.

"Dinner is served, lovely lady." He held the bag aloft.

Sydney giggled, turned her back, and reset the alarm.

He slipped his arms around her waist and nuzzled her neck.

"Oh Silas," she whispered. "You do make life interesting." She leaned into the hardness of his body. "Is that your magic I feel?"

Silas's breath caught in his throat. The brown paper bag fell to the floor. Sodas clattered across the tile. Sidney twirled, lips parted, eyes wide. Her hands slid behind his head, dragging his mouth to hers. Heat flowed through Silas's veins and other parts of his body. He lost himself in the taste of Sidney and the silky feel of her skin.

"Follow me," she whispered in his ear. She took his hand, opened a door on the left, and pulled him inside. "We use this when we work back-to-back shifts."

"For sleep, I hope."

"Not tonight," she purred.

The room was bare except for two twin beds, a nightstand with a small lamp, and a metal clothes rack. Silas caught a glimpse of a bathroom through an open door on the right.

Sydney crossed to the windows and closed the blinds.

* * *

The sound of his phone snapped Silas awake. Sydney was gone. He swung his legs over the side of the bed. A string of clothing led from the door to the bed. He followed the ringing to his khakis, picked them up and pulled out his cell. Four o'clock in the morning. He'd had a few hours of sleep. "Hello."

CHAPTER TWENTY-SIX

"Hey Boss. Sleeping Beauty's awake."

"Is he talking?"

"Screaming like a banshee and threatening to sue or press charges against everyone in the state of Missouri."

"Has he been served his restraining order?"

"That's what set him off. Before that he was just trying to figure out who had his cell phone and how he got here."

"Wonder how the court knew he was there—and conscious?"

"Anonymous caller would be my guess. Of course, I couldn't say for certain." Hadley's voice was gleefully innocent.

"I'm sure you couldn't. I'm on my way." He snatched his clothes from the floor, dressed, and ran to locate Sydney to turn off the alarm and let him out. At the door he kissed her long and hard and raced for the SUV.

He met Hadley outside Morgan's hospital room. Angry red lines crisscrossed the whites of the detective's eyes. A dark mask of beard shaded the bottom half of his face. "You spent the night?"

To the left, Mendez paced the hall. Hadley thumbed in the uniformed cop's direction. "The young'n needed to be kept awake."

"He looks wide awake to me," Silas said, dryly. "Anything new from Morgan?"

"He wants to walk, but he's not an idiot. The CAT scan's been done. If he doesn't have a crack in his skull, he's outta here."

The door to the hospital room swung open and a doctor emerged. He stopped in front of the two men. "Detective Albert. Detective Barker." His gaze took in Silas's artificial hand. "Good to see you alive and well."

Silas read the man's name tag. He felt a twinge of guilt that the name was meaningless. There'd been too many doctors in his life. "I had a good deal of help. We'd like to talk to your patient.

Is that possible?"

"You can. He's getting dressed now. He's not in a good mood. I advised him of the risks of leaving, but I can't hold a patient against his will. A member of the profession himself, he knows a person doesn't recover from a concussion in only a few hours."

"Thanks." Silas said, as the doctor retreated down the hall. "Record every word, and move made in this room," he said to Hadley. "I wouldn't be surprised to see our friend assault a police officer." Silas knocked.

"Come in! For God's sake, what else could you bloodsuckers possibly want now?"

Silas stiff-armed the door open, with Hadley at his heels. Aside from the marks left by fists and the gun's handle, Morgan hadn't changed. The black eye resembled the one Silas had so happily delivered years earlier. The arrogance was there, blatant and deliberate as ever.

"You!" Morgan spat his recognition of Silas. "Get out of my room."

Silas forced a condescending smile. "Why all the hostility, Mr. Morgan?"

"Dr. Morgan to you—you, stupid flatfoot."

"Weell noow, there's no need for insults. Detective Barker and I will only inconvenience you for a few minutes. We'd like to ask you a few questions."

"Go ahead. I'd like to ask a few of my own. Is my bitch of a wife who did this in jail yet?"

"I appreciate your cooperation. I'll make this quick. How do you know Abbey Bryant?"

The man blinked. "Why? Is she one of your girlfriends? Are you going to throw another fit of insane jealousy right here in front of your cop buddy?"

Silas stepped inside the doctor's personal space. "Is that a yes, Mr. Morgan?" He showed his contempt, saw the doctor battle for control. "What about Savannah Peterson? Do you know her too?"

"I don't recognize those names." Morgan's eyes shifted. He wasn't a good liar. "Why are you asking me about these women? I thought you were here to find out who assaulted me and who transported me to this second-rate hospital against my will."

Silas leaned in. "I believe your head injury is causing you confusion. Restraining orders aren't issued in the middle of the night without solid evidence to back them up. For your information, your wife is considering filing charges." He moved closer, almost chest to chest. "But we're interested in something more serious. You've been identified as following these women and taking their pictures. Are these photos your little souvenirs to enjoy after you murdered them?" Silas set his feet prepared for the fish to bite.

Molten heat raged in Morgan's eyes. "You son of a bitch." He planted a hand on Silas's chest and shoved.

The bait taken, Silas set the hook. He gripped Morgan's wrist with his prosthesis, spun the man in place and shoved the doctor's hand all the way to the shoulder blades. Morgan stepped forward to relieve the pressure, and Silas walked him to the hospital bed and slammed him face-down amongst the rumpled bed sheets. He would have preferred a concrete floor, but he hated Internal Affairs, and they were sure to see his actions through a different lens.

"You just assaulted a police officer. Detective Barker is my witness. You're under arrest."

"Screw you," Morgan raged. "Go to the head of the unemployment line. You're the same as fired." Morgan bucked and kicked.

The heel of his shoe skinned Silas's shin bone.

That's it," Silas said. He dragged Morgan from the bed and threw him to the floor. He knelt, jerked the doctor's arms behind his back, and pressed a knee in the middle of the man's spine. "Mr. Morgan just resisted arrest. Detective Barker, read this man his rights."

Hadley stepped forward, cuffs in hand. "You are under arrest for assaulting a police officer and resisting arrest. You'll be escorted Downtown for booking and further questioning in the deaths of Abbey Bryant and Savannah Peterson." He snapped the restraint in place, drew the metal tight enough to make Morgan gasp, and recited the Miranda.

Silas hauled Morgan upright. "Dr. Morgan, do you understand your rights?"

"Yes. One of them is the right to a lawyer." Morgan fixed him with an arrogant glare.

"You are correct, Mr. Morgan. Please understand that you are being charged with a felony. I'm sure you're aware of how hospital administration in this city deals with convicted felons on their staff?"

Winter settled behind Dr. Tyler Morgan's angry stare.

27

CHAPTER TWENTY-SEVEN

Taking command of the eastern horizon, the sun forced a thin veil of violet and rose-colored clouds into submission. Morgan's arrest had consumed the hours before dawn. Silas lowered the sun visor. The flow of traffic on I-70 was smooth, adding a bit of optimism to Silas's mood.

He'd left Hadley and Mendez to book the doctor and lock him up. But not exactly in that order. He'd ordered a cooling off period for the protection of the suspect. Silas's lips twitched. Four hours in a holding cell turned lions into lambs.

At 8:00, Morgan would be officially booked. The delay a minor inconvenience for the prisoner, in the interests of his own safety—of course—and well within the 48 hours allowed by law. By the time Silas returned, the doctor would be out on bail, but there was a satisfaction in knowing the man's ego had been delivered a severe blow. Now it was time Silas manned up and took his lashes from Elizabeth.

He called Elizabeth. On the fourth ring she answered. "Chief Cartwright here." Each word came out choppy as though she was out of breath. A train whistled in the background.

"Good morning Chief. Hope I didn't wake you." He knew better.

Liz was an early riser.

"You didn't, but I'm busy," she said. "I'll call you back."

"Your call has ended." The hands-free technology stated the obvious. What was up with Elizabeth? He was due a severe butt-chewing, but it hadn't come. Maybe she was building steam for a new and improved verbal castration. She couldn't say he hadn't tried to keep her informed.

A dark blue Suburban slipped behind the SUV. Silas remembered a similar vehicle parked across the street from the precinct when he pulled out of the underground garage. His internal antenna quivered.

He signaled, checked his blind spot then eased into the left-hand lane. He sped by the next two vehicles and pulled back into what Lila had nick-named the *old people's lane.* The suburban remained a blue shadow in his rear-view mirror.

At 6:45, Silas exited to Highway 54 at Columbia. In fifteen minutes, he'd be with the warden. If the Suburban followed, the day promised to become more interesting. Silas slowed, attempting to read the license plate. A layer of mud obscured the letters and numbers. In striking contradiction, the body of the vehicle gleamed in the sun. Half-a-mile ahead, he knew he'd be turning left onto No More Victims Road.

The SUV's onboard phone beeped. He tapped the screen open expecting Elizabeth, but the face of his old friend Archie Hamilton appeared. Silas signaled a left turn and checked his mirror. The dark blue Suburban had stopped, not following him onto No More Victims Road. Silas pulled to the side of the road.

"Archie," Silas said. "How are you, buddy? I hear you've been promoted to Special Agent. Who're you holding hostage over there at the FBI?" He chuckled. "Just kidding man, congratulations." Archie and Silas went way back. Archie worked out of the FBI's St. Louis office and appreciated the strengths of The Blackbirds. Through the years the two colleagues had secretly exchanged favors.

Silas shot another glance to the rear. The Suburban waited. Silas unsnapped his holster.

"Hey, Silas. I'm good. Heard you were headed to the big house over in Jeff City. I'm having lunch in that little town of California. I'll be at the Knic Knac Café around 11:00. It's right on your way home. Wondered if we could meet up and share a thought or two?"

"Can you give me a clue what this's about?" Silas trained his gaze on the Suburban.

"Let's just say, we're closing in on a pit of vipers. I need a little *special* help to chop off the big snake's head and shut down a supply chain of opioids. We're close to connecting Russell Beacham to someone in your area."

Silas felt his blood stir. "I hate snakes," he said. "I'll see you at the Knic Knac."

"Sounds good."

Silas started to ask if his boss had been advised, but Archie was gone. The Suburban rolled closer to the turn. One person was visible inside. Silas weighed his options. He slid his gun from its holster and laid it across his lap.

The Suburban executed a slow U-turn and returned the way it had come. No show of guns—no smack of bullets, just a message. *We're watching you.* The why was harder to sort out.

Russell Beacham's world of opioid distribution was the last hornet's nest Silas had stirred by rescuing Carla, the man's wife. The Blackbirds had reported no lapse in security, and they were all accounted for. Dr. Morgan was in jail. So, who wanted to know his whereabouts? And, who didn't care that he knew?

The incident left a *to be continued* residue slithering amongst his senses. Another minute passed before he palmed his phone, tapped in a message for Bertha, and hit send. He shrugged out of his shoulder harness, holstered his gun, and stowed them both in the console. The road behind him remained empty as he finished the drive to the correction center.

Stone-faced guards at the entrance confirmed his appointment with Warden Jasper, and Silas entered the grounds. The place resembled a hundred other prisons, concrete walls, barbed wire, and cold gray metal. He parked in the front row of the nearly empty visitor's lot.

A familiar ring tone caught his attention, and he clicked on Bertha's message. A plan was in place. He acknowledged the computer's strategy with the press of his finger. Four Blackbirds flew across the screen. A big surprise awaited the driver of the blue suburban. He exited the SUV and headed for his meeting with Henry Jasper.

After completing the labyrinth of security checks, a guard the size of a refrigerator, skin the color of ebony, and dark eyes that said *don't mess with me* motioned him forward. "I'll take you to Warden Jasper's office." The man spoke in a tone absent of warmth.

Silas followed the guard down a corridor deeper into the depths of the prison. The Warden prided himself in staying connected to the heartbeat of his responsibilities. Every inmate travelled through his office. He advised them of the rules on their way in, and if they were lucky, he wished them well on their way out. Between those meetings, he tried to keep the men as close to human as possible—sane and alive.

The guard turned left instead of right at the end of the corridor, Silas stopped. "Isn't the Warden's office that way?"

"Nope." The guard never missed a step.

Silas followed, glancing over his shoulder at the empty hallway. If this was a set-up, he was on his own. Another left, then a right, and the guard stopped in front of a closed door.

"Look, I don't know you, but you must be somebody special. The Warden hasn't had a visitor since he transferred into this office." The guard's black eyes bored into Silas's. "He's my friend, if you upset him, you'll be dealing with me. Got it?"

Silas remained quiet, meeting the guard's intimidating stare with one of his own.

The guard's gaze shifted. His stance no longer certain. He opened his mouth to speak, thought better of it, turned and knocked. He opened the door and motioned Silas inside.

Henry Jasper met Silas half-way across the room and greeted him with a hug, the way a father might a son.

Silas returned the show of affection. Henry Jasper had never been a big man, but today the frailness of his body reminded Silas of his sister in the last days of her battle with cancer. A drumroll of dread pounded his temple.

"That will be all, Lonnie. Thank you." Henry nodded his dismissal of the guard.

"Are you sure?" Lonnie's expression tightened, brows drawing together in a look of concern. He jutted his jaw as though he intended to argue.

"Lonnie!" The warden's single word was an order not to be questioned.

Lonnie shot Silas another threatening look and stomped out of the office.

"What's going on, Henry?" Silas hooked his thumb in the direction of Lonnie's fading footsteps. "A bodyguard—since when?"

"Thinks he's my nursemaid." Henry chuckled. "Lonnie is a bit more dramatic than I like, but his intentions are good." The warden pushed the door shut. "Have a seat. Let's talk about why you're here."

The wind from the shut-down topic slapped Silas's face, but he wasn't to be sidetracked. "No, Henry. Let's talk about why you're—*here*." Silas waved his right hand to take in the small office. "This place looks like you've been decorating from a garage sale." He pointed to the old metal desk, a worn executive chair, boasting a cracked vinyl seat, and one visitor's chair. "Where are all your files, and photos of notorious inmates? This is a cell not an office."

A small table hosted a shiny, maybe even new, coffee pot. The smell was enticing. "Appreciate the fresh coffee. Glad to see your promises are still good." Silas stepped over to the pot, poured two cups of the brew, set one on Henry's desk, and slumped into the visitor's chair, holding the other.

Unsteady on his feet, Henry settled behind his desk. The old chair creaked a mild complaint. But somehow, Henry appeared comfortable, maybe even satisfied. He patted the metal desk. "Did you know this desk and chair were the first I ever used in this prison? Seems appropriate I should occupy them in my last few weeks as warden. My replacement has taken over my old office. He's a good man and will make a better warden than I ever did."

"I doubt that," Silas argued. He eyed his friend over the top of the cup. The gray skin tone, and absence of a sparkle in his blue eyes, sickened Silas. He shifted in his chair. "Is the decision to leave yours?"

"Let's just say, God showed me His plan and I am no man to argue with The Almighty. My hope is that I can help you once more before I take my leave." Henry tugged open a desk drawer and retrieved a folder. "Mike Rojas was Norman Shields' cellmate. I've arranged a private room for your interview. It's never a good idea for the other prisoners to know, one of their own is having a friendly visit with the police." Henry handed Silas a folder." Rojas may be less than cooperative. Thought you might want to know a little about him." Henry extended a thin packet of paper. "Here's a record of Shields' visitors."

Silas sipped his coffee as he scanned the Rojas file. "Drugs and human trafficking. This should be an interesting meeting." He handed the folder back to Henry and switched to the visitation list. Carla Gleason. His gut jumped to attention. The woman rescued by The Blackbirds was named Carla Beecham. Could there be a connection? Silas filed the information away to be explored when he returned to The House of Audrey.

Tyler Morgan's name came as no surprise. "Who is Elle Goodman?" The name Elle tickled his memory banks, but he couldn't place why.

"Shields designated her as the person to pick up his ashes."

"A relative?"

"Don't know. Shields' lawyer drew up the papers. After Shields was cremated, he was of no interest to me."

Silas's finger trailed down the log to the name listed more than any other. "Russell Beecham visited Shields like a dedicated wife. The last time, right before Shields was killed."

"I thought that might get a rise out of you. I heard Beecham's been arrested."

"Nothing gets by you." Silas smiled.

"I still have my ear to the ground." A glimmer of the old sparkle had returned to Henry's eyes.

"Was Beecham moving drugs into the prison?"

"We couldn't prove a thing. The in-and-out method remains a mystery. The FBI had only been involved a few days, when another inmate took a shiv to Norman Shields. Couldn't nail anyone for that either."

Silas stiffened. "Did the FBI achieve anything?"

"Not really. I understand recent activities have reignited their interest."

Silas raised his eyebrow.

Henry extended his hands, palms up. "I can't help it when I hear things." The older man grinned. "Shields was not an addict, just a miserable excuse for a human," Henry continued. "After he died, the prison telegraph informed us he'd been short-changing Beecham to pay for an escape."

"Beecham had him killed to appease the man in control?"

"Maybe. In this place with Shields' history, a dozen guys wanted his slice of the drug pie.

A spider crept from beneath Henry's desk. For Silas, spiders belonged in the same category where Hadley placed cats. Silas kept one eye on the arthropod's progress.

"What was Shields doing with the skimmed money?

"Funneled to an unknown accomplice on the outside. His method was either genius, or we overlooked the obvious."

"We arrested Dr. Morgan this morning for assaulting a police officer," Silas said, measuring the decreasing distance between the spider and his own legs. "Evidence is piling up that he's The Surgeon. Do you know why he visited Shields?"

The old chair creaked as Henry shifted his weight. "Claimed he was writing an article on behalf of prisoners who wanted to become organ donors. I was surprised when Shields agreed to do the interview. Then—Shields wanted to be a donor. I figured there wasn't a chance in hell, because of his age, and the fact that he was a killer. Morgan went to bat for him. Touted the rare blood type and how many lives could be saved."

"Are you saying, Dr. Morgan initiated the idea?" Silas cringed as the spider switched to arachnidarting, the final preparation for launch onto a victim. He resisted standing on his chair.

Henry nodded and Silas's gut twitched. His picture of Dr. Morgan and the man Henry was describing didn't match. "Did Shields know Morgan was his son?"

Silas might as well have set off the prison's alarm system.

"What?" Henry's feet slapped the floor. The spider scurried into the opposite corner of the room.

Relief poured over Silas. He focused on his friend.

Henry Jasper surprised by anything inside his beloved prison was a rare thing to witness. The grayness of his skin brightened as though an infusion of health had taken place. "Are you sure?"

"Richard Maeken told me. We're checking Morgan's DNA against Norman Shields' now."

Henry drummed his fingers on his desk. "A successful doctor arranges a meeting with the one person who could damage, maybe even ruin his career if the connection came out—interesting."

"Indeed," Silas said. "Sounds like the good doctor's family jewels were in a pretty tight vise for him to risk coming here. The question becomes, who had a reason for tightening the screw?"

28

CHAPTER TWENTY-EIGHT

Silas took his leave of Henry Jasper and followed a different, but no more friendly guard. The man led him down hallways, turning left and right a dozen times. Silas had no idea where he was when they finally stopped in front of a room marked Chaplain. The guard turned the knob, pushed the door inward, and motioned Silas forward.

Wary, and naked without his gun, his nerves tightened in primal readiness. If the guard followed him, Silas was in trouble. He stepped into a narrow room. The door swung shut. Through a small window the detective saw the guard take up a position in the hall.

Florescent lights hung from a dingy ceiling. One bulb was black on both ends and not lit. Determined patches of paint clung to the walls in a dull yellow. The room's condition drove home a sad message. Henry Jasper was dying. The Warden, Silas had known kept his prison pristine.

"I've been expecting you Chief Detective Albert." The title slid from Mike Rojas' mouth oozing disrespect.

Hands and feet shackled, the drug dealer and human trafficker wore a prison issued orange jumpsuit. His short legs dangled inches above the floor, giving the impression of being suspended in the air. Silas checked twice to locate the nylon strap buried amongst folds of flesh where the man's waist should have been. Hooked to the belt was another band leading between the inmate's legs. The restraint passed through a metal chair hidden beneath layers of fat but connecting to the chains around thick ankles. If the man sneezed, only a miracle would prevent total collapse.

"Rojas," Silas didn't give the man the courtesy of a—*Mr.*

"What does the brass want with me?" Below where the man's chin should be, incredible layers of skin wobbled with each word. "I'm no snitch."

"No. You're not," Silas agreed. "A snitch gives information for something in return. There's nothing for you to gain here except perhaps a clearer conscience." He hesitated, then decided to not pull any punches. "We need your help to stop a serial killer."

The inmate's mouth formed an ugly grimace, that might have been construed as a smile. "At least you didn't give me some line about gaining God's forgiveness. There's no hope for me there. My apologies if you're a believer." His chest heaved followed by a fit of dry coughing. Silas surmised advanced COPD, even though there was no oxygen bottle in sight. Too much risk of being used as a weapon, he guessed.

"In case you didn't know, Chief Detective, a clear conscience doesn't change a thing for a person in here." One finger of the prisoner's child-like hand moved in a circular motion. "Chasing a serial killer led you to me. Why?" Two wiry black eyebrows inched upward, revealing eyes black as coal and gambler keen.

Silas chewed on the request. He despised men like this one, but Rojas had opened the door. Silas took a shot in the dark. "The killer is connected to your old cellmate, Norman Shields. You knew the man better than anyone."

A veil dropped over Rojas' eyes. "Norman's been dead for years, his organs donated, and his body cremated. Is the old Devil operating from beyond the grave?" A giggle, high-pitched and mean, burst from the inmate's bloated face.

"Someone's killing transplant recipients. Specifically, those who received one of Norman Shields' organs. You lived with Shields. He trusted you. Told you things." Silas let the words sink in. "He may have even protected you. Then Dr. Morgan showed up and everything changed." Silas knew he'd struck a nerve when the inmate balled his hands into tiny fists. "How did Shields respond to a visit from his long-lost son?"

Rojas' face darkened. "Norman never took threats well. And he'd had plenty. Stomped around the cell all night. Banged his head into the wall a few times too. Muttered and carried on about giving up everything for ungrateful children. I was ready to kill him myself."

The muscles in Silas's shoulders tightened. *What did Shields' children have to be grateful for? He killed their mother.*

The convict continued as though Silas had left the room. "Norman was tight-lipped about his life before prison. It didn't matter, because I knew what he'd done. But that night, he had the balls to claim he was innocent. The man I knew, wouldn't have taken the fall for anyone. But he said he did. What a joke. Or so I thought." Rojas let loose another giggle. "Don't you know, everyone in this place is innocent, even me."

Silas cringed. Innocence and this low life didn't belong in the same sentence. "How could Dr. Morgan possibly threaten his father? The man was already in prison for the rest of his life."

"Even men in prison don't want to die." A coughing spell robbed Rojas of air and turned his skin blotchy. His mouth hung open as he dragged in vital oxygen. At last he continued. "Norman was a king pin in here. But he wanted out. He planned an escape funded by money he skimmed from his inside deals. But he got in a hurry and took too much. Signed his own death warrant."

"What did that have to do with his son?"

"Morgan wanted his old man to make his final arrangements." A film of moisture gathered in the inmate's eyes. Norman Shields had been more than a cellmate to Mike Rojas.

Blood rushed to Silas's head. "Morgan knew there was a hit out on his father. How would he know that, and why would he even care?"

Rojas frowned. "One question at a time. He wanted Norman to be an organ donor. He said Norman was the same as dead anyway, and a special person needed his heart."

Silas felt his knees weaken. "Who?"

"You're the Chief Detective, don't you know?" Rojas' eyelids drifted closed, hiding a wicked gleam.

Silas knew, and the truth sickened him, but Morgan's involvement didn't make any sense.

What else was going on here? Silas chose the power of silence to obtain more information rather than pounding Rojas with his prosthetic, although he sorely wanted to do the latter. The guard banged on the closed door. Flecks of paint broke loose from the wall and fluttered to the floor, adding to a growing pool of yellow specks. "You about done in there. I've got to take a break."

Silas almost swallowed his tongue. "Call for relief or hold it." he growled.

"You're a cool one," Rojas said, his gaze empty and distant. "And I'm the inquisitive sort. I want to know where this serial killer thing is going. Is Morgan your man?"

"What do you think?"

"God only knows." The inmate tilted his head. "Or, is it the Devil? Sometimes I get the two mixed up."

"I'm sure you do." Silas didn't smile. "I'll say this. Morgan is *a person of interest.*"

Rojas pursed his lips. The room was cool, but beads of sweat covered the man's brow. A sickly cast had replaced the red blotches across his skin. "I'd like to see Morgan get the needle." The inmate's words leaked a coldness that made Silas's skin prickle.

"Chief Detective, you have a reputation, and because you just might be able to get Morgan the death sentence, I'll share the whole story. I have one request. I want to witness the bastard take his last breath in the kill room." Rojas waggled black eyebrows as though he'd asked for the winning card in Go Fish. "What-do-you-say?"

Silence blanketed the room, broken only by Rojas' labored breathing. The outrageous appeal underscored a weird combination of rational thinking and insanity. Silas hesitated, needing the man to think the request warranted consideration. "I'll make your wishes known."

"You'll be more willing when you hear what Norman told me the day his son visited. Believe me it's out of left field crazy." Rojas peeled off another round of giggles.

The sound set Silas's teeth on edge, but he played along. Rojas had the stage. "What did Shields say that was—left field crazy?"

"That was a good line, huh? You dig that insanity shit, don't you?"

A red haze blurred Silas's vision.

"Come on, hit me. I know you want to." The convict rattled his shackles. The metal chair popped as his weight shifted. "Cops love to beat on a weirdo who can't defend himself."

A burst of laughter cleared the red haze. "That would be too easy, and it wouldn't help me convict a serial killer."

The orange clad excuse for a human being, managed to clap his shackled hands. "You, my friend, have a sense of humor."

Friend and Rojas created an oxymoron of ugly dimensions. "I'm waiting," Silas said.

"That night, after his son's visit, Norman bawled like a baby. He swore he'd given up his freedom to protect his children. Now they wanted his body parts too."

"Organ donations?" Silas forced the words from a dry throat.

"I spent most of the night getting that story out of him." Rojas paused for effect. "It seems, Norman's grandchild needed a transplant. The kid was about to die, needed a kidney or something. The father wasn't a match, but Norman was. Don't ask me how Morgan knew that, but he is a doctor, so I guess he has his ways. What a deal. Kid couldn't live without Norman's help, but he had to die first."

Bile rose in Silas's throat. He swallowed it back. "Who killed Shields?

"You're the Chief Detective."

Silas refused to let the remark get under his skin, but he wondered where Rojas was when Shields was stabbed. In prison, a life cost little more than a pack of cigarettes. And there was the possibility Rojas had carried out a warped act of love for Norman Shields. "Just so you know, his death didn't help the granddaughter. She died after a boating accident."

"This one didn't."

For an instant, the floor seemed to drop beneath Silas's feet.

Little pointed teeth, yellow as corn, broke the plane of Rojas' face. "I can tell by the look in your eyes, you didn't know Norman had two granddaughters." Rojas snickered. "How'd you ever get to be Chief Detective? But, since you're so inept, I'll help you a little more. The second granddaughter is a secret love child."

The floor dropped another inch. "The mother blackmailed the father to save her daughter?"

"Good guess, but no cigar." Rojas looked like the cat that swallowed the bird. "The mother is out of the picture. Dead from the big C. Someone else knew about the child, and threatened to expose the famous doctor, ruin his career, his marriage, and get him charged with rape."

Silas's stomach plummeted. He grasped at a straw. "You said the granddaughter was a love child."

"A matter of interpretation." Rojas gloated. "I might have put my own spin on that part of the story."

Silas's face stiffened into cardboard-like layers. His mind flew backward nineteen years. The hysterical call from his sister. His frantic drive to the University of Missouri in Columbia, finding her incoherent, bruised, and beaten. Nine months later Lila was born.

He'd promised to keep his sister's secret. Not even their parents knew. His sister changed her name to Girard, claimed a short-lived marriage, and came home to be a single parent. Then the cancer took her.

The memories punched Silas in the throat. Sheer willpower chained his arms to his sides. For seven years, this scum in front of him possessed the information to put his sister's rapist behind bars and keep a serial killer off the street. Silas forced the fiery need for revenge to a slow burn. Rojas wanted him to lose control, and Silas's history wasn't snow white. But he'd never assaulted a restrained prisoner. He wasn't about to start now.

Silas circled Rojas. The inmate twisted left then right, attempting to keep Silas in view. The detective leaned in close enough for his whisper to bend the hairs on the man's neck. "Picture *yourself* in the kill room." He struck the back of the chair with his fist. "I'm tired of playing your little game. Who has Morgan by the short hairs? I want the name of the person he trusted with his deepest secret, and I want to know why."

"I don't have to tell you anything."

He had him. Weight flew from Silas's shoulders. Rojas knew the name. "No. You don't, but it will be hard to watch what happens in the kill room when you're invited there first." Silas faced the inmate. "How much did Dr. Morgan pay you to kill Norman Shields?"

Rojas winced. His false bravado wilted. "I didn't take a dime." The tone of his breaths deepened, sounding raspy and ragged. "I loved Norman. He didn't treat me like a freak. I did what he asked, not what that snake of a son tried to pay me to do. I'll tell you who it is, but you're not going to like what you hear."

"Spit it out."

"You can trust your deepest secrets with a cop—right?" Rojas clutched his chest. "Especially if you're family." The inmate's face contorted, his body spasmed, and plastic restraints popped under the stress. A screech of failing metal split the air. The chair collapsed. Rojas hit the floor like a load of concrete, creating a miniature dust storm of yellow paint flecks.

Silas shot his hands above his head.

The guard burst through the door his baton drawn. Alarm flared in his eyes.

"Call a medic!" Silas dropped to his knees. Rojas wasn't breathing.

The guard's glance whipped from Silas to Rojas.

"NOW!" Silas ordered.

"Dispatch send a medic to the Chaplain's office—STAT. Inmate 5591 is down. It'll take six guys to get him off the floor. Send them, too."

Silas searched his soul. In his mind he heard his grandfather. 'Don't play God, but don't owe the Devil either.'

Silas tilted the inmate's head. He verified Rojas had not swallowed his tongue. The detective positioned the heel of his right hand on the man's breastbone, interlocked the fingers of his prosthesis with the first hand, and using stiffened arms and his upper body strength performed a compression. He counted to 100 three times before help arrived.

Guards filled the room. A medic continued the chest work. The guard who had escorted Silas into the room offered his hand and helped Silas to his feet.

"You're a better man than me," the guard said. "No way would I do what you just did. He could have been pretending and you'd be dead."

Silas thought of Richard Maeken carrying him from the burning drug house. "Anyone can do what's right," he said.

The compressions continued for several minutes. The medic shook his head. "No response. I think he was dead when he hit the floor."

29

CHAPTER TWENTY-NINE

Two hours later, a guard escorted Silas from the prison. He gulped buckets of the cool April air. The sense of drowning remained. A thousand questions raced through his mind. Another thousand fears thundered right behind.

He arrived at I-70, but he had no idea how. He didn't remember getting into the SUV or putting on his shoulder harness and gun. Comforted by the weight, he no longer felt naked. With a jolt, he realized he'd forgotten his promise to meet Archie Hamilton at the Knic Knac café. He wheeled through a drug store parking lot and headed back toward Missouri State 50.

Rojas was dead. A black cloud swept through Silas's conscience. Trained to rule his emotions with a will of iron, he'd nearly failed. He'd been ready to kill—for a name. Silas hammered the steering wheel with his fist.

I still am.

At least Silas had found out who had raped his sister. An image of Morgan boiled to the surface. For a delicious moment, Silas entertained the idea of permanently altering Morgan's manhood. Lucky for the doctor the confines of the city jail protected him. Lucky for Silas, too.

He forced the firestorm in his head to the size of a small inferno. He had Lila to think of, and a job to do. If he couldn't get Morgan on anything else, soliciting a person to commit murder, carried a hefty penalty of up to twenty years. Silas intended to be there when a judge extended the hospitality of the state to Morgan.

The case against the doctor was stronger with the prison's surveillance footage. But the primary witness's character was flawed. Not to mention he was dead. A defense attorney would tear Mike Rojas' credibility to shreds. The solution lay in nailing Dr. Morgan for the serial killings.

An impatient driver honked and swerved around the SUV. Startled from his thoughts, Silas blinked, stared at the stalled car in front of him, and swore. He could hear Elizabeth now. "You rear-ended a stalled car? How the Hell did you let that happen?" He steered into the moving traffic, thankful the good Lord had taken over the wheel and saved him one more time from Elizabeth's wrath.

A carefree blue sky filled his windshield, diametrically opposed to the upheaval in his brain. A memory of his grandfather sprang into his mind. They'd been sparring on the patio in a boxing ring outlined by chalk. "Study your opponent until you know his weakest point. That's where you throw your hardest punch, and you keep throwing until he begs for mercy." Silas had been ten years old.

From their first introduction, Silas suspicioned deep seated insecurities hid beneath Dr. Morgan's arrogant facade. The man had a need to prove himself. At the epicenter of that drive was the ultimate failure. Not preventing the death of his mother. Power and a successful image had soothed the pain—until it didn't.

Silas frowned. Two things didn't add up. Norman Shields had confessed. And Dr. Morgan liked control. Rojas' last words left the impression of a killer who operated at the beck and call of a cop. A cop who would be a relative to Lila. Silas rolled his shoulders, but the tension remained. Lila's relatives were piling up like driftwood on a wind-swept beach. He'd have to have a week to explain her extended family.

Silas used his on-board technology to ring Sydney. The call went to voicemail. He left a message. "Sydney. I need you to unearth the autopsy report for Norman Shields' wife. Do a double check of the gunshot angles. The examination may have been sloppy due to the confession. I've good reason to believe a Shields did the shooting, but not Norman. I'll explain everything later. Thanks."

He called the war room next. The young man who had identified Abbey Bryant's friend, Margaret Culver, answered. "Anyone know where Chief Cartwright is?" Silas asked.

"She called in for an update but didn't state her location."

"Put me on speaker."

"Listen up, everybody. Chief Detective Albert's on the line."

The room quieted. "Okay folks, things are heating up. See what you can do with a thirty-year-old murder." He explained what his trip to Jefferson City that morning had revealed, and what Sydney Franco was working on. His heart hurt as he exposed Lila's role.

A few choice cuss words filtered through the speaker. Silas understood. Each man and woman on the team knew Lila. When a fellow cop's family was threatened—there was Hell to pay.

"Dig until you find the reports from the murder scene of the mother. Tear them apart word by word. Interview the investigating officers. Use everything at your disposal to identify and locate the other children. I'll be asking the FBI for help. The Surgeon is a sick man, but the cop pulling his strings is worse.

Be discrete if you can. We don't want to scare anyone off. Any questions?"

"No sir." Silas recognized the confident voice of the meter maid turned homicide investigator, Janice Sloan.

"Send a text if you learn anything new. I'll get back to you."

"Yes sir," Sloan said.

The assignment lessened his sense of drowning to one of treading water. He drove the SUV across the Missouri river, murky enough to uphold its' name, Big Muddy. The dark blue suburban from the early morning had been pushed to the back of his mind, buried by the revelations of Mike Rojas. Now he noticed he was being shadowed once again. He nearly grinned.

Driving at a steady pace, he turned right onto Missouri 50. Five minutes later he was in farm country. Traffic was light, only three vehicles behind him—the blue suburban, followed by a white, unmarked police car, flying a small red flag. A gray van brought up the rear, displaying a matching red flag. Bertha had The Blackbirds in place. Including the prisoner transport van was a nice touch. He sent the computer a voice to text command. "Call off The Blackbirds. I'll handle this one. They can make the arrest when I'm finished."

Silas stomped the accelerator and the SUV roared in response. Barreling down the blacktop he slid through a curve, the tires mewled in protest but clung to the pavement. The smell of burned rubber stung his nose and pumped his blood. He flew up one hill and down the other side. In the flat, he spotted what he was looking for. He slowed, pulled off the highway into an overgrown lane. He parked beside an old fashioned lilac bush, the nose of the SUV pointed out. The engine idled and the sweet fragrance flowed into the vehicle.

The blue suburban flashed by. Silas counted to ten, and then rocketed onto the highway. Sixty seconds later, at ninety miles an hour, he lined up behind his unsuspecting prey. The red lights and siren responded to the touch of his finger.

The driver's head jerked. His vehicle veered to the right. One wheel contacted the drunk bumps at the edge of the pavement.

"Shit! This guy really is a rookie."

The man over-corrected. The suburban careened across the highway and slid into a shallow ditch. Both front doors bounced open.

Silas braked to a sliding halt. Time stalled. Silas flung off his seat belt, bolted from the SUV, and raced toward the wreck. A person sat upright contained by the safety restraints and released air bags. Slowing to a cautious walk, Silas unsnapped his holster and removed his gun. "I am Silas Albert of the Kansas City Homicide Unit. Place your hands on the steering wheel and do not move."

The air thickened with energy. Silas approached the rear of the vehicle then inched along its side. The seat belt latch clicked loud as a rifle shot. Silas's pulse throbbed at percussion level. "Hands up. I'm not here to arrest you. I only want to talk."

A flurry of movement exploded from the front seat. The man slipped himself from under the air bags and disappeared from sight.

Silas reached the driver's open door in time to see a figure dressed in dark green, limping toward the woods. Silas fired twice into the air. The escapee limped faster. Silas slammed his gun into its' holster and gave chase. He jumped the ditch and pursued a skinnier, younger man. Counting on endurance, he held his pace for fifty yards dodging bushes and thorn trees. The distance closed. Ten yards, five yards, one yard. At the top of a casual incline, Silas launched himself.

The impact of his body barreled the man forward. Silas drove him into the dirt with the force of his own landing. Air swooshed from his target's lungs. Silas struggled to his feet, rolled the man face up, and strategically placed his foot for maximum results. He scanned the man's figure for serious injury. Blood spurted from one nostril. A splash of red leaked through a tuft of grass hanging from the other. Broken twigs imbedded the man's long dark hair. Skin abrasions trailed down his forehead to his scruffy chin. The man swung his head. He gagged, snorted, and pawed the dirt and grass from his nose.

"What's your name?"

Silence.

"Who are you working for?"

"None of your business."

"Try again." Silas shifted his foot pressure.

A moan rolled through tightened lips. "Stop. Stop. I'm Rusty Ballou. I was hired by a woman—Elle."

A shaft of ice stabbed Silas's chest. Elle Goodman had picked up Norman Shield's ashes. "What did she ask you to do?"

"Keep tabs on you."

"Why?"

"She didn't say." He squirmed under Silas's foot. "Look, I'm telling you the truth. I've never even laid eyes on the woman. A note was left on my car. Sounded like easy money, so I picked up the down payment and started tailing you."

"How long ago was this?"

"Couple of days."

And nights. Silas cringed, remembering how the windows in Sydney's office exposed their movements, before she closed the blinds.

Blood trailed down both sides of the young Asian's face. He

appeared to be early twenties. Only a couple of years older than Lila. "Do you still have the note?"

"Nope. Not a good idea to keep stuff like that."

"How do you give her updates?"

"She supplied me a TracFone. I call and leave a message every two or three hours, never hear her voice."

Silas gritted his teeth. Elle Goodman was careful. "Where did you pick up the down payment?"

"I drove to an old farmhouse out in the country. Some black kid on a bicycle shoved an envelope through my car window. Scared the shit out of me."

"Look, I'm going to let you up, but you'd better be cool. Don't run and don't be swinging at me. I haven't shot anyone today. Don't spoil my good mood." Silas stepped back.

Rusty Ballou struggled to his feet. "I hope I never run into you when you're in a bad mood." One hand dug a greasy mechanic's rag from his pocket. He pressed the cloth against his nose. The other hand gingerly cradled his crotch.

"Now. Walk in front of me back to the highway. Don't talk, and don't trip, I might think you're trying to get away."

A few minutes later Ballou limped across the highway. Silas followed, nodding to the four female police officers standing beside the white, unmarked patrol car. A gray van was parked nearby.

"I thought you weren't going to arrest me."

"I'm not," Silas said, brushing debris from his clothes. Maybe by the time he reached the Knic Knac Café, the damp spots on the knees of his khakis would be dried. "These ladies have jurisdiction. I don't."

He identified himself as though he and the four women were strangers. "Speeding, reckless driving, endangering the life of a police officer, stalking, resisting arrest, and obstructing justice."

Ballou's face paled beneath the angry abrasions and drying blood.

"His name's Rusty Ballou. He might see his way to help with the apprehension of Elle Goodman. She is a person of interest in a case involving the sale of drugs, and murder."

Ballou sucked air.

"Goodman hired Mr. Ballou for illegal purposes." Silas hid a wink from the petrified young man. "In Kansas City, we cut a little slack for those who help us out. Given of course, Mr. Ballou has no other criminal issues."

"We do the same, Detective," an officer wearing the insignia of Sergeant responded. "All depends if the information leads to an arrest." She returned his wink. "We'll take it from here."

CHAPTER THIRTY

Silas took his leave. As he pulled away, Ballou was being assisted into the back of the gray van. The man was in capable hands. Capable of getting information from a rock. Silas couldn't be in two places at once.

He continued along Highway 50 in the direction of the little town of California. The take-down had eased the inferno in his head, but the sense of treading water returned.

Lila was right. Their family was cursed. How many more times could his niece receive heartbreaking news before she was broken herself? And Lila didn't deserve any part of this horror story. And what about Silas's parents? Would they understand the vow he'd made to protect Lila from the knowledge of her mother's rape? His chest tightened. For now, Lila was safe. Only the rapist knew the story and he was in jail.

A sign welcomed Silas to the town of California, population 4,278. He pulled into the Knic Knac Café parking lot. Ten minutes early for his appointment with Archie and well ahead of the noon rush, he parked next to a metallic purple VW beetle.

He retrieved his phone from the console. He visualized a dozen calls from Elizabeth, her level of anger rising after each reroute to voicemail. He opened the screen. Seven messages. An immediate ringing startled him. The name on the screen made him sit up straight. "Hello."

"Detective Albert, James Torrey. Remember me? The Afghan Vet with the prosthetic leg."

"Of course, James, how's your little superman?"

"Being a typical four-year-old."

"That's a good thing. What can I do for you?"

"You told me to call if I remembered anything helpful. I did think of something, but it's kind of weird."

"Weird, how?"

"Well, you know how everyone has an SUV now-a-days?

Silas dragged in a long breath. "I do."

"Very few have a Federation of Police sticker on the back. When you drove away, I noticed yours. I've realized I'd seen the sticker before. Mostly at night. I even saw the vehicle parked in Savannah Peterson's drive."

Silas's heart thumped. "Could you identify the driver, tell if it was a man or woman?"

"Sorry. It didn't seem as out of place as the silver Mercedes. Like I said, everyone has an SUV."

As though proving James's point, a black SUV pulled into the Knic Knac parking lot, parked, and Archie Hamilton stepped out. Silas pointed to his phone. Archie nodded and headed inside the café.

"But that's not the big thing I remembered." James said.

"Tell me you have the license number."

"There was a plate, but it was dirty. I could only make out the first two digits, and I'm not real sure about them. 3V, maybe. At the time, I didn't think it was any big deal, so I didn't do any other recon."

"What else did you recall?"

"Another person visited Savannah Peterson. I know this can't be important..."

"The slightest thing might solve the case," Silas encouraged. "Did you recognize this person?"

"No, but the reason I don't think it's important is because he was a cop."

A coldness slid along Silas's spine. He shook it off. "A cop, how do you know?"

"The uniform. The first time I saw him, he appeared to be talking to the girl about her car. Then I saw him again. This time, they were sitting together on the front step."

Silas swallowed hard. "Can you describe the officer?"

"Not real well. Dark skinned, black hair. Hispanic maybe."

Dear God, not Mendez? Silas's stomach churned. Was that why Mendez had been so upset? He knew Savannah Peterson. Mendez also knew how critical it was to make any personnel connections to a case known. *Didn't he?* Silas shook off his uneasiness. He'd talk to Mendez about procedure when he returned to Kansas city.

"Are you at home?" Silas asked James.

"Yes."

"Stay there, I'll send an officer over to take your report. The officer will have you look at insignia affiliated with police organizations. See if you can identify the sticker you saw. Try to remember any other details about the man on the step." Silas breathed deep. "Thanks James. Sometimes it's the little things that solve a case."

"No problem."

Silas notified his team to collect James Torrey's information. He instructed them to check all department SUV's for the beginning letters 3V. He scanned the remaining messages. Nothing new.

He went to his contacts and pressed Lila's number. The call went to voice mail. He tried Hadley. His friend's voice directed him to leave a message. A rapid drumbeat pounded his chest. Where was everyone?

He'd try again after he met with Archie. He climbed from his vehicle and headed inside the Knic Knac.

He glanced around, spotting Archie in a corner booth, cradling a cup. "Coffee please," he said to the waitress. "Bring the pot." He pointed toward the FBI agent.

"Have a little roll in the bushes on your way?" Archie grinned and pointed at Silas's head.

He ran his hand over his scalp, coming away with bits of dirt and broken twigs. "People at my paygrade have to work for a living. Look, Archie. I don't have much time. How can I help you?"

"I'm short on time myself. The wife's about to have a baby."

"Congratulations. Give her my best."

The waitress arrived. "Anything I can get you two gentlemen besides coffee." She offered a pleasant smile, plunked cups in front of the two men, filled them, and picked up Archie's cold cup. "I'd be happy to bring a menu."

"I'll have a club sandwich. No sides," Archie said.

Silas nodded. "Same for me." The woman hurried away.

"I'll keep it short," Archie said. "Pharmacy delivery trucks are being targeted all over Missouri. They load up at the distribution center and disappear before they make the first stop. The drivers are unharmed, but never see the pirates. We know Beecham is involved. He was smart and careful but not in charge." Archie took a slow sip of his coffee.

"Where is the warehouse?"

"Kansas City."

"I see."

"Jail has handicapped Beecham, but we're not underestimating him. Do you know where his wife is?"

"Yes."

"We need to question her."

"She has been severely abused, mentally and physically. Can this wait a day or two?"

"No. Another truck is leaving tonight. We don't want the driver's life in jeopardy. Have one of your blackbirds talk to Mrs. Beecham—woman to woman."

"What do you want to know?"

Archie dove straight into the deep end of the pool. "We want information on Dr. Tyler Morgan. I understand you have him in custody. I'd like to help you keep him there."

Silas's pulse jumped. "If his lawyer hasn't sprung him already. You think he's the link to the robberies?"

"That's right."

The delivery of their order interrupted the agent's explanation.

"I've got to find the John." Silas said. His head was spinning. "Go ahead and eat your lunch. I'll be back in a minute."

When he returned Archie's plate was empty, and the agent was gone.

The waitress hurried over to the table. "Your friend said to tell you he had an emergency and he would text from the highway." She smiled warmly. "He paid the bill—including pie."

Silas slid into the booth. He bit into the club sandwich. The food tasted good and his last meal had been—he couldn't remember. He waved the waitress over and ordered a piece of cherry pie. Might as well enjoy it, who knew when he might have time to eat again?

Fifteen minutes later he left a twenty-dollar tip under his napkin, took a coffee to go, and headed outside. His phone lit up just as he was about to drive the SUV out of the parking lot.

Archie's message read. "Sorry I had to leave. My wife's having the baby. Wanted to discuss this last item face to face. Morgan is not the king cobra. You have a cop in your department pulling his strings. I'm counting on Carla Beecham to give us a name."

Another dirty cop. Silas wished he hadn't had the pie. He wanted to throw up.

31

CHAPTER THIRTY-ONE

Silas had driven the backroads on his return to Kansas City. He pressed his thumb to the security pad and entered The House of Audrey. A moment later he stood in front of the apartment assigned to Carla Beecham. Exposed to twenty years of rescuing battered women, Silas had learned abuse littered the demographics at every level and age group. The power of the rich created yet another dimension of control over their victims.

Was that all Carla was?

An unidentified woman had called the hotline two weeks earlier, begging for help. A team of Blackbirds had kept the Beecham home under surveillance. They would intervene only if Carla's life was in danger. The Blackbirds had nearly been too late.

Now it seemed, Carla held the key to many secrets.

Silas knocked on her door. "Carla, it's Detective Albert. I need to talk to you."

"Coming."

Silas recognized Lila's voice. A moment later she ushered him inside the apartment. "Everything good?" he asked, scanning her face for indications otherwise.

"Making progress," Lila replied. "Carla's in the kitchen.

Grandma Nancy's been with her most of the day. I'm giving Grams a break."

Recessed into the bare brick walls, the lighting cast a welcoming glow. Carefully chosen colors neither starkly white nor boldly vibrant, created the soothing nature of the sea. Silas followed his niece around a bamboo divider, separating the kitchen from the living area of the apartment.

Carla faced him, poised to dive under the table or throw the cup she gripped in an unsteady hand.

"Hello Carla, how're you managing?" Black, blue, and yellow-ish green bruises painted an ugly history, but her eyes held a spark of defiance. The same spark he searched for in a Blackbird candidate. But it was too soon to explore that possibility.

"I'm better thanks to you Detective. You saved my life. Russell would've killed me this time." The woman relaxed her grip and set the cup on the table.

"Your husband's been arrested. But there's a problem. I've been told over five hundred opioid pills were found in your kitchen. There was also a large amount of cash in an open UPS package on the table. What can you tell me about how they got there?"

The woman hung her head, her face an open book of shame.

"Carla, I know you're afraid." Lila placed a hand on the woman's shoulder. "Silas brought you here for your protection. But he expects your husband to post bail. Put yourself back in control. Help the police keep him behind bars."

Carla raised her head swinging her gaze from one to the other. "Russell's a drug supplier. He sells pain killers to dealers."

Silas's heart rate surged. "From your house, with you there?"

"No." She shook her head. "He has a special phone. The dealer leaves a message. Russell calls back on a TracFone. He arranges the exchange."

Silas was aware of the phones she meant. They were in the hands of the FBI. "Does he make the deliveries?"

"He takes packages to a UPS store. A courier picks them up, makes the deliveries, collects the return package and sends it to another connection who brings it to Russell."

"How do you know all this?"

"At first Russell was very secretive. The more control he had over me, the more he bragged about his perfect system. He knew I'd never have the nerve to stand up against him. And if I did, he'd kill me before I could go to the police."

"How did your husband get the drugs?" Silas asked.

"I never saw that part of his world. But I knew when his supply was low." She pointed to her swollen eye. "About once a month he'd get a phone call. I wasn't sure if the person made him scared or excited. His behavior was different. He paced the floor, and he did something I never saw, except when he talked to this person. He sweat. Then he'd leave for a couple of days. When he came home, he'd have another supply."

"Is he an addict?" Lila asked

"I don't think so."

"Did you ever see him talking to a cop?" Silas pressed for the answer Archie Hamilton needed.

"You mean like a cop in the drug business?"

"Yes."

Carla shook her head.

"How does his source get paid?"

Her shoulders slumped. "Sorry, I don't know that either."

Russell Beecham was indeed a bad boy. But wealth had made him arrogant. Attempted murder and possession of enough oxycodone to addict half of Jefferson City would keep Carla's husband off the streets till his beard turned grey.

"I appreciate everything you've done," Carla said, "but I've got to check on my grandmother." She jumped to her feet, staggered, then steadied herself against the table. "Years ago, Russell promised to kill my grandmother if I ever told anyone what he did to me. I should have checked on her already. Her life's been so bad, I can't let anything else happen to her."

"Who's your grandmother?" Silas asked. "We can protect her."

Carla shook her head. "You can't. Russell has too many connections. He may have already sent someone to hurt her."

"I'm guessing your grandmother's in her eighties, probably can't get around so good." Lila placed a hand on Carla's shoulder. "You can barely stand yourself. How do you plan to defend her?"

"I don't know, but I have to."

"Is she in Jefferson City?" Silas asked. "There's a safe house there."

Carla shook her head. "She lives here—in Kansas City."

"Give me her name and address," Silas said firmly. "Time is critical."

Carla crumpled into her chair. "You're right, I might get her killed. It's just—I—I want to help her. Roles reversed; she would have found a way. That's the way Margaret Culver is—now." Carla face took on a troubled look. "She did find a way. A few days ago, I was depressed and desperate. I called her. I didn't tell her Russell had beat me again, but she knew. It had to be Granny who called the hotline."

Silas barely heard the words after the name, Margaret Culver. He didn't need the address, it was two blocks from the home of The Surgeon's second victim, Abbey Bryant. He studied Carla, as he tapped a Blackbird mission into Bertha's programs. Under the bruises, he recognized similar bone structure, a fine arch to the brow, and the amazing blue of Margaret's eyes. The woman Carla resembled wouldn't be easily convinced to leave her home.

"You look like her," he said.

"You know my grandma?"

"Met her in my early days on the force. Visited her several times through the years. Struck me as one independent woman. She didn't want to accept my help either."

"She wasn't always strong. I guess the loss of her only daughter changed her. You see, when I was two, my father killed my mother. I was Carla Shields then."

The air shifted. Silas pictured the war room and its overhead screen of red and blue connections. His blood raced as he mentally added the new information and intersected the colors.

Lila twisted a chair toward Carla and sat. "Shields," she said. "Is your father Norman Shields?"

"I'm afraid so. The system gobbled me up, adopted me out, and turned me into Carla Gleason. My adoptive father is a lawyer. When I was twenty-five, I wanted to find my biological parents. My adoptive father hired a private investigator. What a revelation. One parent was buried, the other in prison for her murder." Carla's words rang with bitterness. "My grandma's the saving grace. The PI found her too."

"That's terrible," Lila said in a hushed voice. "Why didn't the court let you live with your grandma?"

"She said no. Too scared, I guess. She feels bad about that. You know, history repeats itself in the ugliest of ways. My grandpa was an abuser, my father was an abuser, and my husband's one, too. Granny blames herself. She knew Norman was hurting my mother, but Grandpa Charlie wouldn't let her interfere. Beat Granny up for suggesting Mom leave my father. After Mom's murder, Granny was afraid to bring me into her home because of Grandpa Charlie. But it didn't matter, I added Russell to the cycle all by myself."

"What about siblings?" Silas said.

Carla's honey colored brows drew together. "Granny says I have a brother and a sister. Can't remember them, my mother either for that matter. I visited my father in prison once, hoping he would help me find the rest of my family. Claimed I wasn't his daughter. He said he didn't have any children. But someone picked up his ashes."

Silas leaned forward. "How do you know?"

"The prison notified me when Norman died. I checked about his ashes. Don't ask me why. It didn't matter, they'd already been collected."

"By who?" The question was a shot in the dark.

"I didn't want to know. I had all the closure I needed, and who would want a killer's ashes?"

"Do you know Elle Goodman?"

A frown pulled Carla's brows together. "No, should I?"

"She picked up your father's ashes."

Carla startled. "Granny called my sister Elle. Could it have been her?"

"Maybe, I've got people working on it."

Lila rested a hand on Carla's shoulder. "Have you tried to locate your brother?"

Staring at fingernails chewed raw, Carla drew a shaky breath. "I wanted to. Russell wouldn't let me have the money to search, and he isolated me from anyone who might have helped." She raised her head, blue eyes beseeching them to understand. "I haven't seen my adoptive parents for over a year. I was scared to death for them."

"That must've been tough. Didn't they try to see you?" Silas asked, sure he already knew the answer. Russell Beecham had followed a classic pattern. His charm hid a jealous, manipulative, and controlling personality. He had used fear to keep Carla isolated.

"They tried." Moisture glistened at the corners of Carla's eyes. "I'm so ashamed. I've hurt them so much." She swiped at the dampness. "I pretended to hate them. I said some very mean things to keep them alive."

Lila gently grasped the woman's hands in her own. "We'll let them know what's happened. They'll understand." Lila's words feathered the air, soft and reassuring. "Maybe you can talk to them later tonight."

Silas checked his phone. Five blackbirds flitted across his screen. "A team is on the way to check on your grandmother. I have other work to do, but I'll let you know when she's safe."

"Thank you."

"I'll sit with you for a while," Lila said. "Then I'm going to spend some time with Grams. I sent her a text. She said it would be okay."

Silas nodded. His mother was Lila's safety net. "That sounds like a good idea." He kissed her on a slightly damp forehead.

She made eye contact, as though to say. *I'll be fine.*

Silas wasn't so sure. The worst was yet to come.

32

CHAPTER THIRTY-TWO

A dark grey van rolled to a stop, beneath the skeletal cover of trees, three blocks from Margaret Culver's house. A single streetlamp's sparse fingers of light battled poorly for control of the shadows. The driver scanned the street. Her thermo head-scope, detected a slinky opossum and a three-legged dog. She pressed the van door's electronic release.

Soundlessly, the door slid open. Five women from The Black-birds reviewed the plan in low whispers. Each team member synchronized her electronic device. A thumbs up indicated, *team ready.* Red Bird disembarked. At designated drop points, Hawk, Owl, Canary, and the team leader—Eagle left the van, melding into the darkness.

North, south, east, and west, block by block, bush by bush, the team swept the area approaching Margaret Culver's house. Thirty yards out, Owl sent a signal indicating she had a visual of a trespasser. The team leader acknowledged. Thirty seconds passed. Fifty dragged by. One minute was the mark for Canary to move in to assist. At fifty-nine seconds, Owl notified the team that the situation was in control. Eagle released her breath. Owl had subdued the suspicious visitor.

The team leader signaled to advance the probe. Thankful for the moonless night, she darted to the left, stopped in the darkness of a shrub, surveyed the landscape for the object that didn't belong, and repeated the exercise to the right. Nothing.

She crept forward, each step shrinking the perimeter. The house loomed ahead. The outline of a tree shifted. Eagle froze.

A'choo!

Thank God for spring allergies. Eagle sent a visual contact signal to the others. Using the distraction, the sneeze had caused its owner, she closed the distance. The barrel of her pistol bumped against the lookout's temple. "Don't move."

"What the ..."

She shoved the gun's bore harder into the man's skull. "How many more like you?"

"You're a woman?"

She clicked off the safety. "One, two..."

The man slumped. Eagle twisted aside, dodging the defensive backward thrust of the man's head. The misguided move carried the thug past the team leader. A quick foot to his ankles, and he thumped to the ground. She dropped beside him and slammed her gun into his back. "Don't be a fool," she said. "How many?"

"The old lady's dead by now."

Eagle shifted her weight. "You'd better hope not."

"Two others," he croaked.

Eagled checked her wrist phone—forty seconds gone. She snapped self-locking ties into place and yanked them tight. Pulling a rectangle of fabric from her pocket she forced the gag inside the thug's mouth. At fifty-five seconds, she transmitted, *situation secure.*

Where was Redbird?

Eagle crouched beneath dripping trees. The sound of a scuffle came from her left. Despite her self-control training, her heart rate increased. She wasn't a killer, but if she didn't get the proper communication in fifteen seconds, she would go to Redbird's aid—no holds barred.

The team leader held her screen close to her face, willing the message to come. She had taken half-a-dozen steps when Redbird fulfilled Eagle's wish.

Again, Eagle signaled to move forward. A single lamp cast a glow from what appeared to be the living room. She tapped Margaret's number into her communication device. Inside the residence no one answered the persistent ringing.

"Entering the house." Eagle spoke softly into her phone. She prepared to pick the lock, but the handle turned easily in her hand. Her muscles tightened. An eighty-seven-year-old woman shouldn't leave her home unlocked. The cool April air whipped through the trees, making the team leader shiver. Or was it the distinct feeling that she was not alone?

She waited for a Blackbird to reposition behind her. At the signal, she assumed a defensive position and opened the door. A flash of black darted past. Only years of training kept her from taking out a cat headed straight for the food bowl marked Tommy.

"Where's your owner?"

Tommy rudely ignored her whispered question. She left him to his meal. In the kitchen, a few dishes sat draining in the sink. The living room was unoccupied. An old-fashioned purse sat on the floor beside a beat-up recliner.

Not surprised to find the bedrooms empty she issued instructions. "I'm almost finished in here. No sign of Margaret. Red Bird, check the garage." She continued to poke into closets and the bathroom. She found nothing unusual for an older person living alone.

Retracing her steps, she paused in the living room. Tommy crouched under an end-table a black swatch of cloth between his paws. "Come here Tommy," she said, bending to give him a stroke.

Tommy slapped at her gloved hand knocking his play toy from under the table. The Blackbird team leader stepped back. At her feet lay a mask. The construction was unique, and identical to those worn by The Blackbirds, certain units in the military, and Homeland Security. What in the world was Margaret Culver doing with one in her living room? Eagle's phone lit up. She identified the sender as Red Bird. "Talk to me," she said.

"I've found Margaret Culver."

"Is she alive?"

"Barely. Looks like a stroke or heart attack." The sound of the Blackbird's breathing burst through the phone in fast puffs. "I'm administering CPR."

"I'll be right there." The team leader raced from the house. "Hawk to the garage." Half-way across the yard, the smell struck her. Decaying flesh. Inside the garage, she stripped of her backpack and mask, at the same time scanning the scene. A badly decomposed cat lay near a shovel at the edge of a hole. Margaret Culver appeared to have been in the process of digging a grave.

She switched places with Red Bird and began chest compressions. Eagle could hear the 911 conversation in the background. Her gaze strayed to the cat. Her stomach contorted. The cat's paws were missing.

"Ambulance is five minutes out," Red Bird said, breaking the 911 connection. She knelt beside the team leader.

Hawk burst through the door. "I'll take over," she said.

The team leader relinquished her position. She jumped to her feet and spoke into her phone. "Canary, abort mission. Final pickup in four minutes." She stuffed the black clothing and her gun into her backpack and tossed it to Red Bird. "Get out of here. Hawk will join you in three minutes."

Eagle tore her gaze away from the shallow movement of Margaret Culver's chest long enough to send a voice-to-text message to Bertha. Breath coming in short spurts, Eagle continued her inspection of the garage. Why would an eighty-seven-year-old woman be burying a cat in the middle of the night? A cat with no paws.

Eagle strode the short distance to the end of the garage. A stack of neatly folded clothing lay on a rickety white picnic table. The colors of fabric corresponded to the current spring fashion. They also matched the description of what Abbey Bryant was wearing before she was found nude and very dead. Smears of reddish brown stained the white tabletop.

"Change of plans," the team leader said. "We have a crime scene." She pointed to Red Bird. "Go! Now! I'll do CPR until the ambulance turns down the street.

33

CHAPTER THIRTY-THREE

I approach the house from the east. My destination will be to my left. Abbey Bryant's last moments were in that building. From the corner of my eye, I glimpse movement. I am not alone.

A man steps from the shadows and peers through the living room window. Light from a lamp inside spills over his broad shoulders. A steady hand balances a gun in an experienced and dangerous fashion.

My gaze follows the trespasser to the back door. He tries the knob. A moment later, he enters the house. A clunking sound comes from the garage. My heart races, and my mind flashes back to the moment earlier today, when I realized I was missing a mask. Retracing my steps since I wore it last has brought me here.

That day I had used a recorded meow of Abbey Bryant's missing cat to lure Abbey into the garage. I don't care if someone finds two amputated cat paws. They can't be linked to me. But the mask will have my DNA.

My instincts tell me the intruder has a buddy.

"Lucas, come on in." The man speaks from inside the house. "The old lady's gone."

No response from the invisible Lucas. The sound of footsteps approach where I crouch. The door swings out. I allow him one step. I bring the edge of my palm across his throat in a voice stopping blow. I grab his arm and twirl his body to meet the forceful thrust of my knee to his diaphragm. He drops the gun and falls in a writhing pile to the soft ground. I press the chloroform-filled rag to his nose. He stills. I roll him under an evergreen bush.

The scuff of a shoe's sole sends me into the shadows. My muscles draw tight as I wait for the intruder's partner, Lucas, to appear. I expect Margaret Culver to bang on the garage door at any moment.

Disturbed air brushes my face. I stiffen, not breathing. The barest impression of a person glides past me. Light from the window exposes the intruder pausing at the door. Words whisper into a cell phone, but I cannot understand what is said. Inside the house a telephone rings and rings and rings. The black clad figure wiggles the doorknob then slips inside the house.

Where is the man the intruder called Lucas, and why is Margaret Culver so popular in the middle of the night? My plan to drop in, retrieve my mask, and disappear into the night is bungled.

The garage door opens as if an invisible hand is on the latch. Light bursts into the yard. I lean forward. Margaret Culver is prone on the dirt floor. My heart thumps. I didn't want her to be hurt. Another black clad figure is bending over her. I hear the words CPR and 911.

I fade deeper into the darkness. The mask is no more than an irritation. I have ways to make it disappear even from the confines of an evidence room. Minutes later, the sound of emergency sirens split the night air. An ambulance turns down Margaret Culver's street. The vehicle's lights pass over where

I hide. The earth's April dampness seeps through my clothes. I can't make myself leave.

34

CHAPTER THIRTY-FOUR

The freight elevator carried Silas skyward. Inside the apartment, he headed straight for the shower. He draped his dirty clothes across an already overflowing laundry hamper and removed his prosthesis.

He turned up the pressure of the shower head and for the next ten minutes forced all thoughts of drug lords, criminal cops, and serial killers from his brain. He stepped from under the pelting water, dried, grabbed fresh clothes, and dressed. Lastly, he prepared his stump and attached the prosthetic. He was ready for the next battle.

Bertha's unique hum indicated that might be right around the corner. His pulse picked up. "Hello."

"Team Leader Eagle has reported."

"Go ahead."

"Margaret Culver transported to the hospital. Possible stroke or heart attack. Hawk confirmed the garage as the crime scene of victim, Abbey Bryant. Police contacted. All Blackbirds accounted for. No security breached. Will there be a reply?"

"No thank you, Bertha. Goodbye." Silas said. Abbey Bryant was Margaret Culver's friend. Any investigator worth their salt would have swept the older woman's garage. Mendez was a good, maybe even exceptional officer. Yet he had not checked. There had to be a valid explanation. He also had not made it clear he knew Savannah Peterson. There was not a good enough reason for that.

Mike Rojas's last words surfaced. *He has a relative who's a cop.* Silas shrugged. Mendez fit into that scenario as well as sauerkraut on an ice cream sundae. He hurried to the garage.

Inside the SUV, Silas called Lila. "I need you to give Carla some not-so-good news."

"Okay," Lila replied.

He shared Bertha's update from the Blackbird team leader. "Soon as I know which hospital, I'll text. I'm on my way to the scene now, may be gone all night. Be sure Carla understands the team did encounter intruders. Arrange an escort for her to visit her grandmother." He trusted Lila to handle the situation. "Don't let her go alone."

"I'll do the best I can," she said.

A sense of pride rose in his chest. She was the best.

Silas sped through the city streets, siren and emergency lights flashing. Mist, or in Lila's words 'angel spit,' speckled the windshield. He flipped on the wipers. Hadley called as Silas approached the I-70 freeway.

"Tell me somethin' good," Silas said.

"Sorry, no can do. Our man Morgan put the pressure on. The mayor arranged for the good doctor's release. All that upstanding citizen of the community baloney."

"What time was that?"

"About five o'clock. He checked into the Raphael on the Plaza. We've got three undercovers tacked to his backside."

"Where's Mendez?"

"Home, I guess. He was a walking zombie."

"That's good." Silas ground his teeth together. He didn't want to speak what was on his mind concerning Mendez. Questioning an officer's methods left a residue that polluted the department's air. He had to be careful. The distance between destroying trust and making a department stronger was razor thin.

"I smell a big BUT coming," Hadley said with zero humor in his voice.

"We've found the Bryant woman's murder scene in Margaret Culver's garage. An anonymous 911 caller asked for an ambulance for Margaret. The responders found Abbey Bryant's clothes and her missing cat. The cat was very dead and absent paws. We knew Margaret was Abbey Bryant's friend. Mendez interviewed her, but, for some reason, he didn't search her garage."

"Not like Mendez at all. Maybe she didn't give permission."

"Hard to believe that charmer couldn't get permission. He also didn't let us know he had a connection to Savannah Peterson. Chief's not going to be happy." Silas signaled and then blended into the freeway traffic headed east.

"Cartwright's smarter than that. She knows he's a good cop, he's just green."

"She does," Silas agreed. "But she has a job to do. And, so do I."

"I'll talk to Mendez. He's not going to be a happy camper. But he knows how things work. I'll get to the bottom of what happened."

Silas could almost see his partner twirling a pen between his fingers, an incessant habit that drove Silas crazy. He wanted to question Mendez himself, but Hadley was a better choice, and Silas faced a full night ahead.

"How's Lila?" Hadley changed the subject.

"Putting on a good face in her typical Lila way. She's sitting with the shelter's latest guest." Silas told Hadley of the connections he'd uncovered in Jefferson City. Knowing how much his friend adored Lila, Silas held back the story of his sister's rape. He didn't need Hadley murdering the bastard.

"The good doctor might as well reserve his room at the Death Row Hotel. I'll be planning an injection party in his honor." Hadley said snidely.

Heavier rain pounded the windshield. A tsunami from the wheels of a transport truck slammed the SUV. Blinded, Silas hit a chug hole dead center. The impact jarred his teeth. "Listen, I want you to keep this on the down low." He told Hadley about the drug robberies. "We're going to be working with Special Agent Archie Hamilton. The FBI has reason to believe Beecham is only a link in the supply chain. They want the man at the top. We're going to assist."

"Are we trading efforts. Will the FBI be helping us solve the serial killings?"

"That's the plan."

"How far on the down low am I supposed to go."

"The FBI thinks the man at the top is a cop."

"Shit."

35

CHAPTER THIRTY-FIVE

Margaret Culver's street was blocked off. Silas parked the SUV and climbed out. He dodged puddles left behind as the rain traveled east. Holding up his badge to the posted cop, he stepped inside the yellow crime tape. "Not the best weather for doing our job, huh?"

"No sir."

Silas approached an unmarked crime scene van and a police paddy wagon parked near the garage. He recognized the smell of decomposing flesh. A big man dressed in stained jeans and a worn Chief's sweatshirt stood near the van's open door. Hands cuffed behind his back; his head drooped. Oily black hair curled around his ears and spilled over his collar. Two other men lay on the ground trussed up like pigs ready for the spit. A male officer waited inside the van, while a female officer readied the cuffed suspects for transport.

"Are they talking?" Silas asked.

"Oh yeah." The female officer said. She pointed to the man on the ground. "The little one's spilling his guts. The big one's promising to kill him for being so helpful. That one over there is the smartest, he's keeping his mouth shut."

"Helpful how?"

"Claim they were hired to abduct Margret Culver. She's the woman transported to the hospital."

"Which hospital? I know her family."

"North Kansas City."

"Thanks." Silas stepped aside and sent a quick text to Lila. When he turned back, the big man was gingerly climbing inside the police van. Every move brought a moan and a colorful adjective exploding from his mouth. Seconds later the suspect was seated, his ankles shackled.

Silas helped the female officer remove the lock ties from the remaining suspects and assisted them into the van. "You mentioned these guys were hired. Did they share who was paying, and why?" He asked, waiting for the prisoner's shackles to be resecured.

"We've got a name, but it's nobody big. Red Jorgensen, a small-time drug dealer from Northeast. Guys like these don't care about the why of a job."

"I know Red. Maybe he'll cough up somebody bigger. What did you find when you arrived?"

"Very strange scene. The little guy was lying back a few yards under a tree, hands and feet restrained, just like you see them. He had a gag stuffed in his mouth. The second one was in the rear of the house bound the same way. The big guy was under a bush, unconscious." She pointed to an evergreen near the back door. "I recognized the sweet fruity smell. My father is a doctor."

Alarm bells clanged inside Silas's head. "Chloroform? Are you sure?"

"Positive. I hated the smell of chloroform as a child, and I hate it now. He has a bruise across the throat, too. A karate chop causes that kind of mark."

"The small guy didn't smell—like chloroform?"

"No sir."

"What is your conclusion?"

The officer shot him a glance, as though no one had ever asked for her opinion. "Well." She hesitated. "The styles of subjugation are different, but each indicates experience, perhaps even sophisticated training." As she spoke, her demeanor changed. She stood straighter, dropped her slang, and looked him straight in the eyes. "Chloroform is the anomaly. My gut says there were multiple aggressors, two, maybe even three different agendas. More than likely they didn't know each other."

Silas mentally accounted for two agendas. He understood the purpose behind the hired thugs. The Blackbirds had been the opposite kind of mission. Lightening split the sky in the east followed by a clap of thunder. Silas carried a limited respect for superstition. He didn't see the nature show as a good omen.

"Are you thinking the killer has the third agenda?" He asked the officer.

She nodded. "They often return to the murder scene—for kicks, I guess. But this feels different. I'm thinking he's accidently left us a souvenir, one that can't be explained away. He was on a retrieval mission."

"Do you often rely on your gut?" Silas asked. At this moment his was turning inside out.

The woman stiffened, her eyes narrowing.

"I'm not mocking you." Silas rushed to reassure. "Use every tool you have," he said. "I do."

She gave him a searching look. "I collect facts to back up my instinct. If they're there, I move forward."

"Ever been wrong?"

Her gaze shifted toward the dark perimeter of the crime scene.

CHAPTER THIRTY-FIVE

"Once."

Silas sensed the officer's discomfort. Yet, she hadn't dodged the question. She deserved her privacy. "You been inside?" He nodded toward the open garage door.

"No sir," she replied. "Based on the information from dispatch, my partner entered the building. I backed him up, waited for the ambulance, then executed the first sweep of the exterior. We tried to minimize interference with the crime scene. I'm afraid the paramedics have different priorities."

"Rightly so," Silas said. "Life should take precedence over death."

"Indeed." The woman agreed and slammed the van's door shut. "We'll be on our way."

Silas crossed the short distance to the garage. A photo tech and a redheaded evidence tech were working the building inch by inch. They didn't need him in the way. He turned toward the house.

A path covered in pea gravel disappeared around the corner. Back when he knew Margaret Culver's life might be in danger, he remembered following her down this same path. He had pleaded with her to accept his help, but she had promised her husband was not a problem.

The house was small, and a few steps carried him to its northern corner. The light dimmer here, he paused to let his eyes adjust. Clay pots heaved sideways by the freezing and thawing of the soil held the withered remnants of last summer's blossoms. Geraniums he thought.

Damp leaves cushioned the sound of his feet as he left the path and meandered across the yard. The uneven rhythm of moisture dripping from tree branches played softly in his ears. He mulled over the female officer's theory, plausible except for one major problem. The prime suspect was under surveillance.

Was Morgan guilty of domestic violence, and soliciting a murder, but not the serial killings? The thought didn't answer why the famous surgeon was taking pictures of the victims.

A rock structure materialized in the dim light. Silas recalled Margaret Culver's beautiful lily pond. A few steps brought him to the containment wall. A dog growled from the shadows. Silas lowered himself to a non-aggressive position his artificial hand at the ready. Better a damaged piece of technology than his other hand. The animal waddled into sight. Silas breathed. Too old and too fat to run, the dog stopped to sniff the ground. He growled again, turning his big head toward Silas in search of approval.

"Good boy." Silas said. His ears caught the whisper of movement. He tilted his head. A powerful kick to the chest knocked him backward. Silas rolled sideways. A dark figure leaned forward from the low rock wall. Silas sensed a body slam. He scrambled to his feet and swung his artificial hand. He connected with air where legs should have been. The taunting echo of running feet hinted at the existence of a real person.

"Stop!" He shouted. "Stop or I'll shoot." A wild shot in the dark was the last thing he intended, but the suspect didn't know that.

Silas chased the sound of crunching gravel at a full run. The police spotlights disappeared behind him. If he remembered correctly, this part of the path would take them to the mailbox and a small wooden bridge connecting to the road. His eyes strained to keep the dodging and darting figure in sight. Low hanging limbs raked his cheeks. Where were all the neighborhood guard dogs when you needed them? One would come in handy right about now. But then again, how would the dog know Silas from the suspect? He didn't like the idea of being brought down by a mouthful of gnashing yellow teeth. He increased his pace.

The insanity of pursuit in the near dark at a flat run entered his mind. The thought evoked an unpleasant image of his body lying in the dirt the victim of a clothesline decapitation. The bridge loomed. Ahead, the slap of shoes against wood told him he was closing in.

Silas hit the bridge at a fast clip. Then the world turned upside down. He skidded out of control arms flailing left and right in maniac fashion. He grabbed for the handrail. Too late, the law of gravity, balance, or the devil himself took control. He was airborne.

He landed flat of his back, sliding. The rough planks plucked at his jacket, but the weight of his skidding body carried him under the handrail and over the edge. His right foot struck ground at an awkward angle. He pitched headfirst into the concrete bridge support. Slimy water spattered his face. Pain shot up his leg like a high voltage electric current. Consciousness hesitated, ready to beat a fast retreat. A dark figure returned to the bridge and peered over its side. Silas waited for the searing pain of a bullet. His sight blurred, and darkness took over.

36

CHAPTER THIRTY-SIX

"Here! Over here. I found him." The voice seeped through a steel curtain in Silas's brain. "Sir, can you hear me?" Bright light penetrated his eyes sharp and painful as slivers of glass. He tried to knock the light to the ground, but his arms failed to cooperate.

"Is he alive?" Another person yelled.

The sound of running feet, and more shouting. Close by, the sound of a person in pain. He realized the moaning was his.

"He's groaning. Looks like he was knocked off the bridge."

Hands gripped him under the arms and lifted him from the cold muck. "My ankle," he moaned.

"Get a stretcher down here! Detective Albert's injured."

Minutes later, the four CSI techs circled the stretcher, their faces grim. "Where did the guy come from?" one asked.

Silas's foggy brain failed to provide an answer. "What guy?" he said. The redheaded tech gently wiped his face. The cloth came away red. He touched his forehead relieved to find he still had one eyebrow. At the base of his scalp, he located the source of blood.

"How bad is it?" Silas asked the tech.

"I'd say about a two-inch gash. Not bad on the outside. Are

you nauseous?"

"No, but I'm about to shoot whoever's running that jack hammer in my head. What about my ankle?"

"Don't look. It *will* make you nauseous. A bad sprain. You need an x-ray. Also, you'll want to get your hand cleaned up." The man pointed to Silas's mud caked prosthetic. "I've read about that sophisticated technology. It doesn't handle dirt well.

A patrol car cruised down the street. The search light scanned yards and buildings. "That's a waste of time," Silas said. "The person I was chasing is long gone."

"Precaution. He might come back to finish the job."

"Too smart for that," Silas said.

The CSI who'd dragged him from the ditch approached. "There's been a big pile-up on I-435. A bus and a semi. There'll be a big delay on the ambulance. We'll transport you to the hospital."

"No," Silas said, authority ringing in his voice. "We have work to do here. Dig me out a superman-size Band-Aide and an Ace bandage. Something to clean this up with too." He pointed to his artificial hand.

The men glanced at each other. "All right, but we have to load you inside the van," the redhead spoke. "You need to stay warm—concussion—you know."

"We're wasting precious time," Silas said, rising to one elbow. "Find me something to use as a crutch."

They jumped into action. A packet of moistened towelettes landed in his lap. "Perfect," Silas said.

The first aid kit produced a box, showcasing various human joints wrapped in elastic. Through gritted teeth, he endured the binding of his ankle. He followed the redhead's earlier advice and didn't look.

"You won't be wearing a shoe any time soon," the tech cautioned.

"My dance partner will be disappointed," Silas retorted, frowning at the adhesive pad, the size of a bed sheet, headed for his scalp. He bit back a curse. A chemical cold-pack and a blanket came next. Then, as if by magic, a set of aluminum crutches appeared.

"Guess none of you are carrying a bag full of oxycodone?" His remark brought smiles. "Damn the luck," he said. "In that case, get your asses busy and find some evidence. We need to catch a killer, and we don't have all night."

A few moments later, he was in the front seat of the van. "One more thing," he said. "Thanks."

"No problem, Sir. I left the keys in the ignition, in case you need to start the engine to keep warm," the tech replied.

The door slammed shut. Silas eyed the bench seat, wanting to put his foot up. Instead he unfolded the blanket over his body and collapsed against the backrest. His eyes roved the interior of the van. A clock blinked away red minutes.

At 9:45, the van door flung wide. "Detective, you need to see this."

Startled, Silas slammed his body rigid. Big mistake. His head exploded in throbbing pain. He took deep breaths, blocking the pain the way he had when he lost his hand. One of the techs assigned to the house stood in the door's opening, palming a phone.

He frowned. His head must be screwed up for sure. What did a phone have to do with Abbey Bryant's murder, or Margaret Culver's intruders, or anything, for that matter? "What do you have?" he asked.

"A baseball bat, the barrel's matted with dried blood and hair."

The CSI crawled inside the van and handed Silas the phone. "I've seen enough crime scenes. I'm sure that's human hair. Look at these pictures."

"But Abbey Bryant wasn't bludgeoned to death," Silas said.

"No, but I'd bet my firstborn, someone was."

Silas's first gut reaction had centered around Mendez's interview with Margaret Culver after Abbey Bryant's murder. A new thought occurred to him. Maybe his premonition didn't have anything to do with Abbey Bryant's murder. He thumbed through the tech's screenshots of a bedroom and a closet filled with dated men's clothes. Shoes lined up in pristine order were cracked from a lack of care. A person could write their name in the thick layer of dust. The bat hung from a leather strap hooked over a nail inches inside the closet door. A half-dozen cell phone images showed what the tech was talking about.

His temples hammered. He recalled the stubborn woman who'd refused his help twenty years earlier. Never once did she admit her husband beat her. During a later conversation, she claimed her husband abandoned her. Margaret Culver's husband left her and his clothes behind. Not the behavior of an abusive, controlling person. "How close are you to finishing inside the house?" Silas asked.

"Couple of hours, at least."

"Look for items a man wouldn't leave behind."

"Like a wallet?"

Silas shot the CSI a look. "A wallet would be good."

"Page backward about ten shots."

Silas thumbed the screen to the left. There it was, a black leather billfold worn at the corners and checked with age. Another shot showed a Missouri driver's license long since expired. He enlarged the image. The owner's name snapped into view—Charles

Eugene Culver, Margaret's husband.

"Good work," Silas said, returning the CSI's phone. "This property is more than likely a murder scene from years ago. Advise the team in the garage we're calling in a cadaver dog. You guys will be on scene protection duty until we know what we've got." He hesitated, "What's your name?

"Doug."

Give me your number so I can message you if I need you."

"Yes sir." The tech gave Silas the number and hurried off to pass along Silas's instructions.

Silas knew the head nurse at North Kansas City Hospital. He selected her number from his contact list. When she answered, he asked about Margaret Culver. The nurse placed him on hold. Moments passed, and she was back.

"She's stabilized but, her condition remains serious. Strokes always are. The danger is multiple strokes."

"Can she speak?"

"Not yet. She did recognize her granddaughter, at least her voice. That young woman's face is a mess. Her own mother might not know who she is. I hope you've arrested whoever did that to her."

"Carla Beecham is there—in the hospital?"

"Yes." The nurse's voice faltered. "Your niece brought her, so we thought that was alright.

Red bloomed behind his eyes. He should've known this would happen. *Lila and her big heart.* "Don't let anyone else in," he said. "Carla Beecham's husband is a vicious bastard. Russell Beecham's in jail. Even from there, he sent thugs to hurt Margaret Culver. There are other security concerns too."

"There's a guard at her door. I'll make sure he knows. Not quite sure how your niece found the patient. Access to our admission records are blocked in the computer. Must be a data glitch. I'll report the breach to information security."

"Thanks for the update. I'll be in touch." Silas called Mort Kultiveck, the dog handler. "Mort," he said. "Silas Albert here. We've got a situation. Is Rags ready to go?" He explained the situation.

"Rags is always ready," Mort said. "Be there in an hour." The phone went silent. Mort was a man of few words.

Before he could pocket the device, it rang again. *Sophie Morgan.* "Hello."

"I've been in Tyler's office. It's bad. Please come. I'll meet you at the front door."

The words simulated a siren slicing through Silas's brain. "I'll be there in ten minutes." He messaged Doug the CSI, advising he'd be leaving for a while. He would check in later.

37

CHAPTER THIRTY-SEVEN

Cool damp air blew across Silas's face. He lowered himself to the ground, supporting his weight with his good leg and the crutches. Wrapped in a thick bandage the injured ankle felt bulky and foreign. He tested his balance, then set off for the SUV. Swing, step, swing. After a jerky start, he established a reasonable rhythm that carried him to the street.

Bare tree limbs created a dancing labyrinth of shadows on the sidewalk. A sense of being watched made his skin prickle. He couldn't be more vulnerable. A one-legged man swinging aluminum crutches might as well shoot himself.

He was sweating when he reached the SUV. He threw open the door, tossed his crutches across the seat, and dragged himself inside. He settled his good foot on the accelerator and twisted the ignition. The engine started on the first try. If he wasn't a mess? An artificial hand, a split head, and another limb that hurt like hell. He sped off down the street. The headlights exposed no sign of an assassin dressed in black, hiding in the trees or anywhere else for that matter. Silas trusted his senses with the same confidence he counted on the sun rising tomorrow. Someone had been there. Watching.

The gate was open when Silas arrived at the Morgan house. He drove between the two-foot, square metal posts and rolled to a stop in front of the brick mansion. He pocketed his phone, grabbed the crutches, and shoved open the car door. The pale orb of Sophie's face peered through a window.

She met him at the top of the porch steps. "What happened to you?" She pointed to the crutches.

"I lost a footrace, but what are you doing here? I thought you and Hunter planned to stay in a hotel."

"We are. I left Hunter asleep."

"Why didn't you call me? You shouldn't have gone in there alone."

The toll of her decision bent her shoulders. "My husband is not a nice person, but he is the father of my children, and at one time we had a good life together. I needed to know what was in that office." She choked back a sob.

"You are a brave woman, Sophie Morgan. What did you find?"

She stiffened as though she faced a fierce wind. "Follow me, I'll show you." She halted in front of an open elevator. "It's mostly pictures. I only looked at a couple." She turned to him, her face stricken. "I don't know how to tell you this." One hand clutched at her throat. "One of the pictures is of Lila. I think he's planning to kill her too."

"This may be what we need to stop him."

"I pray that you can."

Silas followed Sophie into a walnut-lined elevator. She pressed the number three. Seconds passed, a soft bump, and the doors opened. He dug a latex glove from his pocket and slipped it on his right hand.

"If this evidence points to the commitment of a crime, I will need to call in additional investigators. For my own protection, and yours."

Sophie swung to meet him. "Do you have to involve that Elizabeth Cartwright woman?"

The unusual question threw him. "She is the Chief of Police and my boss. I have a responsibility to keep her informed."

"Of course, you do." A grimace slashed Sophie's face. "You weren't wrong that night you punched him in the face. There is something between them." Bitterness edged her words.

She stepped off the elevator and turned right. They passed an open door. Silas glanced into a workout room equal to the one he'd installed at The House of Audrey. Silas remembered Sophie at the Mayor's ball, the man at her elbow a perfect candidate for the cover of GQ magazine. Elizabeth having an affair with Tyler Morgan didn't sit well, and now there was a major conflict of interest.

Sophie paused and waited for Silas. "In there," she said, tears glistening in her eyes. "I replaced the shrouds exactly the way I found them."

"Was the door locked when you came up here?"

"Yes."

"Wait here."

Light from the hall filtered into an otherwise pitch-dark room. He edged inside and used the end of his cell phone to flip a switch. The hulk of a walnut desk consumed the center of the expansive office, backdropped by a wall of windows. Thick black paper covered the glass. A shiver crawled under Silas's skin. Easels covered in fabric surrounded the perimeter of the room. Five were covered in black, seven in white. One set slightly away from the others.

Silas's mouth went dry. He turned in a circle, scanning the room with his phone. He needed evidence of the room's state before he touched anything. A sense of dread built in his chest. What he discovered here could have the power to destroy or to save. He thrust his crutches forward and swung toward the easels draped in black.

Swing, step, swing, step. Willing his boiling emotions under control, Silas lurched to a stop. He hesitated, then raised the foot of his crutch, and flipped the fabric into the air. An object dropped to the floor. Silas froze. A middle-aged woman smiled at him from a portrait sized photograph. He didn't recognize the face. His gut told him she was a victim of The Surgeon.

His gaze shot to the item knocked to the floor. Enclosed in a clear plastic bag was one earring in the shape of an owl. He shifted back to the photo where a matched pair pierced the woman's ears. A trophy.

The second and third easels, exposed strangers. A man's image surprised him. But he knew from Lila's experience, organ matching crossed sexes and races. The trophy bag held a smattering of dark curly hairs. The act of murder ripped away a human's modesty. Still, Silas hoped they were chest hairs.

The fourth photograph confirmed his fears. This room was not a shrine, but a gallery of kills. The killer had captured the kind expression in Abbey Bryant's dark eyes. In the easel's tray, Silas recognized the grim exhibit collected to satisfy a sick mind. A cat's paws.

Swing, step, swing, step. Pausing in front of the final black shroud, he checked the time. Mort and his cadaver dog would arrive at Margaret Culver's house in thirty minutes. He flicked his crutch. Fabric dropped to the floor. The close-up of Savannah Peterson waving to the camera took Silas's breath. Savannah knew her photographer.

Silas's pulse thumped. Savannah's list of acquaintances hadn't included Dr. Morgan.

A spot of gray fur caught his attention. His mind produced an image of the cat in Savannah's trash can. His gaze returned like a shot to Abbey Bryant's easel tray. Two paws there. Savannah's cat had all four paws amputated. Where were the other two? And where was victim number one's second owl earring.

Silas hobbled across the room. He disrobed six of the seven remaining tripods. He prayed Sophie was mistaken and he would not see Lila's face. One by one he revealed strangers. The crutch wavered as he lifted the white cloth away from the last photograph. A groan rose in his throat. The window of the Studebaker framed an image of a smiling Lila. When had Morgan taken a picture that personal?

The eyes of the other targets bored into Silas. Innocent people needed help to escape this monster. The Surgeon had every intention of gathering more trophies. And Morgan had a distinct advantage. He knew their names, addresses and daily schedules.

Silas threw his weight into the crutches and propelled himself behind the walnut desk. He fumbled through a stack of folders. One thing his artificial hand didn't do well, was shuffle paper. He studied the drawers. Locked. He looked closer. Electronic.

His ankle throbbed. But something else bothered him more. The attack in Margaret Culver's back yard couldn't have been carried out by Morgan. Even the famous doctor couldn't be in two places at once.

Silas weighed his next move. The CSI crew chief would call him when the cadaver dog finished her work. He needed a crew here, in the Morgan mansion, and he needed to keep Lila safe. He shot a glance toward her photograph. She wouldn't leave Carla and the two of them were at the hospital with Margaret Culver, where there was a posted guard.

CHAPTER THIRTY-SEVEN

"Call Hadley." Silas spoke into his phone.

"What's up, Boss?" Hadley answered.

"We've got enough to charge Tyler Morgan as accessory to the murder of Savannah Peterson and Abbey Bryant." Silas explained what Sophie had discovered. "I'm sure one of the remaining five is the Denver victim, Gloria Sweeney." For once his partner didn't waste time on smart remarks.

"Can a lawyer get him out this time?"

"God, I hope not. The judge should consider him a flight risk."

"Do you think Morgan will give up his accomplice?"

"I've got an idea of how to force his hand." Silas laid out his plan.

"I'll beef up the surveillance at the hotel. He won't flick an eyelash without us knowing." Hadley's voice thickened. "Remember to think like a defense attorney."

"You do the same." Silas disconnected.

Hadley's words ringing in his ears, Silas turned. There would be surveillance equipment here. If he made one wrong move, anything uncovered in this room would be inadmissible. He called the department dispatch and ordered a CSI unit. His stomach tightened as he thumbed the screen, punched the Chief's direct line, and waited for Elizabeth Cartwright to answer.

"Chief of Police, Elizabeth Cartwright. Leave a message."

Silas hesitated. He had no right to be bothered by who Liz had an affair with, but he was. Morgan was such an arrogant ass. Liz was a better judge of character than that—wasn't she? "Elizabeth, call me. You need to be brought up to date on new developments regarding the serial killings. You may want to consider holding a news conference." There. His bases were covered.

He called his homicide team. "Put me on the speaker," he said, pausing to gain the group's full attention. "Twelve photos will be coming your way. Pull out all the stops to get these people identified. Two are confirmed victims of our serial killer. Three are probable victims. Seven are in grave danger." Silas identified the man about to be arrested.

"The bad news is—the killer has an accomplice. Also..." He cleared his throat. My niece Lila is one of his targets.

A cacophony of cuss words shot through the speakers. "Calm down," Silas said. "Focus. Work as a team. I pulled this group together, because you're the best at what you do. Now I need you to prove me right."

A pall of silence then the phone exploded "Yes sir." His team replied as one voice.

"CSI will forward all information to the war room." He disconnected, letting his eyes scan the room one last time. He wouldn't give his right arm to have the first look in the doctor's desk drawers, but he'd seriously consider sacrificing one finger of his artificial hand for the privilege.

For evidence leading to death by injection he'd easily give the middle finger.

38

CHAPTER THIRTY-EIGHT

Lila sat with Carla alongside the hospital bed. Machines and monitors hummed and beeped in the uneasy rhythm of a hospital. An oxygen mask covered Margaret Culver's face. Her chest rose and fell at a steady pace.

After being made aware of her grandmother's stroke, Carla insisted on coming to the hospital. Lila wasn't about to place the fragile woman in the hands of a stranger. She'd driven Carla here in the Studebaker.

Margaret was conscious and had squeezed her granddaughter's hands in response to her questions. She recognized Carla, and yes, she had been the one to call the hotline. The old woman was resting now.

The door swished open. A nurse strode in carrying a small plastic bag. Her gaze lingered on Carla's battered face. "These are the clothes Mrs. Culver was wearing when she arrived in the emergency room. Are you family?"

"I'm her granddaughter" Carla replied.

"Then I'll leave these with you. You may put them in this closet if you want." She pointed to the door next to the bathroom. There was no purse, but the 911 caller identified her." The nurse smiled and handed Carla the bag. "The doctor will be in soon to give you an update."

"Thank you." Carla smiled in return.

The nurse checked the monitors, made a few adjustments, and left the room.

Carla shook the contents from the bag. A well-worn sweater, housecoat, and slippers dropped to the bed. She gathered the sweater and hugged it close to her chest then slid her arms inside the sleeves. "The last time I visited her, she was wearing this." Both hands slipped naturally into the pockets.

"What have we here?" She frowned, extending her open palm to show a business card and another item.

Lila's heart slammed against her ribs.

Carla gave her an odd look. "Are you okay? You look like you've seen a ghost."

"I'm good, tired I guess."

Carla slid the two items back into the pocket, removed the sweater, and draped it across the foot of the bed.

"I need something to drink," Lila said. "Do you want a soda, or a coffee?"

"Coffee sounds good."

Lila hurried to the cafeteria, purchased a small soda and an extra-large coffee, and returned to the room. She sipped her soda and made small talk with Carla. Fifteen minutes passed. Lila squirmed in her seat.

At last, Carla stood. "That was a *big* cup of coffee. I've got to use the bathroom."

Lila smiled. "I understand. Works that way for me too. You can use the one here in the room."

The door barely closed behind Carla. Lila jumped to her feet. She grabbed the sweater and plunged her hand inside the pocket.

Her fist closed on the familiar item. She raced out the door, stopping long enough to advise the guard a water sensor alarm had gone off at home. She asked him to let Carla know where she was and to call Hadley Barker when Carla was ready to return to The House of Audrey.

Lila's heart pounded as she rushed down the corridor. Only one person could explain how this particular item came to be at The Surgeon's crime scene. And Lila intended to find out why.

39

CHAPTER THIRTY-NINE

Silas swung into the hall. Sophie stood at the end of the corridor, staring out the window. Noticing him, she hurried in his direction. Her face was grim. His own emotions roiled like a raging river.

"I've called the Crime Scene Investigative Unit. They should be here any minute. In the meantime, I need your help. My department has your husband under close watch. We believe he has an accomplice. With your help he should lead us to that person."

Sophie bit her lip, then looked him full in the eyes. "What can I do?"

"I'll give the CSI team their instructions, and then you and I will make a phone call."

"Tyler won't do anything I ask him to do."

"He doesn't have to do what you ask. He only has to believe what you say."

The sound of vehicles in the drive interrupted the discussion. "That will be a team of investigators." He pivoted toward the elevator. Swing, step, swing step. "There is an electronic lock on your husband's desk. Do you have the password?"

"No." She matched her pace to his.

"Do I have your permission to have the lock picked?"

"I—I guess so." She stumbled but righted herself. "This can't get much worse."

They reached the elevator and stepped inside. "Your husband built this brazen gallery of victims and targets using a list of organ recipients from one donor. Having those names would save time and lives."

Back in the living room, Sophie stopped. "Was my daughter the donor?"

"No. The blood type is different."

Sophie looked startled that he would know her daughter's blood type. "Do whatever you need to do. I pray to wake up from this nightmare."

"My feelings exactly," Silas said. "Get your purse and your cell phone."

She nodded, grabbed a hand-tooled leather bag from a sofa table, and pulled out a phone. "I forgot. Tyler took my phone. This one's Hunter's."

"Better yet."

Silas turned to the CSI team, issued the directives, took Sophie by the arm, and led her to the SUV. He drove across town, explaining what she needed to do. He parked in front of a small trailer house. "This is a special FBI unit used for different types of undercover work. You'll make the call from here."

Sophie looked skeptical.

Silas knocked and then entered the trailer. The last time he was here, the furniture was sparse and ratty. That hadn't changed. Silas took in the putrid green sofa with split seats, a drunken recliner covered in some fuzzy red material, and a long table loaded with electronics. Three wooden kitchen chairs faced the table.

A man who looked more like a high school student than an FBI agent maneuvered his wheelchair from behind the table. Silas handed him his police identification. "Archie Hamilton sent us."

"Been expecting you," The agent said.

Silas shook the man's hand. "This is Sophie. What do we call you?"

"I'm working through the alphabet. Jim works today." He flashed a charming smile, captured Sophie's gaze with his own, and shook her hand.

Another Hadley. All about the ladies.

"Sophie, please sit there." Alphabet Jim pointed to one of the chairs at the table. "I need the phone." Sophie obliged without a word and alphabet Jim connected the device to a small, black electronic box.

For twenty minutes the agent worked with Sophie. Silas's blood pressure rose with each rehearsal. He found the coffee pot. Three cups of black congealed liquid later, his nerves threatened to play The William Tell Overture.

"I'm ready," Sophie said. She appeared calm and determined.

Silas called Hadley. "We're initiating contact."

"We'll be actin' like stick-tights on a border collie." Hadley replied.

The agent rolled his wheelchair back, and Sophie went to work. Silas prayed the plan worked.

As she disconnected, a smile of pride parted her lips. "He took the bait."

"Good job. You're a born actress." Jim grinned, too. "This little device connects, behind the scenes, to his phone's camera. It doesn't even have to be on. We'll see what his camera sees." He held out his hand to Silas. "Give me yours, I'll make it do the same." He tapped the black box. "A hard file is retained here."

A moment later, Silas recognized the Mercedes insignia in the middle of Morgan's steering wheel. "I feel a little like James Bond. Is this admissible in court?"

"When a Federal crime has been committed."

"Now we wait." Silas swung the length of the trailer on his crutches, flopped down in the fuzzy red chair, got up, paced again, made a pot of coffee, and paced more. His ankle throbbed with every jerky motion.

The agent scowled. "For God's sake, man. Stop. You're making me twitchy."

Silas's phone pinged, once, twice, three times. *What the Hell, is everyone on the same wavelength?* Sydney, Janice Sloan, and the missing Elizabeth Cartwright demanded attention.

He hobbled into the bathroom. "Sydney."

"Hi Silas. Took me a while to retrieve the autopsy report on Norman Shields' wife. You were right, it's a mess. Sloppy pictures, poor measurements, etc. etc. But bottom line. Rojas told the truth. Norman did not kill his wife."

"One of the kids?"

"We need to call in an expert, but the angles and points of entry support that theory."

"Do it. I'll figure out how to get Elizabeth to pay the bill."

"The DNA results came back."

Silas gulped, realizing he hadn't kept Sydney up to date.

"I'm sorry, Silas. Norman Shields is without a doubt Lila's organ donor. I have more bad news." She hesitated. "Dr. Morgan is Lila's biological father. How is that even possible?"

Silas's mouth went dry. "My sister Audrey was raped while she was away at college. She never saw the attacker's face. You've confirmed what Mike Rojas told me this morning."

"Oh Silas...does Lila know?"

"No." He paused searching for the right words. "My parents don't even know. I was hoping you would help me work through this with her."

"Of course. Just say when."

"Lila is with Carla at the hospital now. We need to tell her tonight. Before the media creates a sensationalized nightmare."

"I'll wait for your call. Be safe." Her voice was soft, warm, and caring. He held those vibes close to his heart. He needed Sydney as much as Lila.

Before he could review Janice Sloan's message, Hadley's name appeared on the screen. "What up?"

"The doctor's on the move. Exited the hotel in the silver Mercedes. We have a tracer on his car. He's turning east on Brush Creek Boulevard."

Silas slammed open the bathroom door. The knob cracked into the wall with the sound of a rifle shot. Wielding his crutches like a mad man, he thrust himself past Jim and Sophie. "Morgan's on the move. Jim, can you arrange for Sophie to get back to the hotel?

"Sure."

"Sophie. Don't worry. We'll help you and Hunter work through this mess."

He was out the door before she could nod her head.

40

CHAPTER FORTY

By the time Silas intersected Hadley, the Mercedes was headed north. He fell in behind the unmarked Honda Pilot. Morgan drove fast. Silas heard Hadley inform dispatch to advise all police to let the Mercedes through.

The caravan of police rolled north, then turned back east. The scenery degenerated with every block. Vacant buildings covered in graffiti lined the streets. Streetlamps highlighted broken glass between layers of leaves and trash. The silver car slowed, making a sharp turn into a private lane.

Hadley drove the Honda beyond the turn-off then pulled to the side of the road.

Silas stared into the timber lined tunnel as the SUV rolled past the overgrown lane. He called Bertha. "Send a drone." He gave the computer the address. "Forward the photographs to my phone. Identify the owner of the property and advise."

He pulled alongside Hadley. "I've called in a drone. We'll have overheads soon."

Hadley cleared his throat. "Now we have supersonic drones able to navigate in the dark?"

"Latest technology." A Blackbird lived less than a mile away, and she was very adept at operating the newest night surveillance.

"Oh yeah, I forgot. Your FBI friends."

Silas didn't correct him. "I've never been down that road over there, have you?"

"Nope, but Morgan acted like he knew where he was going."

They turned their vehicles around. Hadley joined Silas in the SUV. Hadley had replaced his detective garb for black, weather-proof tactical clothing.

Silas explained the gizmo that *alphabet* Jim had rigged up to work through Silas's phone.

"Wow!" Hadley muttered. "I want to play with the FBI."

Silas brought up a computer enhanced map of their location. The lane twisted and curved, disappearing into a grove of trees. An old house stood in a clearing, nearly consumed by the brush and brambles. A barn from another century loomed near the lane's exit on the far side of the property.

The remainder of the police caravan found an inconspicuous location and waited for Silas's direction. Silas retracted his window in time to hear the familiar hum of the drone. Morgan could be driving out the other side by now. He mentally counted the seconds. At two minutes the drone returned. One minute later, Silas held his phone where Hadley could see and thumbed through the overheads.

"Shit!" Hadley cursed. "That's Lila's Studebaker." He pointed. "See right there behind the barn."

Silas stared at the familiar outline of his niece's car. "Dammit. She's supposed to be with Carla Beecham at the hospital. God Almighty! Why can't she ever be where she's supposed to be?" He punched his niece's number, prayed for her to answer, but knew in his bones she wouldn't or couldn't.

"Hi. This is Lila. Leave me a message."

Silas went cold inside. "She's meeting Morgan. She's made this personal."

Bertha's signal interrupted. "The identified address is owned by Elle Goodman. Purchased for delinquent taxes in 2001."

Elle Goodman, Tyler Morgan, Carla Beecham, his own sister—Lila—the red and blue lines of connecting information swirled in Silas's head.

Hadley's phone beeped. "Janice Sloan."

Silas nodded, but remained quiet.

"Detective Barker."

"Detective, I'm calling you from a private office here at the station. We've uncovered the current identities of the Shields children, and—well this is highly sensitive. I don't know what to do."

Lila was in grave danger, and seconds mattered, but Janice Sloan was not a woman of indecision. Silas bit his tongue.

"Go on," Hadley said.

"You know two of the children. Carla Beecham the youngest and Dr. Morgan the oldest. The middle child was formerly Elizabeth Shields, adoptive name Elle Goodman, legally changed to Elizabeth Cartwright. Sir. I'm sorry, but our Chief is the suspect's sister."

Janice's words collided in Silas brain. *Elizabeth.* His head threatened to split into two pieces. *Why? Why? Why?*

Janice cleared her throat. "There's more."

Silas jerked back to reality.

"Go ahead." Hadley said.

Silas steeled himself for disaster.

"The team interviewed a dozen people present at the Shields crime scene. Neighbors, first-on-the-scene officers, EMTs'. At eight years old, Elizabeth Shields most likely shot her own mother."

Silas's brain froze.

From a distant place Hadley spoke. "Good work, Janice. Anything else?"

Janice continued. "Mort Multiveck's cadaver dog alerted in Margaret Culver's garage. CSI found skeletal remains buried under the picnic table. CSI thinks it's Margaret's missing husband."

"Call the prosecuting attorney give him everything you have," Hadley ordered. "We'll sort this out later."

"What if Chief Cartwright comes in?" Sloan asked.

"Hold her for questioning."

"Oh—well—of course, sir—I can do that."

Hadley disconnected. "Sorry man, but your life just got more complicated."

Silas forced the gears of his brain to grind into action. "Let's go. Lila may be in trouble." He opened the door, grabbed his crutches, and slid to the ground. Hadley joined him at the front of the SUV. Silas handed him his phone. "Carry this and tell me what Morgan's seeing. Stay close so I can hear you." In full SWAT mode now, icy control claimed Silas's body. He gathered the other officers who had followed Morgan and issued instructions.

Silas unsnapped his holster, leaving his gun free and accessible. Hadley did the same. Swing, step, swing, step. Silas entered the lane. Hadley matched Silas's hobbling gait. The other officers spread out through the undergrowth to the left and right. A brisk breeze stirred an earthy hint of decay. Overhead, a cat's eye slice of moon slipped through the clouds, dappling the ground in unpredictable but welcomed light.

A steady pace brought them to the curve in the lane. The windows of the old house glowed through the grove of maples. Abandoning the road, they moved into the trees, and nearly broadsided the parked truck.

Hadley cursed and shined the light from Silas's cell over the exterior of the green, four-wheeled drive Ford. The driver's door had a dent the size of a basketball.

Silas gasped.

"What's wrong?" Hadley whispered.

"Dad's truck—this is my Dad's truck!"

"What? That's not possible. What would your dad's truck be doing here?"

"I don't know, but I know it's his. I put that dent in the door."

"Damn. Which side of this family reunion does he belong on?"

Silas propelled himself to the front of the truck. He touched the hood. "He's been here a while. The hood's cold." He turned toward the old house. "Is Morgan's camera showing us anything at all?"

"Not much. Elizabeth is talking to a person I can't see. I don't see the doctor, Lila, or your dad."

"That thing's worthless." Silas thrust his crutches into the ground, catapulting himself forward in an uneven run. He heard Hadley click his gun's safety off. As they crossed the open area, he could see the front door hanging open. At the porch, he abandoned his crutches, drew his gun, and clicked off the safety. He belly-crawled across the rickety wooden floor to a window and raised his head above the sill.

The room was small, showing two entry points, the hallway and a door opposite Silas. Elizabeth sat in a wooden chair, her hands tied, back to the hall. Dr. Morgan was on his knees, hands secured behind his back, a 9mm semi-automatic Lugar, straight out of The House of Audrey's weapons room, pointed at his head. Silas's father held his finger on the trigger.

"Now that I've got you tied up all nice and neat, let me introduce myself. I'm Clifford Albert. You killed my daughter."

Rage transformed Clifford Albert's face into one Silas barely recognized. "She died of cancer, but when you raped her you might as well have stuck a knife in her heart. I promised her I'd get the one who caused her so much pain."

"I'm sorry. I didn't mean to hurt her," Morgan babbled. "I'd had too much to drink and I thought she was playing hard to get. She slapped me. Things got out of hand."

Sardonic laughter rolled through the open door. "Don't play me for stupid, or I'll shoot you now. My daughter never knew who raped her. She never saw your lying face. But somebody else knew what you did—your sweet little sister. Did you know she was setting you up to take the fall for her work as The Surgeon?"

"Shut up." Elizabeth ordered.

Silas froze.

"You're a crazy old fool," Morgan shouted. "My sister would never sell me out. I know too much."

"Tyler, don't say another word." Elizabeth's voice was high-pitched and tight.

"Yes, Elizabeth, you had it all figured out. You're the Police Chief. Who would doubt you when Dr. Tyler Morgan, The Surgeon was killed during an arrest? Your brother is a lowlife son-of-a-bitch, but you're the devil. I'm sorry my granddaughter will know who her father is, and that her aunt is a serial killer.

Silas drove himself to stand.

His dad's tirade continued. "Elizabeth, you loved my son. I'll give you that." He waved the gun in her direction. "You were willing to do anything to make him happy. In the beginning you wanted to help him take care of Lila."

"Yeah, and a lot of good that did me," Elizabeth sneered. "I loved Lila like my own daughter, but Silas pushed me away when her heart failed."

"So, you located the perfect donor. Your own father—Lila's grandfather. It took murder for hire to accomplish your wishes and your dear brother was happy to help you out." Clifford brought the gun back in line with Dr. Morgan's head. "How convenient."

"She threatened to have me arrested for rape."

"Shut up, Tyler. They can't prove a thing."

Silas gripped the door jamb. "Oh Elizabeth, I think we can." The gun weighed heavy in Silas's hand. He pointed the bore at Elizabeth's chest. "Your own brother's words have condemned you both."

Silas hobbled through the door. "Hello, Dad. Looks like I'm just in time to give you a hand. Do you think maybe you could give me that gun, or at least point it at the floor? I want this bastard to make it to a jail cell."

Hadley entered the room behind Silas and handed him his crutches.

"I wasn't going to waste a bullet on his dumb ass. I was just holding him for you." Clifford dropped the angle of the gun but remained close to his prisoner. "Bertha clued me in there was a problem. I knew I could get here faster than you or a Blackbird."

"I want to believe that's true." Silas swung on his crutches to a table near the kneeling doctor. "This yours, Doc?" He pointed to a phone.

The doctor's gaze followed the direction of Silas's finger. "Yes."

"Dr. Morgan, I want to thank you for leading us to our killer. You even recorded for posterity." Silas displayed the device then stowed it in his pocket.

"I'll notify the other officers this situation is under control."

Hadley angled his body away from the group and spoke into the radio attached to his shoulder.

Lila stepped from the darkened hallway. "Hello Elizabeth," she said, trudging into the woman's line of vision. She held a dragonfly earring in her outstretched palm. "I believe this is yours."

Elizabeth stiffened, studying Lila's face. "You heard everything?"

Lila nodded. "How could you do this? I loved you. Respected you," her voice hitched. "You killed all those innocent people. Even your best friend's daughter. Why?"

Elizabeth's face could have been cut from stone. "Simple. I couldn't let my father's evil live on through them. You were the only one meant to live. You made Silas happy. I planned to kill the others from the beginning. I knew they didn't have Silas to make them strong. Make them good—like you. I gave them a few years. Just like my father gave me, before I failed him, and he began to hurt me."

"He hurt me too." Morgan protested.

"Shut up, you coward. At least I tried to stop him."

"Elizabeth, your father failed you in almost every way. But he confessed to killing your mother. We know you shot her. Elizabeth, he covered for you. He protected you."

Elizabeth laughed. "My father never did anything for anybody but himself. The shooting was an accident. My mother had called the sheriff. He was going to jail for child molestation and dealing drugs. They fought. He dropped the gun. I picked it up, and she got in the way. He knew the special attention other prisoners gave convicted child abusers behind bars. He was scared to be on the other side of that pain. He promised to keep my secret if Tyler and I kept his."

"Why didn't you tell the sheriff the truth?" Silas asked.

"Even as children, we understood our father being in prison wouldn't keep us safe from him. If we had told the truth, no one would have believed us. He wouldn't have gone to jail."

"I'm so sorry, Elizabeth," Lila said, her face drawn and sad. "He turned you into a monster."

"Monster!" Elizabeth's face contorted with rage. "After I saved your life, that's what you think I am?"

Silas swung between Lila and Elizabeth. "Elizabeth Cartwright. You have the right to remain silent..."

"You, ungrateful son-of-a-bitch!" Elizabeth erupted from her chair. She spun on the balls of her feet and punched Silas in the neck with her elbow.

Silas clutched his throat.

Elizabeth grabbed one of his crutches. Holding her bound hands above her head, she hurled the weapon across the room. Hadley moved to get a clear shot. The projectile smashed the detective in the mouth. Blood flew and Hadley fell. Hunks of plaster dropped from the ceiling.

Silas choked and spat dust. He tried to bring his gun to bear, but Lila dove for Elizabeth, blocking his line of fire. Elizabeth dodged Lila and spun, landing a kick into Clifford's chest. Clifford and his gun dropped. The sound of a gunshot split the air.

Both women screamed. One in pain. One in sorrow.

41

CHAPTER FORTY-ONE

Silas's heart ached as he placed a white rose at the base of the simple granite headstone. There would be no celebration of life for Elizabeth Cartwright.

Silas had helped Archie Hamilton and the FBI connect the dots between Dr. Morgan, the opioid thefts, and Russell Beecham's drug ring. Those charges plus accessory to multiple murders would send the doctor to prison for the rest of his life. Some would say Elizabeth's death had spared her from paying for her crimes. Silas had no answers for those comments.

The body in Margaret Culver's garage proved to be that of her husband Charles. Margaret had confessed to his murder then proceeded to have another stroke. The prosecuting attorney had taken the old woman's health and age into consideration. He had refused to prosecute.

It turned out that Mendez had been interested in Savannah Peterson. He admitted not revealing his connection was a mistake. Silas had let internal affairs deal with the young officer's error.

Silas did worry about Hunter. The young man was hurting too. Silas counted on Lila's healing nature to help her reach out to her half-brother. But, she would need time to adjust first. Sydney was the stabilizing force, helping both he and Lila work through their issues.

Silas took Lila's hand. "Losing Elizabeth has made me realize something."

Lila looked up at him. "What's that?"

"I think it's time we made The House of Audrey's heart stronger."

"How?"

"There are children the system can't reach. Like Elizabeth and Tyler were. We need to find a way to help them."

"Are you thinking it's time to expand the skills of Big Bertha and The Blackbirds?"

"Exactly."

Lila faced him. Her gray eyes darkened. "I think Great Grandpa would like your idea." She smiled. "A whole new way to keep the promise."

Silas's phone buzzed. "Hello."

"Silas. This is Archie Hamilton. I'm sorry to bother you, but the FBI has a new job for The Blackbirds."